Whispering in French

Whispering *in* French

SOPHIA NASH

WILLIAM MORROW

An Imprint of HarperCollins*Publishers*

This is a work of fiction. Names, characters, places, and incidents are products of the author's imagination or are used fictitiously and are not to be construed as real. Any resemblance to actual events, locales, organizations, or persons, living or dead, is entirely coincidental.

P.S.™ is a trademark of HarperCollins Publishers.

HarperCollins books may be purchased for educational, business, or sales promotional use. For information, please email the Special Markets Department at SPsales@harpercollins.com.

FIRST EDITION

Designed by Diahann Sturge

Library of Congress Cataloging-in-Publication Data has been applied for.

ISBN 978-0-06-247178-9

17 18 19 20 21   LSC   10 9 8 7 6 5 4 3 2 1

This book is dedicated with love and gratitude:
to my parents, Marie-Solange Leglise and
G. Richard N. H. Nash, who taught me
courage by looking fear in the face;
and to my editor, Carrie Feron, who taught me to dream.

"What is essential is invisible to the eye." —*Le Petit Prince*

"Fall down seven. Stand up eight." —Old proverb

Whispering *in* French

Prologue

A lady of stone sleeps atop the peakery of the Pays Basque, each foot in a different country. Her dark hair spills in valleys carved from green, green mountains tumbling into the sea. As storm clouds scud above her tranquil profile crowned by martyrdom, dignity, and solitude, she dreams of trials suffered, won, and lost. Indeed, sometimes I wonder while walking in the valley below these mountains what she would do if she ever wakes up, breaks free of the roots that bind her, and finds her way far from the fog of the Cimmerian years that shroud her. Or will she continue to slumber, and slowly dissipate under the weight of the years until she melts into the granite core and nothing hints of the lost potential under the verdant spring grasses?

I also sometimes wonder if I'll ever wake up.

Chapter One

In a night sky salted with stars, the waxing moon unspooled its light over the jet's wing. Inside, disconnectedness settled over the passengers of the Air France night flight to Paris. And in those murky hours after the food carts lurched down the aisles, the die-hards began a third film, exhausted infants surrendered to sleep, and the travelers in business class retreated ever further into the luxury of elbow-room anonymity.

I don't belong here. The bonhomie of economy is my standard. But Antoinette, during a familiar mother-daughter dance, with guilt and obligation as accompaniment, had asked me to handle a family matter in France and had eased her maternal conscience by putting me beside people of a class of which she almost approved. But I knew the other truth. Antoinette had likely purchased the upgrade because she thought I'd become like an egg past its expiration date, and there was less danger of me cracking and leaking noxious fumes in the cocoons of Espace Business.

So far, not a soul had dared intrude upon my solitude. After picking over a tray of curried something and chocolate something else, I settled into half-reading a book, half-watching a movie, and glancing at other distractions.

My marooned neighbor's hand shook as he raised a double whiskey to his night-shaded profile reflected in the window. Well, of course his hand shook. That was the life aim of back-to-back double whiskeys.

It was hard to judge his age. There was no way to study him to make it out. It would only invite conversation. I vaguely remembered graying hair, a starched white collar, and a weathered face. Turning away, he fixated on the darkness beyond the porthole. Thank God he too was unwilling to exchange niceties with someone he'd never see again.

I'm sorry. Perhaps you were expecting me to be kind, indeed, even beautiful in spirit if not in face, and heroic—yes, perfectly imperfect with an amusing assortment of eccentricities. But you see, I'm none of those things. Not sure I ever was. The faster you understand this, the better you might like the story.

Like so many trotting down the track, I'm nothing more than a battered soul, whose metal has been tested and proven to be the commonest ore despite a golden youth lived by a firm belief in the opposite. Yes, I'm as uncomfortable in my skin as a hermit crab looking for a new shell on the Skeleton Coast beyond the vast Namib, or a black mamba as he consumes an animal three times his size—all of which I'd seen in vivid detail alongside my father, whose sojourns to Africa were long and legendary.

At least I've finally come to accept that this sensation will never go away. Not that I'm complaining. I'm explaining—an uglier action as it implies guilt. This is what all modern therapists suggest, and since that is what I am, I must spout it as if I believe it. I never tell my clients that if there is a religion to follow, it is the one my father advised, "Don't cry if you end up crying." Life is far less complicated if you follow this one rule. Of course, this goes against the cardinal rule of therapy, "Let it out."

By now you may have surmised I'm not a very good psychologist—or life coach, my newest, more marketable professional title. But here you would be wrong. I know how to bite my tongue and listen with the best of them. It's the token wisps of advice-giving that pain me. But, you see, well schooled in the "let them burble on until they figure it out for themselves" technique, I rarely need to offer advice. We need only to prod and point the unhappy in the correct direction during a forty-five minute window of concern and eventually they start listening to their oozing helter-skelter. In ninety percent of the cases—six months to six years later—they either become so disgusted paying two hundred a pop to unload their shite that they change, adapt, grow, and live slightly less unhappily ever after, unless fate has something nasty in store, which it always does, or they give up and choose not to change, in which case fate might deal them a new, great hand—proving, once again, that fickle fate holds all the cards.

Either way, their Visa card balance is lighter each month.

And the ten-percenters? The narcissists, the good and bad psychopaths, sociopaths, and the total screw-ups (of which I am a card-carrying member)—those dear souls? Why, they never change—no matter how many times they wallow in front of someone like me.

So much can happen in this unit of time. Good things. Terrible things. And looking back now on what happened in the next forty-five minutes, I regret not biting my tongue. I'd blame it on the Veuve Clicquot, but we both know I wasn't in Espace Premier, and that treacle they serve in business isn't fit to be called champagne.

The flight attendants, tired of serving us with false but efficient smiles, turned off the cabin lights and prayed we'd quietly incubate before the jarring return to reality by way of a stale, rude excuse for a breakfast. A push of three buttons slid me into an awkward tilt for which 1A through 3F passengers pay double to avoid.

And there it was again. The shudder of my neighbor's fingers, peeking just beyond his seat.

For Christ's sake, I was off duty.

This was not the telltale tremor of Parkinson's. Nor did it appear to be old age, for he just didn't give off an ancient vibe. God, I hoped it wasn't a precursor to something for which I'm ill trained—cardiac arrest or stroke, or . . . "Are you all right?"

His hand went still.

I counted to fifteen and closed my eyes, my duty done. "I'm

well. Perfect. Excellent." The man's halting monosyllables penetrated the engine drone.

I said not a word.

"But, may I ask your opinion on something?"

Why, oh why? I rose to my elbows.

"I'd prefer not to discuss this face-to-face."

It was to be a confession then. I lay back down.

"It's a simple question, really."

"Yes?" It was never simple. Indeed, when someone said it was simple it was always a thousand degrees in the opposite direction. And I was no good at math, degrees, or directions.

"Is there anything that trumps someone's word once given?"

You see? I told you it wouldn't be simple. "Your word?" Repeating often jogged loose more information.

"When you make a promise to someone, is there anything that justifies breaking it?"

"It depends, of course, on what the promise is," I replied.

"It depends," he echoed. "That's not an answer. I require a yes or a no."

I remained quiet, waiting. It always amazed me that nothing made people continue talking more than utter silence. People are hardwired to fill awkwardness.

But no words rushed from his side of the great divide. Well, at least his hand was no longer shaking. I closed my eyes. Five minutes of ill ease dogged me before I relaxed. People had to own their shit before I would put on a show of empathy.

"Look, I realize the question is rude." He stopped.

I waited, letting silence do its dirty work.

"I guess the real question is if it's ever right to gamble with a family's happiness and security or is martyrdom the only right course?" The rush of words slowed to a drip. "Sorry. I'll stop. Forget it."

Heartburn. Yes, that was what curried Thai chicken, beet salad, and chocolate cheesecake on a plastic tray did to you. I could do this too-close-to-the-bone issue under the sterile layers of the vault of my office, but not blindsided on a jet. "What matters more is what you believe. You don't know me. How can any answer I give be of value? I could have the moral fiber of an ax murderer for all you know."

He said not a word. After such intimate revelations, I wasn't surprised. I never told anyone what I truly thought anymore, especially when I'd spectacularly fallen down in this corner of life. So, why not provide the generic, one-size-fits-all answer? "Actually, I believe in a person's right to do anything as long as they are of sound mind, and it isn't criminal."

"Ah. The right to pursue happiness."

"Yes," I said. "But, this is a subject beyond right and wrong." I was tightfisted with my memories as well as my words. I wanted to scream that you couldn't protect anyone from everything their entire life. "I can't give you an answer."

"Or won't answer."

"Same outcome."

"Please," he whispered in the darkness. "Do you have a family?"

"Yes," I replied. *Sort of* was the more correct answer.

"Well, how do you calculate risk and fallout when every option hurts someone?"

"I've taken an oath to do no harm." Oh, the impossibility of that promise. "And I am not the person to give you advice."

"You're a doctor."

"You requested anonymity and I'm keeping it."

A moment's silence.

"I fear I've intruded on your privacy long enough," he finally said.

His hand retreated from the space beyond his lowered seat and he shifted away from me. Ill ease raked the corners of my mind. Unhappiness and ill fortune dog the heels of every living being on this planet. When would people learn that happiness is but a fleeting gossamer thread woven into our lives like fool's gold, which cannot endure throughout the course of our lives? Our best option is to embrace the concept of change, our ever-evolving paths, and endure the good and the bad. Or just become numb. I was one to muse. Only work kept one sane. The loftier called it a sense of purpose. Oh, and hope? That saintly word? Forget hope. Forget Oprah and Dr. Phil. Just learn to endure. With a sense of purpose. Or not.

Because really, we, each of us, are born alone and die alone.

My therapist (and yes, therapists do sometimes go to therapists, albeit special therapists, who can smell bullshit better than a bluetick pointer on a covey of grouse) suggests I am depressed. We quibble on one issue only. It concerns the words *possibly, mildly, moderately,* and *severely.* He refuses to buy my opinion concerning the beauty of existentialism, and the gold standard of nihilism. Cynical humor, according to him, who I'm convinced last laughed in 1983, is my favorite defense. So he thinks me only mildly unhinged and prescribes slow-release Ambien in impressive quantities. He says he's not worried because I don't have an addictive personality. Little does he know. I have my reasons for being a chameleon—and why spoil it by saying more?

A few minutes passed and I raised my seat to glance at my neighbor's still form beside me. He'd find his answer on his own. He was merely uncertain in a healthy sort of way. No one else could make up his mind nor should they.

Of that I was certain.

I picked up one of the newspapers and switched on the light. News of the ever-churning turmoil in the Middle East flooded the page. My gaze jumped to my book, and then to the mini screen ahead. Lack of focus and distraction had lost its charm many months ago. I turned off the light and lowered my seat again to rest an arm over my eyes. Sleep still eluded me as time floated in the eerie space above 39,000 feet.

Involuntarily, I finally gave an answer. "I used to think promises and sacrifice were the currency of family." I paused. "And that you could protect the ones you love by giving your all if necessary." Wow. This newfound level of Hallmark drivel deserved a halo. Hollow bitterness stepped in. "Now I know it's impossible to protect anyone from the trials of life. Follow your gut—good or bad."

Slumber must have come, for suddenly my mind zapped back to reality when jarring lights illuminated the cabin. Attendants jostled down the aisle with bitter coffee brewed twice over. Buckled and prepped for reentry, I refused to glance at the man beside me. He was clearly of the same mind.

The baggage carousels at CDG were as slow as the horrendous crocodile of travelers inching their way through the taxi lane. I would miss my connection at Orly, halfway around the Paris *périphérique*. It was steadily raining, the annual state of the weather for Paris in April. Insufficient heating in a taxi awaited. There'd be a few more hours reprieve before stumbling into my grandfather's crumbling house on the coast of the Pays Basque. Secrets and lies lurked in every corner of that ivy-covered villa since the first sand-colored stone had been laid three hundred years ago.

A long, dark blue Mercedes pulled in front of the taxis and an immaculately suited driver exited, heading toward the trunk. Others in the taxi lane looked on with bored interest. A moment later, the man who'd crossed the Atlantic beside me, Mr. I Have A Question, strode past onlookers and slid into the cool darkness beyond the door the driver now held open. As the dark, expensive car pulled away, the man's eyes found mine for a fraction of a moment.

Had he heard me? No. The entire interaction had been oddly normal in my world of the mentally disordered. But still. Had I changed the course of a family's life? Had I instilled guilt where none should be? God, I hoped not. I now wished I could take back those stupid, whispered words.

And then I was at the front of the line, jostling into a dirty Parisian taxi driven by a bearded, heavyset, smiling immigrant.

He grunted and hoisted my bag into the trunk, but I refused to give up the carry-on, filled as it was with two laptops and the files of a couple of the more stubborn clients, who'd refused to be handed off to a colleague for the coming month or two. Skype, that lovely invention by someone who assumed women loved to smear on makeup at any hour in the name of professionalism, was to be the only tool in the mad sandbox now. Half my clients were in LA, where the lure of an escape from driving in traffic, had produced more Skyping clients than the in-person appointments in Manhattan. Well, if I'd thought NY-to-LA videoconferences were taxing, I'd bet my backup power sources that I was in for a rude awakening to the oddest of odd hours now that that laggard, America, was in my rear-view mirror.

What had I been thinking? Clearly, not clearly at all.

Beaten yet again by that beast called family obligation, I got into the car, one step closer to six weeks in Gallic purgatory.

God, I hated Hallmark moments.

Chapter Two

I'd forgotten the erratic toll of the church bells. Situated on the steep hill on the other side of the Route Nationale, St. Nicholas's two access roads had signs that read *Accès Interdit*. No access. What would Jesus say? No one had ever been able to explain why the bells pealed five to twelve times a day, eight to eighty-seven clangs each time in this corner of France where I'd been packed off to my grandfather each summer. The July I was twelve—too old to enjoy netting shrimp in the tide pools with Magdali, the housekeeper's daughter, yet far too young to be part of the mysterious adult world that involved alcohol and the hot beat of the nightclubs—I'd counted and notated the peals while it rained. The following dry, hot July, the mildew receded, and all interest in church bells had been replaced by a fascination for surfing. The obsessions had fluctuated, much like the tides, for fourteen summers until I stopped going to France entirely.

There was only so much of the French an American should have to endure, my father used to say. It always made people laugh and forget the original question. But the unspoken fact I figured out years later was that, more likely, no one could afford an airline ticket to send me that summer. My father had lost his shirt and things of far greater value, such as our house, to that wild rodeo known as the commodity market, where pork bellies, beef, sugar, and gold—among other mysterious things—bucked and fell without much rhyme or reason to my childish mind. It was only too bad my father hadn't embraced my entrenched thinking in the end: Don't risk what you can't afford to lose.

Instead, he played the stock market's version of a slot machine from hell, and my mother, Antoinette, and I had no choice but to hitch our cart to a wagon driven by an amusing, fearless driver interested solely in the fool's gold of the future, which, in fact, had an 85 percent chance of complete failure.

But at least he was fun. He insisted upon it. And as long as you were willing to play his game, his way, life was a grand adventure. My mother was eager to play. For a while. Me? I learned the game's rules and strapped myself in for a tumultuous ride.

Head reeling with fatigue and clanging bells, I forced myself from my great-great-grandmother's lumpy horsehair bed, which was so short my feet dangled off the end by six inches. The faintest dark-rose-and-jasmine hints of Patou's Eau de Joy infused the matelassé coverlet embroidered with my forbearer's initials.

The screen of my cell read 3:48 and in the fog of jet lag I wasn't sure if it was day or night in the darkness of the shuttered room. My toe caught a suitcase as I stumbled toward the windows. The oblong handle groaned its annoyance as I wrestled and pulled open the vertical panels to unlatch the dark blue shutters before throwing them wide.

A briny cold wind instantly buffeted the T-shirt against me and I shivered. The haunting beauty of an endless stretch of small bays and beaches extended all the way to Spain in the hazy distance. Heavy, fast-moving clouds roiled over the Pyrenees, promising a pelting of the herd of surfers, who looked like seals in their wetsuits, far below the cliff. Swells undulated the sea as the paddleboarders battled with the surfers for ownership of each wave.

Immediately below the window, the budding plane trees' leaves threshed the air and cast shadows on the pea gravel, which surrounded the ivy-covered villa Madeleine Marie, named after two maiden aunts with too many *great*s before *aunt* to reference.

A delicate, caterpillar-like strand of greenery had snuck its way into the window well, and tiny vine hairs had first latched onto and then delivered primordial glue into the pitted cream stone. Indeed, the ivy would outlast the stone, just like the stone would outlast the people within. Only time and the elements were the winners in the end—ever marching on, leaving husks and carnage in their wake. A gust of wind parted a stand of fern and an odd-looking little animal disappeared under the hydrangea.

Bolting the window and dressing quickly, I felt my stomach churn with the same ill ease that had taken up permanent residence a while ago. A spiral chestnut staircase led from the third- to the second-story landing and the stairs creaked as they always had. Now it didn't even help to avoid certain parts of each step.

A tall, slim biracial woman of regal bearing, marking her noble Namibian heritage, emerged from the front salon. She turned and stared at me, her familiar eyes ageless and knowing, just as her mother's had been when she'd cared for me during my childhood. Magdali's mother, Nadine, had been my grandfather's housekeeper until she'd died more than a decade ago, and her daughter had assumed the position. Magdali bowed slightly and looked as if she would say something but stopped herself.

I hurried down the last of the staircase. "Magdali?" Impulsively, I hugged her rigid form to me. I forgot that hugging was uncivilized on this side of the ocean.

She pulled away. "Madame." Her wide-set, curious, dark hazel eyes studied me then lowered.

"Oh no. Don't you dare. I'm not madame to you."

Her pause was a beat too long. "As you wish, Kate."

Oh, it was as awkward as I'd known it would be. Twenty-odd years of silence after a short, intense childhood friendship such as ours cast a gut-hollow echo in the pit of my stomach.

"I'm glad you've come," she said quietly. "And I was sorry to hear about your daughter. And of the divorce. So sorry."

"Thank you for your letter." I prayed she wouldn't ask me what everyone wanted to ask.

The silence between us pulsed in waves, and the words that I should have said remained stuck in the back of my throat.

"Your grandfather is impatient to see you," she finally said. "*Dîner* is served at eight o'clock. Promptly."

"Some things never change."

"And some things do," Magdali replied before she straightened her spine and turned to leave. Her proud bearing spoke of her mother's Himba ancestors who tended the sacred fires of long ago.

Something clattered to the parquet floor beyond the heavy door. Turning the brass knob embossed with an ancient Basque cross, I faced down the man who was so cold, so impersonal, so formal, he'd never used the informal *tu* when addressing his own mother.

His face was gray, his eyes large, pale blue, and rheumy. "You've grown even taller, Kate," he said, his gaze appraising every inch of me. "Must be the American genes."

"I think the statute of limitations for commenting on my height expired thirty years ago," I replied.

He reached for his cane, which had fallen to the ground beside his cushioned chair. "Well, at least you've grown a backbone. Perhaps."

"Backbones are overrated."

His watery eyes narrowed. "I'm not leaving and I'm perfectly fine, *merci*. You can go right back across the ocean if that's why you've come." He murmured something in French, but it was impossible to make out.

"Good to see you again too, Granddaddy." Well, at least he wasn't blubbering some sort of condolence. Neither one of us would be able to stand it. "Jean," he said. "Only children should call someone Granddaddy."

"Sorry, *Jean*," I muttered. "Never read that part in the French family rule book."

He motioned for me to come closer. "I see you've forgotten your manners. Not surprised, living with heathen for over two decades."

I crossed the large room, heel clicks breaking the stillness of the blue salon. Ovals and rectangles of a deeper blue dotted the cracked plaster walls, revealing the grim financial truth. The paintings of landscapes and exotic animals that once graced the walls had disappeared. Only a handful of family portraits remained, their ageless eyes staring at me with what seemed to be disdain. Likely because I was of the generation who would sell out as opposed to their generations who had earned and safeguarded it.

"The heathen are happier. Usually." I bent down and brushed a kiss on each of his moist, cold cheeks, which smelled of the familiar eau de cologne he'd always applied a little too liberally.

His hand clawed and gripped the chair's arm instead of mine. "That's the thing of it, Kate. Life is not about being happy."

"So I finally learned."

"I didn't mean—well, you know I wasn't referring to that

business of last year. It will smooth over. Everyone will forget what hap—"

"Oh no," I interrupted, my bones suddenly heavy. "No need to discuss that. We'll go on as before. Far better. We always operated better with misunderstandings. And don't worry, I won't be here long."

"How long?" Turning his face toward the bank of long windows, his pale irises constricted until his pupils were pinpricks.

"Six weeks? Antoinette asked me to put the household in order and find a more permanent solution"

"To be *installé* in that mausoleum up the hill or in a little mushroom of an ugly hut in Urt? *Non, absolument pas*. I'm not selling our family's villa."

Old age was a bitch. No question about it. And my relatives had never embraced the notion of aging gracefully. "But the nuns are so kind. Just think how much fun you'll have tormenting them."

Color flooded his cheeks.

I always forgot the French don't appreciate irony. You know wit is on its last leg in a place where Jerry Lewis is considered the saint of comedy.

"You forget the other option," he thundered.

I would not rise to the bait.

"The one where I'm planted under the church."

"Well, that is an option," I replied. "But consider the centuries your soul would be plagued by those bells. Personally, I'd go with the nuns."

"I see your sense of humor hasn't improved."

"Must be the French genes," I said.

"Enough." He rattled off an order in French for whiskey and a blanket while tapping his cane on the floor.

"Please speak English," I said, walking back to the door.

"Why Antoinette never taught you French properly is a travesty."

He said something else but it was lost on me as I poked my head out the door to ask Magdali for tea and a blanket. I'd be damned if I'd let him have a drink before seven. I retraced my steps and scooped up his cane. "My mother never taught me because my father wouldn't let her."

"Of course not," he muttered. "He was determined to make you American. And he succeeded."

"He had faults like everyone else, but I'm grateful to live in America—the land of the free, the brave, and the decent job."

"But you're French," he whined. "The food, the wine, the culture—and your family. You should live here. My great-granddaughter . . . Lily should live here."

"No." *No* was such a great word. I loved the slightly bitter tang it left on the tongue, like arugula. It was an acquired taste learned too late in life.

He wouldn't let up. "But you love the sea. Nature. You hate cities. And that awful plastic food they prepare and eat in haste. They have no idea how to live. All work, no leisure."

I would have almost felt sorry for him if I hadn't seen the old steel of condescension lurking in his watery eyes. "Where is Uncle?"

He glanced toward the yawning marble fireplace stained with centuries of soot. "In Paris." He could have said Hackensack with more excitement.

"When will he return?"

"I don't know."

Pulling answers he didn't want to give was an endurance test. "When did you last see him?"

"A while ago."

I waited.

"When he came with M. Reynaud."

"Who is . . . ?"

"The estate person."

"Estate person?"

"The one from Christie's who took the paintings." He scratched the back of his liver-spotted hand.

"Did you tell Antoinette?" The concept of frank communication was always lost on the French.

He waved a hand above the armrest. "Jean-Michel said he would call her."

The likelihood of my uncle doing anything unless it involved money going into his pocket was the same likelihood of my mother doing anything unless it involved business or an amusement. And the likelihood of my grandfather facing the truth about his offspring was about as likely as me facing the truth about myself and my daughter.

It was obvious things were far worse than my mother knew or had let on.

Magdali entered, tea tray in hand. She set it on the glass-topped table, her elegant, slender arms graceful in their movements. She refused to meet my eye. My grandfather said not a word of thanks, befitting his class. Or maybe he was just furious the whiskey was absent.

"Thank you." I went through the motions of serving tea and burnt my fingers on the silver teapot. Magdali faded into the shadows near the overcrowded bookcases. She had that silent, floating footstep of old-world, ingrained servitude.

"You haven't forgotten M. Soames is coming to take tea with us tomorrow, Magdali?" Grandfather continued without waiting for a reply. "You are to join us, Kate. I should like you to meet him, and his relative, who is visiting. Do not forget those biscuits he likes, Magdali."

"*Oui*, monsieur," she replied. "About the pâtissier's account—"

"We'll have no mention of that," Jean interrupted.

"Magdali, does the house have Internet?" I breathed in the ancient smoky pine tar scent of the Lapsang Souchong. "A Wi-Fi password, perhaps?"

"Of course not," Jean said. "Why would we have something so unnecessary?"

"Because we're in the twenty-first century," I retorted, catching the birth of a smile about Magdali's mouth as I offered a teacup in her direction. "And some of us require it. To work. And by the way, could we turn up the heat? It's freezing in here."

"Magdali," Grandfather said without looking at her, "you may leave us."

She looked at the offered cup, shook her head when I started to open my mouth, and left without a sound.

The gravelly voice that had ordered my childhood three months a year took on a clipped tone. "I'll ask you to keep your ideas to yourself, Kate. And I shall remind you that you are under my roof. In case you have forgotten, we do not speak freely in front of servants. Ever." His long nose rose an inch. "It breeds impertinence."

"I don't think Magdali could be impertinent even if her life depended on it. And by the by, you might want to reconsider your ideas. I'm not the one who has trouble finding and keeping employees." I held up my hand when I saw him ready to burst. "Enough. I'm not here to argue with you. I'm here to help."

"I didn't ask you to come and I don't need your help," he said.

The old bugger would never give over. "Of this there was never any doubt." Reverse psychology was the answer. I was not above using it. "But you're absolutely right. You have everything in order. I should leave. I'll look into rebooking flights tomorrow."

Contrariness won over pride every time in our family. "I forbid it," he replied.

I stood up. "Well then, I shall arrange for Internet. And pay for it, don't worry." I hurried toward the door before he could object. "Sorry, I really must find an Internet café and check email."

"Dinner is at eight," he boomed. "Promptly."

"Got it."

Magdali was on the other side of the door, waiting. I touched her arm. "How much does he owe the baker?"

"Two hundred seventy three euros," she replied.

"And the others?"

She sighed. "Almost three fifty to the butcher. And about five hundred to the corner *marché*."

"And?" I encouraged.

"He owes the electrical company, water company, and the gardener has stopped coming. None of the restaurants will serve him. He's stopped going out anyway. He has only his military pension for food and a bit of electricity and, of course, water."

"And you?"

"I have my room and one for my daughter when she is here," she replied. "And my savings."

"How much does he owe you, Magdali?"

"Seven months." She whispered a figure that was shamefully low.

I nodded. "All right, then. I'll go to the bank in the morning. And I'll see to the biscuits and more if you give me a list. No one will remember me in the shops, anyway." I stopped. "Yes?"

She brushed an invisible piece of lint from her skirt. "I would not count on that."

"Why?"

"You've forgotten the ways of a village. Everyone knows you're coming. And everyone will recognize you. And be wary."

"Why?"

"They know your arrival means change."

Of course. Gossip and news was the lifeblood of this chic seaside village.

"Paying off debts is not the solution." She continued, tilting her regal head. "It's a waste of money. It will bleed you dry."

"Then, what do you suggest?"

"I don't know, but I can tell you what everyone else thinks. Except your grandfather and uncle."

"Sell the house," I replied for her.

"Yes." The rhythmic whine of the crickets rose and then fell as a buffeting wind pierced the hollowness of her voice.

"And I'm guessing my uncle is trying to guilt him into living in poverty so that he can inherit it and then sell it himself, right?"

She nodded.

"Although, how he means to cut my mother out of this remains to be seen."

"I would not underestimate him." It was not in Magdali's nature to say something like this. I paid attention.

"What do you think?"

Her sloe-eyed expression held no emotion, save for her mouth, which twisted. "I don't know the solution. I only know it will take a small fortune to save the villa."

"Right." And suddenly I felt my throat and chest tighten. I immediately breathed through the constriction. It was ridiculous. Automatons don't feel anything, especially not feelings concerning crumbling houses.

I was leaking emotion at the oddest of moments, remembering. It was all so long ago. The near-suicidal secret slides down the four-story staircase railing, the peace of reading by a fire in the blue salon as a storm raged outside, playing hopscotch with Magdali on the endless expanse of black and white marble tiles in the foyer, and the feel of my grandfather's large, leathery hand taking mine as we closed the villa's massive door and walked to the beach. But that was a past era and it was time to move on. Nothing good came of living in the past.

And I should hate everything this dusty relic represented to boot—ancestors gone astray, profligate living, cowardice, even Nazi occupation. Magdali would get a pension, Jean would be settled somewhere very comfortably and as miserable as he wanted to be until the end of his days—and uncle? Well, uncle would just have to suck it up and take it like the man he was not.

"Don't sell it," she murmured.

"What? This place is nothing but a money pit haunted by ancient memories of frivolous living by past generations who mean nothing to me. Or you. My grandfather treats you and everyone else he *doesn't* pay like an indentured servant of three hundred years ago. Always has. Why have you stayed?"

"He employed my mother before I was born when no one else would and she was desperate."

"Twenty-plus years of your hard labor paid off that debt. And countless more by your mother." Sweetest woman who ever lived, in my book. Magdali's mother had always been so kind to me when I was a child.

She turned as if to walk away but stopped and looked over her shoulder. The low wattage hall sconces cast a sheen over her expressionless dark face. "It's called loyalty."

I crossed the space to stop her leaving. "If you have something to say to me then just say it."

"If anyone can figure out a solution, you can. You're the intelligent, practical person in this family."

I relaxed. "I guess that means you've decided to forgive me."

"No, you shouldn't have stayed away so long," she replied. "It just means that you should use the gifts you were given, otherwise it's just a waste and it's ungrateful. Not that I—"

"I get it."

I'm not sure if she shut up because of my words or her ingrained, ridiculous notion of servitude.

"So what kind of biscuits does my grandfather's friend like? And who is he?"

"M. Soames likes the ones with the chocolate on top. He's a British expat who lives a five-minute walk up our cliff road. Don't you remember him?"

I shook my head.

"He used to play on the golf tour with your grandfather. Now they watch golf and the Tour de France on the *télé*, and reminisce."

"And his relative?"

"His great-nephew. In the military."

"And?"

"Well, I overheard M. Soames telling your grandfather he was very concerned. Something about post-traumatic stress. I think they want you to help him."

Yet another sick puppy. So I was to figure out a permanent solution for my grandfather, deal with the finances and the natives who all had their hands outstretched, sell a house that was falling apart at the seams, and analyze an officer in the British Army, who probably had zero interest in having his clock examined.

And all within a month and a half. Then I could escape to Espace Business with only a few more cracks etching my shell.

"Anything else, Magdali?"

"Don't forget the chocolate biscuits."

Chapter Three

Whispers from the Garden . . .

*In a fourth attempt to find tranquility beyond yet another fence,
I, a small creature of many quills, had found a little slice
of paradise. An unkempt garden, free of any animal larger
than myself, except for those vicious Barkers that were always
navigating an invasion beyond the chain link of the neighbor,
and a slow-moving Shelled creature I'd seen day fifteen of my
personal nightmare. Fewer bumbling Two-Leggeds intruded
here, but they left revolting charred white sticks on the ground
that one could and had mistaken for a delicious Slug in the
middle of the night.*

*The other irritation was the Wing Beaters. Their inces-
sant cooing during the day from the bower of gnarled together
branches of strange trees would surely drive me mad. How was*

a fellow to take a decent lie-down with all the din? I suppose I could put up with the cooing and crapping if the nightly forage continued to prove so deliciously fruitful. But what were those incessant clanging sounds? It was enough to make one go in search of new lodgings.

It's been a trying time since the last full moon. I'm not sure what happened still. For as long as I can remember, I lived in a small walled garden by day and a wire cage in a cottage by night. Oh, it had its advantages. My pet, a short Two-Legged with long brown hair that was sometimes tied back with little red ribbons, provided a never-ending source of very bland dry tidbit food. It was merely annoying that the Two-Leggeds had not a clue about the importance of keeping day and night hours. Why must there be light coming from those infernal switches at every hour of the night? Did they not know that the dark was to be savored as it swirled its inkiness throughout the land, leaving behind a trail of dew as it cringed and finally withdrew from the east? And all the while, the Call of the Slug wafted through the cottage's windows. Yes, in my world, all things returned to the elusive, heavenly Slug.

But I digress. This nightmare began a fortnight ago when the little Two-Legged with a penchant for ordering my days and nights to her liking, took me on a long trip across a frightfully wide body of water and left me in a foreign garden. In her excitement, she failed to examine the fence for gaps. Of course, it was the first thing I did. Freedom from the light switches and the limpid vegetables whilst on the run was divine. I slinked and snuffled my way through rusting foreign borders and gardens until even I wasn't sure how to return. I realized I'd possibly made a grave mistake when I saw the size of the mashers on those Barkers, and so settled into my new life in the wild on the non-canine side of the Maginot Line.

What? How do I know about the Maginot Line, you ask? Why everyone in my world knows history. It's about the only thing we know apart from survival. But then isn't history the ultimate survival guide? Our sole goal is to pass down history and survival tips from mother to offspring, very unlike the Two-Legged, who seem ridiculously preoccupied with turning night into day and day into night, as well as yapping and tapping on little devices. Not that I do much socializing, you understand. Not in my survival tips from Mum.

I snuffled the ivy at the base of this crumbling pile. Something was off today. There were far too many lights piercing the glass squares of the structure. And far too much noise. I blame the new intruder, who left two long grooves in the pea gravel with a wheeled monstrosity. This spelled change, which always spelled trouble. I'm very good at spelling by the by. It's certain names of living, breathing creatures that complicate everything. Except the Slug. I was born knowing that word. Indeed, my brother, sister, and I used to fall asleep in rumbly-tumbly balls as Mum ignited our other inherent traits with Slugenly historical chants.

Ah, a delectable, plump little offspring, the size of a pearl, gleamed in the light of the waxing moon. And where there was one, there were certain to be more. This would take the edge off my—

Yurump! A swipe from behind knocked me over. *Bloody hell. My drawstring muscle constricted, and I tucked my extra bits inside the ball of spines. If only I could see what hit me. Its scent was peculiar, not at all like the Barker.*

It batted me about the garden until dizziness set in. But, crikey, its scent was heavenly—sweet and wild—and nearly had me letting down my defenses. And then, finally, the scent undid me. I unfurled myself. She was palest orange in the moonlight, with only the end of her tail twitching as she gazed at me with what looked like an evil grin framed by a pair of white whiskers that would surely intimidate the dead. I flexed my quills and stood my ground. It's easy to be fearless when you are intoxicated. I would have even endured the promise of claws and worse if it meant imprinting that scent.

She yowled and then licked a paw, obviously injured by a quill. Then she stared, almost as transfixed by me as I was with her. I think. What in bloody hell? Finally she turned, and slunk away, favoring her left paw.

Clawing Yowler—0. Me—1.

And then her scent hit me again. It was coming from my quills, where she'd had the audacity to swipe me. I felt saliva rising on my tongue and was helpless to fight the urge to self-anoint with the perfume left behind by this damned creature.

How ridiculous. I do not like Yowlers. I do not like anyone really. And now I am sure I especially don't like this new land. It was enough to make me want to find the red-ribboned, short Two-Legged, and become partial to switches in cottages.

Almost.

There's a saying here. If you can see the Pyrenees in the distance, it's going to rain. And if you can't see them, it's raining already.

Today, it hailed.

The baker pushed out his lower lip and shrugged his shoulders, a Gallic reflex instilled at birth. *"C'est normal."*

Normal? Everyone else in the northern hemisphere was surfing a late spring heat wave; AC cranked to the max.

He refused to meet my gaze as he twisted the ends of the paper around three baguettes. A beribboned box of biscuits sat beside the flour-dusted register plastered with advertisements for everything from babysitting and lodgings for rent to surfboards and guided yoga—all in French, Spanish, and Euskara, the Basque language of which there were many different dialects, with almost no similarities. Of course.

This from a mysterious people who counted seven provinces in a nation they'd been trying to wrest from France and Spain since the Paleolithic period. No one knew where they'd come from. Even they didn't know. Or maybe they did, but refused to tell anyone. The ETA tended to let their bombs speak for themselves. If the code-loving Nazis had just promised them a Basque sovereign nation in exchange for the secrets of their dialects (which as far as I could see had as many x's and z's as there is butter in croissants), we'd all be speaking German. It's said that the devil tried to learn Basque for seven years and gave up.

The baker scratched his ear and appeared embarrassed to bring up the subject of the family's debt. *"Et ben, madame . . ."*

And so . . . The heavy Basque accent poured over my senses and warmed me as much as the heat from the ovens. "*Alors,* M. Gaina," I replied, "this should settle the account." I handed over three hundred euros.

He studied me in the way a thief examines a gull. And then he scratched his hairy ear again and broke into a broad smile. "*Et ben, merci, madame.*" He reluctantly handed over the change, obviously doubtful of ever seeing another euro from the family.

The shop door's bells jangled and an elegant, birdlike old woman queued behind me. Madame la Comtesse de Bergerac with the same pinched, haughty expression she'd worn two decades ago. It was the quarter hour before shops closed for a civilized little three-hour lunch. The lure of earning more money would never make a Frenchman forgo *déjeuner.* That would just be unpatriotic.

But the way M. Gaina blushed and stole glances at the aging countess behind me, I would have bet my last *sou* he was trying to work up the nerve to butter a baguette with her as soon as I left. He didn't stand a chance. Class and station were as impenetrable here as they were not in the States.

Turning to leave, I darted a glance at the countess.

Well. Clearly the countess had a sweet tooth that was blind to social standing.

Four hours later, I learned Mr. Soames did, indeed, like chocolate biscuits. His relative did not. Major Soames did not like tea either. But there was something he disliked even more than the former and latter.

Me.

It was ridiculous. Everybody liked me. Except me, of course. If there was one thing I knew how to do with strangers—albeit obviously not strangers on planes—it was to be likeable. It was the most important requirement of the job: gain trust. It was the great perk of *active listening*, my favorite oxymoron. Become fake friends or a pseudo good parent. Whatever. It was easy to do with a little practice and it came in handy in forced social situations. Except, apparently, when taking tea with a recalcitrant British major.

"So what is it you do, Mrs. Hamilton?" Boredom wafted off him like the scent of mothballs in wool. While he was younger than my forty-two years, the parched gray of his expression made him seem far older.

A spidery feeling always curled up my neck when I came across someone who had flirted with the stickiness of malevolence. Narcissists, psychopaths, sociopaths, and the like oozed a morass of charm glue over everyone in their path before they went for blood. Major Soames exuded nothing. And yet, my neck was clammy. "What I do? Why, like everyone else, major, I exist." When kindness fails, go for the unexpected.

"I told you, Edward," his great-uncle said. "Mrs. Hamilton does social work. Well known, indeed. Excellent article in *Psychology Today* last month. Something about self-sabotage?"

"Self-doubt in children of narcissists," I said.

He turned to Jean. "You must be very proud."

Jean concerned himself with a chocolate biscuit.

"You are a psychologist," the major clipped.

"I prefer life coach. Less stigma." I popped a chocolate petit beurre in my mouth.

"But she also does social work for the poor," Mr. Soames almost pleaded.

The major flexed his fingers and leaned back in the dilapidated pale yellow chair in the salon overlooking the sea. "I see."

"And what do you do, Major Soames?" I couldn't help myself.

"Construct infrastructure. In sand." He paused. "But mostly kill and maim."

"Edward—" his relative said sharply.

"No," I stopped him. "It's all right. We're among friends. I understand—"

"I'm sure you do," the major interrupted. Abruptly, he unfolded himself from the cramped quarters of the chair and stood up. "Must go. Thank you for tea, M. du Roque, madame."

"Edward," his great-uncle said. "Don't go. We've just arrived."

But he was already at the door, pressing the brass lever. "Excellent tea. Thank you so much." And then he was gone.

I gazed at his untouched teacup.

Grandfather absently tapped his cane.

"I don't know what to do." The ridges in Soames's forehead were deep with worry.

My grandfather stopped the comment on his lips when he looked at me.

"I think he's going to kill himself. Eventually." The older man said it so quietly, I almost missed it.

"*Arrêtez*, Phillip. Stop," Grandfather said.

I stood up and went to the window. The major bypassed his family's brand-spanking-new black Range Rover parked on the pea gravel and strode through the dark enameled gates to turn left on the road perched on the sea cliff.

"I'm so sorry, Mrs. Hamilton," Soames continued. "My great-nephew was impossibly rude—the opposite of how he used to be. I'm certain you have no desire . . . I wouldn't dream of imposing on your time, and surely you wouldn't consider helping him . . ." His words trailed to a stop. Grandfather had the decency to remain silent.

I turned from the window. "I can only help someone who wants to be helped."

"But perhaps you could just work on him a little," Grandfather said. "Drop by Phillip's house from time to time. Become friends. The villa is not far."

There was such forlorn desperation in Soames's eyes.

"I've never worked with someone in the military."

Soames clenched his hands. "His wife, Claire, has gone back to London. Taken the children."

"Children?"

"Yes, he has a daughter, Winnie, who is eight. The light of his life—just like him really. And a son, Charles, seven." The rest of the story gushed from the old man like tea through a broken strainer. Five tours in Bosnia or the Middle East, a leave of absence, threats of divorce, late-night pacing, drinking alone, silence. The full panoply of denial and depression.

I looked back through the window. The wind had picked up and the sea was roiling, playing havoc with the surfers, most of whom were paddling toward the shore. Only the stand-up paddleboarders were hanging tough. "Mr. Soames?"

"Yes?"

"My grandfather tells me you're a betting man."

"Indeed. I like whist very—"

Grandfather cleared his throat and I turned to observe the two elderly friends.

"Oh, all right. I play a bit of vingt-un at Le Casino in Biarritz from time to time."

"From time to time," Grandfather said with a straight face.

"Well, I would not bet on my ability to lure your nephew into therapy. And I won't be here for more than a few weeks myself. I'd have to refer him if, by a long shot, he agrees to see someone. How long is he staying with you?"

"Indefinitely. He will not discuss why he is on leave. No idea of the why or the how of it." He rushed on. "He's very dear to me, Kate—I may call you that, may I? He and his sister are my only relations in this world apart from their parents. He is a good man. A very good man. I can't imagine him ever doing anything wrong intentionally."

Oh, the innocence of those who had never faced down a weakness lurking in the soul and lost.

"Of course he did not," Jean said.

"I would pay for your—"

"No, Mr. Soames—"

"Phillip."

"Phillip," I continued. "I won't accept anything unless your nephew agrees to seek help. And like I said, it would end up being someone other than me. Please remember, the chances are slim."

"But there must be something . . . I'm a businessman by trade. Now retired, of course. I've never found that people give their best effort without a check."

Curiosity reared its tail. "What was your profession?"

"Headhunting. Soames Headhunters of London?"

And of USA, and every major city in the world. I reined in the smile. "Why, Mr. Soames, it's said that your company is responsible for the success of half the industries in the Western world."

"No. Not at all. It's the people who make those companies successful."

"Phillip is far too modest," Jean added. "His specialties were in the oil, mineral, and communication industries."

Phillip Soames smiled. "I had the best job in the world because most of the business was conducted on the golf course or in the club afterward."

"I see. Well, would you agree to a barter? I'll attempt to talk to your nephew if you attempt to find a caretaker for my grandfather. Agreed or—"

"I don't need another damned nursemaid feeding me gruel and wiping my derriere. *Merci* but no," Grandfather interrupted.

"I think he means hiding the wine and helping him with his bath," I explained.

"Done," Phillip said, smelling a deal and knowing when to close it. "It will be my pleasure."

TWO STEPS FORWARD. Three steps back. I had forgotten the bureaucracy of the French government. French bureaucrats in notary offices, post offices, banks, and, worst of all, mayors' offices had all (I was convinced) taken a secret oath to demand documents from innocent citizens and noncitizens (especially) that would and did destroy entire rainforests every year. In triplicate and embossed with meaningless but impressive-looking stamps. Particularly unimportant documents were additionally adorned with tricolor ribbons. Yes, the Dark Ages were back, and nowhere did they seem more officially documented than here in the Land of the Beret Basque.

On this third Monday in May, the fifth attempt to get into the bank after one of the two hundred–plus saint's day closings, lunch closings, and someone being sick, and the funeral of someone's eighth cousin seven times removed, I was ushered past the faded-burgundy-velvet-roped lines to the hushed, carpeted confines where real money loitered. M. Landuran gave me a pinched look, shook my hand, and motioned toward a hard-backed chic white leather chair that swiveled with the slightest provocation.

"*Enchanté, madame*," he said, smoothing his copiously oiled gray hair. He picked up a Montblanc fountain pen and carefully unscrewed the cap.

"Thank you for seeing me," I said, attempting to keep the sarcasm at bay. My grandfather's finances were in a shambles and yet they hadn't thrown him in the French pokey, where likely they'd serve rations of brie, baguettes, and Brouilly during two-hour lunches, followed by a solid afternoon of watching *le foot* (soccer to you and me) on the *télé*. At least, after my visit to Orange, the French version of AT&T, I was certain they'd be denied Internet. But after five months of good behavior they'd probably qualify for *la cure*, that epic stay at a thermal spa, for which French health insurance pays with gusto so the French can simmer in mud baths just like their Roman conquerors. That and the thirty-five-hour workweek were perks most diehard workaholic Americans could learn to love. Obviously, the socialist government found it more financially prudent to keep people out of jail than in. It almost made one want to explore criminality for a living. And perhaps Grandfather, or rather, Jean, could be talked into a little thievery if he continued to be averse to the nunnery.

As if he could read my wayward thoughts, the banker cleared his throat. "*Mais*, madame, *la famille* du Roque 'as been a client of ours for almost *cent ans*."

A hundred years. You would think they would at least give a toaster for that kind of loyalty even if we were in the red.

"It's only natural I should—how you say in America?—*make time* for such an important client." He perched a pair of thin wire glasses on the end of his long Gallic nose and in his elegant hand scratched out a notation on a Rhodia pad of lined paper. His handwriting looked like a daddy longlegs crawling over the page.

"So—" I crossed my legs and inelegantly jerked forward when the chair began to twirl. "Pardon me, M. Landuran, but may I be blunt? What is the state of my family's, or rather, my grandfather's, finances? I'd like to ensure all is in order before I return to America shortly."

He peered over the top of his glasses, glanced at me, and returned to his spidery notations, which no doubt was nothing more than a love note to his mistress, or the draft of a new holiday he was cooking up for the bank. "I would have thought, madame, that there are the same rules of privacy in America than here in la France."

I clasped my hands together and placed them between my legs. "Of course," I replied. "But I'm more worried about the laws that might compromise my relative's ability to continue in his house."

"May I ask after your mother?"

What? "Umm, Antoinette's fine." Likely planning a trip to Capri or Martha's Vineyard, given the cyclical nature of her set.

His gaze traveled from the top of my head down to the hands in my lap.

"You are not like her," he said. "Yet very beautiful."

That was the thing in France. Everyone thought it their right to comment on everyone else, especially their appearance. Gossip and flirting were noun and verb one. And extra points if you could do it to their face. I smiled against my will. God, I hated to descend to their level. "Monsieur, my mother has always spoken so highly of you. Said you were a man of

distinction and would be the only one to see in this matter."
Liar, liar, pants on fire. I pulled out my Bank of America checkbook to lure him. "Will two thousand suffice for the immediate shortage?"

"That is not *la question*, madame."

"Five?" My roller ball was poised over the pale blue check.

"The question is when will your family sell the house, madame. And to whom."

Well, at least he'd be an ally in my goal to sell. "We shall see,
monsieur. How much is it worth, do you think?"

"Bien, madame, that is not for me to say. I can refer you to
an excellent *agence*, but you must get the approval to sell from
your grandfather first."

"And you don't think he'll agree."

"*Non.*"

"Why?"

He studied me with narrowed eyes like a school principal
sizing up a truant. Blowing his nose with an actual cloth handkerchief, he handed down his verdict. "Your uncle is an esteemed
client here as well, you must know. And I keep all confidences.
But I suppose I may tell you that your grandfather fully intends
to honor the tradition of handing down the villa to the eldest
son as has been done for centuries. Your grandfather, madame,
will never sell. Even if the walls or roof collapse—something
that may happen soon from what M. Colas informed me."

"M. Colas?"

"The best carpenter and mason in Biarritz. A good friend."

"I see."

"But that is if the pipes don't fail first, according to M. Matxinbordakorbidea."

"I'm sorry, but was that a name?"

"But of course, madame. The best *plombier* in the Pays Basque. Everyone knows him. You will too. Soon."

"Plumber?"

"*Exactement.*"

"Could you please write his name and number down?" I inhaled deeply. "Anything else?"

"Well, of course there is the matter of *la falaise* . . ."

"The cliff?"

"*Oui, madame.*"

"What is wrong with the cliff?"

"Why, it is always falling a little here, a little there. Surely you've noticed. Mme Jaragoltxe, a master engineer, of course, says the cliff must be reinforced, or else."

"Or else?"

"It will collapse one day. Taking Madeleine Marie with it, *bien sûr.*"

Of course. "When?"

He shrugged. "Maybe today, maybe next month, maybe in ten years. Who knows, madame? The situation is delicate and complicated, *non?*"

"Indeed. I'll need the spelling of the engineer's name too."

He shook his head and carefully wrote out all the contact information.

Well, the bank may close to celebrate every saint's day but I had to give it to them. They kept an eye on the choice property of their clients.

"And if I may be so bold?"

"Yes?" *Lord, there was more?*

"Do take care with your neighbors." He leaned forward as if plotting a takeover. "Pierrot and Maïte Etcheterry are Basque, and do not take kindly to foreigners taking up residence on land that Basque separatists believe they own."

"What? Are they going to bomb a villa that's been in my grandfather's family for over three centuries just because his granddaughter is visiting?"

He chuckled and extracted a Dunhill cigarette from its elegant pack and tapped one end on his desk. "Of course not, madame. But an American, who might convince her grandfather to sell to a foreigner or somehow"—he glanced at my checkbook—"appropriate the property herself—"

"I assure you I have absolutely no intention of staying or living in France whatsoever."

He shrugged in almost a feminine way and lit the long, thin cigarette with a heavy gold lighter. Clearly the tobacco industry was alive and still partying in this part of the world. He blew a long stream of smoke discretely to one side and finally relaxed his mouth into a smile that had never seen an American orthodontist. "Ah, but you must not worry so, madame. You will find a solution." He paused and glanced toward a bookcase housing tomes that had likely never seen the light of day. "And if you don't, your uncle will take possession and sell it for you. Yes, that might be the best solution."

The damned banker was shifting loyalties as fast as a Vichy collaborator.

"At least you are here, as any proper granddaughter would be, to take care of your grandfather. Most importantly, please give your lovely mother my very best regards." He paused for a moment, darting a glance at my checkbook. "Six thousand two hundred fifty-seven US dollars and twenty-three cents should balance the account in euros, madame. And do not worry. The bank has canceled M. du Roque's *carte de crédit* so there will be no further *factures*."

Well.

I filled out the check, thanked the elegant banker for his time, and walked through the cobblestone streets of Biarritz, toward the Grande Plage. I wondered if I would ever see a euro of repayment from someone in the du Roque family. Antoinette would likely repay me, I knew, if I could not recoup the money from the sale of the villa. So much for that week in London I'd been plotting on the way home to get the Francophile taste out of my mouth. Oh, who was I kidding? There was nowhere on this big green planet that was far enough away for me to leave behind my life.

Settling into a metal and wicker chair in front of Dodin, my favorite childhood pastry shop, I ordered *pain grillée et beurrée*— grilled, buttered toast—as well as a hot chocolate, brimming with the unforgettably potent and molten flavors I'd savored as a child.

For the hundredth time that week, I pushed back thoughts

of Lily, always swirling in the outermost reaches of my mind. There was nothing more I could do for my sixteen-year-old daughter that I hadn't already done. She was safe, or as safe as she could be given the situation. Miss Chesterfield's was one of the best boarding schools on the East Coast and had even traded in its old stodgy ways since the year I'd been imprisoned there. The current teachers and headmaster appeared, in my jaded view, to actually care and help students find their potential. Lily wanted nothing more to do with me. I'd failed her and she knew it. I'd been the last line of defense, and I'd not been there when she most needed me.

And now, once again, I was in an impossible family situation, where no good solution presented itself. Someone was going to end up in tears. My grandfather, my uncle, a hundred dead, wailing ancestors . . . yes, all of them would hate me before I was finished.

Then again, I was perfect for the job. I'd make all of them face the brutal financial facts, be brave little du Roque soldiers, and get on with disposing of the relic. And I was the best person to do this because I just didn't care about any of it. I was the antisavior, who excelled at cold, hard failure by looking disaster and bullies in the eye and trusting diplomacy instead of a big stick. My recent swing in the opposite direction was, at best, ineffective.

But the damned villa was nothing more than a mildewed, disintegrating millstone around all the family's necks. It was only a matter of holding good old *Jean's* feet to the fire until he capitulated and sold Madeleine Marie to the highest bidder so they could all retire to a small modern house in the country to live out their lives modestly in peace—if I couldn't reconcile him to a life with the nuns with a nice sum to Magdali to start a new life.

Almost four hundred years of passing the relic from father to son would stop here. Now. My uncle's inheritance be damned.

Something I knew all about.

From my little café table under the shade of the red parasol, I glanced to the right of the Grande Plage, toward the pink-and-white Hôtel du Palais, a formidable five-star hotel originally built by Napoleon III for his Princess Eugénie, who had spent her childhood summers here. The court had followed the royal couple and erected magnificent houses up and down the coast. Each and every one of these buildings had evolved, passed from one family to another, to host hordes of different families, royal and not.

Madeleine Marie would do the same, and would likely receive a much-needed facelift by new owners. The only question was if I could withstand the childhood memories that lay coiled in every mossy corner of this epicenter of familial disharmony until I managed to sell it. Or were these memories so well buried, and I so far removed from caring, that I'd remain immune to all? Only the whispers of my ancestors who had entrenched themselves behind the limestone walls and endured the battering weather of history taunted me.

A gust of the prevailing southwest wind, which had gathered force as it wound through the Pyrenees beyond, fluttered the edges of the parasol. The chocolate high dissipating fast, I glanced at *la note*, and slipped a few euros onto the small silver tray.

I motioned to the waiter and stood up.

What was the point of remembering the past? It would change nothing.

Chapter Four

There were the strangest noises coming from outside the window of the bedroom. It sounded as if the most inept burglar in the world was loitering in the drive or ET was snuffling about in the hydrangeas. Clearly my imagination was running amok. Must be the pastis combined with the recent visit to the nuns, or Skyping clients at all hours of the day and night.

But for some reason, I felt rested and alert.

There was something about watching the days drift into night or the nights fading to day all awash with the hypnotic sounds of the ocean rising and falling in a cycle off by about an hour each day. It felt like I was being force-fed a curriculum of ethereal nature and peace. Thank God I had a stable of clients back home to keep me rooted in the level of insanity I felt most comfortable. At the desk overlooking the window, Skype's blue screen cast an eerie light in the room as I waited for the first client to call me.

It was four A.M. and under the haloed yellow glow of a nearby streetlamp, I could see the chunky arms of the baker, pumping up the cliff road toward his shop. Soon, very soon, he'd be shoving the first *boules*, followed by baguettes, into an oven so hot it left his arms hairless. Those black rags he used to wick moisture from the baguettes looked like ray skins fluttering in the breeze when he dried them outside each day. The natives here speak of crust texture with as much gusto as American politicians promising to solve the debt crisis a week before Super Tuesday.

Skype's melodic ringtone bleated before the nasal voice of Max Mulroney's assistant zapped me back to the moment. Max took it as a point of pride to pay double for the privilege of booking seven o'clock appointments in LA.

"Doc, the film is tanking. Can't get it into one damn festival. Not even in some unheard of piece-of-shit festival in Cyprus. Where the fuck is Cyprus anyway? Isn't there a war going on there?" Max Mulroney's laugh was deep like he was having a warm gurgle of whiskey. Which he was. A fat glass of Chivas neat tilted in his hand.

"No. That's Syria," I replied, and glanced at his drink again. "How are you dealing with the stress?"

"Stress?" Max Mulroney repeated. "Who the fuck has time for stress? I'm just hanging this one up as a complete fail and locking in the money for the next before it dries up. It's a shark-eat-dolphin world out here in Malibu-bu."

A disturbing half smile blurred the bottom of his face for a moment and then caught up to real time.

"And you're okay with this?"

"Sure. Hell, it might be an epic fail—but I was in it for the *journey*, like you always suggest. Just can't have too many journeys in a row, ya know?"

I nodded. As far as I could tell, Max Mulroney was the healthiest, nicest narcissist in Hollywood. The sole reason he arranged weekly sessions was because everyone who was anyone in the film industry had a shrink, but he couldn't be bothered to get on the PCH in his Carrera to meet someone face-to-face. *Journey*, indeed.

"You really should invest in the next one, Katie. A romance *á la Titanic*. DiCaprio is set to lead. Trying to tie down Sandy Bullock. Set in Italy. Kind of *Titanic* boy meets *Miss Congeniality*. Get it?"

"Intriguing. So. How are you and Kelly getting along?"

He laughed. "Same old. She makes demands, I refuse. She charges up the Amex, I explode. It's just damn tiring."

I sighed.

"I know, I know, Doc. Hey, you know I'm just kidding, right?" He pulled up a sock on the other side of the world. "Well, halfway kidding."

"How do you think Kelly feels about it?"

"Doc, I know you want me to care about how she feels, but why should I? Relationships are business transactions. But you know I'd never be anything less than a good guy. I always give them a fat little golden parachute."

"And that makes you happy? To have women attracted to your money?"

"I'm always happy. How could I not be? Living on the same block as Caitlyn Jenner for Christ's sake. Communing with goddamned nature here in frigging paradise. And you should see my new yoga teacher. Comes here to teach me downward dog and Shiva twice a week."

"I think you mean shavasana. Do any of them throw the money back in your face?"

He nearly choked with laughter. "Not when it's a check with five zeros after numero uno."

For the next forty minutes, I heard a litany of first-world problems.

Maybe I should break up with Max. Or maybe we should speak daily. I wondered how much he'd hand over to the only woman he'd allowed into his sphere for longer than a year, albeit the only one whose naked body he'd never seen. But still. Maybe it would be enough to keep the house from falling off the cliff before a solution could be found.

On the screen, he looked over his shoulder toward the door and then swung around in a blur. "Hey, you can keep a secret right? We've got something like attorney-client privilege and all that, right?"

I nodded. "What's wrong?"

"Nothing." He smirked and scratched the back of his balding, red kinky-haired head. "Okay. So I'll give you a little stock tip. Invest as much as you've got in Limerack. Big payout guaranteed next month. Then give me a fifty percent discount for our sessions. Hell, just deduct the cost of our pep talks from your earnings. I like you, Doc. Maybe I'll try to get you some IPO the next big opportunity from Marty Friedman's group."

"Max." I sighed. "I appreciate it, I do. But let's stick to talking about you."

"That's what I like about you, Doc. It's always about me."

Had to love Max. He was quick on the uptake. A few minutes later, Max cut out to take an incoming call from his stockbroker.

The bakery's yeast and flour scent flowed into the room upon the wind rustling through the plane trees beyond my window. And for the first time in a long time I felt simple and true hunger, irrespective of the hour, rise from my belly to my throat. A few more minutes and then it was time to regroup before connecting via the ping-pong ringtone to Gillian St. James, a divorced Manhattan lawyer contemplating marriage to a pathological liar and cheater.

She was a two-time offender already. It always amazed me that the most intelligent, sharpest people on Earth didn't get it. That we keep making the same mistakes, and then blame everyone else for our lack of courage to choose a new way. Therapy is so simple. It's a two-act play. Act one is easy. The person replays their life from the very beginning. They feel the hurt, free the tears, connect the dots, and see why they made the choices they did. Act two requires jumping into the deep end of the future without the leaky flotation toys we've clung to in the past. Instead, we have to learn to swim by ourselves, using a self-made manual written in a language we don't understand, using a process we absolutely don't trust and violently loathe.

And with the new method? Why, the chances of not drowning only improve about 15 percent.

It takes a kind of faith. Or a touch of insanity. Kind of like navigating the loopy Amalfi Coast without headlights and trusting Google Maps to keep you from falling into the ocean. Sadly, Gillian was hell-bent on gripping the wheel of misfortune and careening out of control with bad boy number three, despite the proverbial beacon of light illuminating a safer route I attempted to provide.

I finally stood and stretched before taking a few steps to the window. There were just a few moments before my last appointment. The distant lights from the little Spanish town of Fuenterrabía winked through the mist covering the many small bays arcing the coast like a string of black pearls. The first rays of dawn broke over the Pyrenees in their daily flight toward the sea.

And suddenly I wished Lily was beside me. Not the Lily of today, but the Lily who was still innocent of the pain in the world. When her small hand had fit so perfectly in mine, and she had looked at me with such raw, pure trust in her clear eyes as we laughed together. I could feel the memories balling up and rushing, pushing to fall out. I stopped breathing, sealed my lungs, and harnessed the primal rush to close down. There was no time for this. I crossed to my small desk.

I glanced at the time on my laptop. Five forty-five. When

most normal people were prisoners to an inchoate dreamland. But Anne Bishop of Washington, DC, was a special case. She was on the cusp of courage. Maybe. I just had to get out of the way as she healed herself. It was heading toward the shortest pro bono case in history.

"Thank you for talking to me, Kate. I know it's crazy early for you. You sure it's okay?"

"No, Anne. It's perfect. I'm a morning person anyway." I squeezed my nails into my fists to keep from yawning. What did it matter? Morning, evening—I had lost the ability to keep regular hours a long, long time ago. "How are you doing? How was your week?"

Anne spoke of the trivialities of life, walking the walk so many clients had to do to finally feel the warm cocoon of intimacy with me before they could really dig deep and face their fears. "Anne, you're doing so well, you are. But tell me, how are you feeling?"

"I'm good. Well, I'm . . . I'm . . ." She put her head in her hands, and her body shook.

I waited a beat. Let her get a grip. "What's going on?"

"You know how you said I should dig deep and dial into my anger?"

"Yes."

"I did. And I figured it out. All this time I've confused sadness with anger. And mixed up happiness, with just not being scared. And thought drama was normal life."

"And?"

"And I'm done with it all. I know you want me to sort through everything, look at my childhood, see where my parents failed, but I think I've just got to do one basic thing and everything else will fix itself."

"And what is that one thing?" Maybe finally someone would give me the answer.

"I've just decided to stand up for myself. Damn it. I don't want to feel sad anymore. I've just got to decide to do that. No one can do it for me. I don't want to heal or be taken care of or be a victim or martyr. I just want to take a stand. Be myself, by myself. And not care what anyone thinks anymore. Except me. No one else is living in this bag of skin except me. I don't have to please anyone except me anymore. It's my damn life and I will live it the way I choose."

And there it was. Raw grit scratching its way to the surface. It was a rare sight to behold. "Go on."

"And . . . and . . . and I'm going to start paying you, Kate. It won't be much at first if that's okay."

"You don't have to pay me, Kate. You're part of the program for which I volunteered."

"I don't care. I'm treating right the people who treat me right and kicking to the curb everyone else."

"And Ron?" Her rich, alcoholic husband had left her and their three boys without a cent but now wanted back in.

"I'll never take him back. No matter how much he and his family bribe me. I will, I will . . ."

"Yes?"

"Well, I'll figure out the rest as it goes along."

"You will," I said quietly. "I know you will."

"I get it, Kate. It's what I think you've been trying to get me to figure out myself."

"What's that?"

"I don't have to worry about trusting others. I just have to trust myself. To trust that I'll do the right thing."

"And if you make a mistake along the way?"

"No one is perfect," she said and buried her face in her hands again.

"What's going on?"

"It's just . . . It's just that I know the answers. Everyone knows these clichés. I just have to do my best. Get it. But everything is such a disaster in every direction." She stared back from the screen, tears of anger trembling on her lashes but refusing to fall.

"You're doing an excellent job in a miserable situation, Anne. When you're ready, the career counselor will help you make job choices. Okay?" Digging up her past that had led her to make poor decisions would have to wait until the next time.

"How do you do it?" She gripped one of her hands with the other.

"What?"

"Hold on every day," she said quietly and broke our shared gaze.

"What do you mean?"

"I overheard the assistant director talking about you. What happened last year to your daughter?" She broke eye contact.

"Anne?" Blackness edged my vision.

"Yes?"

"Remember how you said no one was perfect?" Oh, the cloying sweetness of that cliché. How I hated it.

"Yes."

"Well," I examined the keyboard and brushed a crumb off it, "I'm the poster child for showing you that a degree or two or a bookcase of knowledge does not preempt mistakes."

"But it wasn't your mistake. They said it was—"

"Anne," I cut her off. "I'm here to help you not vice versa. Focusing on others is what got you into this situation. Not that that is a bad thing all the time. It's just that there must be balance. Our time together is for your needs, not mine, got it?"

"But how do you cope? Do you focus on what makes you happy?"

I watched my hand hovering over the red *end call* button. How I wished I could press it. Two minutes to go. "Eleanor Roosevelt once said, 'Sometimes you must do what you think you cannot do.' She was right. Don't you agree? Um, we've only a few more moments." *Thank God.*

The rough staccato of a *mobylette* making its way up the cliff road rushed to fill the silence. Anne's image appeared frozen on the screen until she pushed her hair behind one ear.

"I'm sorry I brought anything up. I would never want to make you feel bad," she said quietly. "You've done so much for me."

"Anne," I replied. "It's completely fine. No need to worry. Really. Shall we Skype again next week? Same time?"

A moment later she nodded and I mouthed a few more pleasantries before I escaped.

Walking to the window, I relatched one of the shutters, which was dangling from its rusted hinges outside. The rust had wept onto the stone walls, leaving tear stains of age and neglect under the veil of ivy. I doubted the hinges would survive another season of salt and storms. Closing my eyes, I breathed deep and then opened my eyes and exhaled all thoughts of sadness. It was a trick I'd learned in the worst of it last year.

The ancient spinster who lived next door, Mlle Lefebvre, was walking slowly up the road, a baguette peeking out of her basket. She was thin, still perpetually all in black, and her gait was sure but uneven, as if one leg was shorter than the other. Her massive marmalade cat, tail twitching, sat next to the black iron gates watching her mistress ascend.

I remembered Mlle Lefebvre from my youth. She'd been old then, and looked remarkably the same all these years later. Those baguettes clearly had antiaging properties in them. A swarm of German bicyclists appeared from around the bend and shouted out *guten Morgen* as they passed. She ignored them, merely shaking her head. I wondered if she and Jean were speaking to each other or at daggers drawn. There had never been any gray area between them. Love or hate, that's how they operated. The French had a loathing for anything approaching friendship between the sexes. She'd been a lawyer at some point, probably when surfboards were made out of wood and gentile women did not go out and earn a wage.

My grandfather had never been so uncouth as to earn a single French euro or franc, old or new, unless it was at Le Casino or in a golf competition. He'd merely accomplished what his male ancestors had done before him: excelling at a gentleman's sport, as well as partying, gambling, drinking, and laughing— except during World War II, when he'd done his duty, but then he went right back to the good life. And my never-seen, mysterious grandmother? Why, she'd divorced him after two children and three years of marriage. Sophie du Roque had arranged an annulment and run off to South America with a railroad baron, avoiding the war altogether.

Two additional wives buried, one neighbor his on again off again mistress, my grandfather was still playing cards, drinking, and reminiscing. Was there any wonder my family was as dysfunctional and unpredictable as the bell in the church?

I yawned, nearly dislocating my jaw. There was something about the air here that was finally making me remember how delicious sleep could be. Slumber had become my foe the last two years. You never know how precious sleep is until you can't succumb to it; and this was always learned at a point when you most needed it.

The bed in Connecticut had become a thing to fear. It had become my private hell six hours a night or much less. Even after I'd ripped off the canopy—an ugly, dusty floral thing that had witnessed seventeen years of marital loneliness—I still hadn't been able to easily fall off the precipice of consciousness. When I finally had, any chance of peace was immediately doused by the barrage of nightmares on the other side of reality. Sadly, my memory never failed in the morning.

I walked to the tiny, sagging bed more suited for a child and smoothed the matelassé. Perhaps just a little snooze before a late breakfast. Perhaps just a—

A knock on the door and Magdali peered inside.

"Yes?"

"The person sent from the *agence*—the new man? He just left."

I couldn't comprehend.

"He quit. I think he knew your grandfather was about to fire him anyway."

"For?"

"Something about *son toilette*. His morning ritual. Said his bath was always too hot or too cold, that he wheeled the chair too quickly, that the man did not earn his wage. And . . ."

"And?"

Magdali hid a smile well. "Your grandfather kept telling him that he dressed like a peasant and smelled like a . . . a—what is the word for *pute*?"

"Whore," I replied. "Or gigolo in this case."

So much for a few hours of sleep. "Let's hope Mr. Soames finds us someone soon. Is Grandfather dressed? Had breakfast?"

His voice boomed up the staircase, demanding something so muffled I couldn't make it out.

"*Oui*," she replied.

I grabbed a sweater off the cracked veneer of the bureau and pulled it over my head. "Okay. Would you mind making a tea tray? This might be—oh, who is kidding anyone? The conversation is going to be painful."

"Bien sûr," she said. "Of course."

I headed to the door but paused. "Magdali, you know him far better than I do. How am I going to get him to sell? What will motivate him?"

The surface of Magdali's dark skin was coated with the soft sunlight of early morning. Her eyes sought out mine. "That's not what is important."

I dragged a brush through my hair. "Really? Then what is?"

"He's not going to live forever."

I just didn't know what to say.

"You have to try, Kate."

"Try? Try? You want me to try? What exactly?"

"To love him." I opened my mouth, but she continued softly, "My mother always said, where there is love there is no darkness. And there is hope." Her solemn expression shadowed the tribal wisdom of her words.

I carefully placed the brush on the bureau and turned to her. "You of all people know his character. The same character of this entire family. We don't stand up for each other or for the truth. We're poor judges of character, and most of us are just plain weak. At least I'm willing to own up to it. Darkness? The entire living du Roque family and their ancestors are the personification of darkness. I figured that out the last time I was here. And you know it too. I'm leaving as soon as humanly possible."

"Then why are you here? Why not just let nature take its

course—the house falls apart, or your grandfather dies, and your uncle sells. We all manage to scrape by. So why did you come?"

"I don't know why I agreed." There it was. The truth. "I don't know why I do anything anymore."

"Since when?"

"Since the day I found Lily after she ran away, and she would only agree to return with me if I sent her to boarding school instead of living with me."

"Kate," Magdali said quietly, "why?"

"Why did she want to get away from me? Because I failed her. Because, *au fond*, deep down, I'm a du Roque. As much as I'm loath to admit it and as much as I've tried to distance myself from anything and everything associated with this family."

"What happened?"

"That is the question," I said evasively. "But right now, I must talk to Jean, as we both know."

Age-old hurt swirled in her sage eyes. "You don't have to tell me."

"Good," I replied. "Because there's nothing that can be done." I walked past her, and descended the staircase.

Jean was seated in the lumpy sofa in the front salon, fumbling with the ancient television's remote control. He looked up at me, his faded blue eyes hard with suspicion. "Don't look at me like that."

I crossed the floor and sat in a massive armchair opposite him.

"I'm not leaving. And I'm not selling." He mumbled something else into his faded yellow handkerchief.

"All right," I replied. "And what will you live on?"

"That's not your affair. Not your concern."

"I agree. So whose concern is it?"

"Mine."

The blue sky beyond the French doors seemed far too pure and filled with happy promise compared to the scene in here.

"And what about Magdali? Who will take care of her? And who will pay her daughter's boarding school next year?"

"Your mother. She promised. Even if she refused to spend *un sou* on Madeleine Marie. But Magdali . . ." He said her name with an unmistakable hint of sadness. "She will have to find another employer, I've supported her long enough."

"Your loyalty is unparalleled."

"It is," he said quickly. In a rare effort, he hobbled to his feet, waving away my efforts to help him. Step by step, with his cane wobbling, he made his way to the window to stare out.

"And if she leaves, who will take care of you?"

"I told you, it's not your concern."

"I hope you're not counting on my uncle."

He turned to look at me, his face shaded by the halo of sun behind him. "Of course I am. He is my heir as is your mother. You still don't understand the beauty of our system here, do you? Americans think independence is king. It's not. Family is all. We might hurt each other, but we take care of one another. You know nothing about that."

I swallowed the bile in the back of my throat. *Do not rise to the bait. Do not* . . . "All right," I said, "and after Jean-Michel sells all the paintings, followed by the silver, and any antiques of value, what then?"

"Then I shall be long dead, I am sure."

"And then?"

"I will have done my duty. I will have raised my family, served my country, had my share of pleasure and pain like everyone else, and I will have preserved the family legacy and passed it to the next generation."

"And will Jean-Michel do the same?"

"That is his concern. And Antoinette's."

"Not yours?"

"Not mine."

"I see," I said, not seeing at all. "And if Jean-Michel found a way to keep Madeleine Marie and not sell it like every person has hinted to me since I arrived, who would he leave it to?"

"Why, to you, of course."

I was not often at a loss for words.

"Unless, of course, he marries again and finally has a child. But I would not count on it."

"Jean . . . As much as I wish I could let you continue to believe in this lovely fairy tale, we can't afford it. Your son will sell Madeleine Marie the minute he can, and Antoinette will be relieved."

"Don't be so sure of that," he murmured. "Every heir has thought about selling at some point. But we never do, and we never will."

I forced myself to breathe deeply several times. "Well, I will promise you this, as much as I wish I could protect you from the truth, if Jean-Michel and Antoinette manage to hold on to it and pass it to me, we will be lucky if Madeleine Marie isn't blown up by Basque terrorists since, according to some, they're convinced I'd sell it to a rich foreigner. The Basques in the region would never let that happen. And that's the nice version of this villa's future."

I had to give him credit, my grandfather didn't argue with my vision of the future.

"Go on all you like," he said, wiping his nose with a tissue, "you would never sell it."

I shook my head, which was as thick as Jean's. "I made an appointment with Sotheby's and they're coming on Tuesday to give us an estimate. You can either be involved or not." So much for trying to love him. Maybe I could get him to hate me as much as I hated myself. At least it would be a feeling. Any emotion was better than none. And what better place to start than with anger? That whirling, churning molten lava in the mind where all things are rendered charred and broken, and something new is born. Some say anger is the truest emotion we possess. I've never seen it lead to anything good, but there was still time to dabble in the dark arts.

Jean du Roque turned his visage back to the window, revealing that beak of a nose all du Roques possessed—even the Americanized ones. Resignation—the grayest of states— flooded him, and his shoulders drooped.

Chapter Five

Whispers from the Garden . . .

Sometimes one had to eat one's vegetables instead of the earthy velvet of Mr. and Mrs. Slug. Sadly, spring grass was on the menu today. Then again, it's what one got when one overindulged. It had been such a delightfully fruitful period the last dozen moonrises. The sun had shone, the moon had waxed to its fullest before slowly melting into its backbone.

And I was blissfully alone. I'd forgotten how lovely solitude was.

I was even learning to bear the cycle of the Wing Beaters, who, aside from their blasted morning revelry, settled to groom their feathers in the gnarled branches of the plane trees during the heat of the day. It had been a Season of the Slug like no other. Gleaming little tidbits had awaited me every night under the tender calla lily leaves. Yes, it was paradise.

I keep trying to hold on to memories of before I came here, but they have become so gray and small and sometimes curl into the air and float away. The only thing I remember with clear-cut precision is that orange Yowler. Or rather her scent.

It was hard to say if that was a good thing or a bad thing. I had no desire to see her, but heaven above, how I liked her interesting perfume. Self-anointing only lasted so long. Have you never experienced the confusion of involuntary behavior? No? I have it every time some scent overtakes the boundaries of my brain. I loathe dealing with anything or anyone. We are alone all our lives, so why become embroiled with anyone or anything else . . . unless it involves Master Slug, our inborn duty to instill our history on others, or the whimsical, destructive little nasal obsessions known only to my family. No one is perfect, right?

Turning over a dry iris stalk, I spied none of the telltale trail of holes of my favorite breakfast, elevenses, lunch, and dinner. It was ridiculous. The sky was brightening and, Lordy, a respite in the shade of the slate hidden beyond the scarlet bougainvillea seemed delicious. I gnawed on a few strands of grass and felt very sorry for myself. Well, at least I could stop worrying about my girth getting in the way of my drawstring in the event of an attack from the Barkers next—

Dear Lord. That perfume swirled about, leaving me dizzy and nauseous. Turning too quickly, my head felt like it was still spinning when I saw that orange swath of velvet padding toward me. Dropping down on her haunches a few feet from me, her diamond eyes narrowed, and those whiskers twitched in a rhythm completely at odds with her tail.

"Y-hello," she said, unfurling her tongue to lick her neck in a leisurely fashion.

Transfixed; my drawstring flickered and failed to deploy.

"Can't you speak? I thought you more intelligent. At least above an insect," she continued, not looking at me.

"I-I . . . of course I can speak," I replied. "What's an insect?"

She ate a blade of grass or three. "How can you not know what an insect is?"

I stood my ground.

"Very well. It's anything with six legs and usually four wings. You know what legs and wings are, don't you?"

"I'm not an idiot."

"Well, then how can you not know what an insect is?" She sniffed the ground and then made a most impolite yakking noise. "You do know what I am, right?"

"A Yowler," I answered instantaneously.

"Mon Dieu," she said. "Do you know what you are?"

"I'm me, of course."

"No. Your breed. Your pedigree. Your station in life. Your raison d'être. It's very important to know these things. How can you not know these things?"

A peculiar feeling washed over me. Something dark and discomforting lurked in the gap between what I knew and what I ought to know. I dug in my thin, little heels. "I'm me and you're you and that's all that's important."

"Hmmm . . ." she purred. "Okay. But I'm a cat. And I'm a very rare type. You're a hedgehog, or hérisson *in French. I'm trilingual. Fluent in Animalese, French, and English. Again, very rare. I have an enormous IQ."*

Hedgehog. *It sounded so familiar. I didn't want to be anything but me though. And who in hell knew what an IQ was? "What's your IQ?"*

"My pet, who is merely fluent in French and English, keeps telling me I have an IQ of a moron. And everyone knows morons are brilliant."

Whatever a moron was, I didn't trust it. I don't trust anything anyway. Except an unusual scent. I trusted that 150 percent. I took a step closer and sniffed the air as inconspicuously as possible. I was beginning to feel that burning sensation on my tongue and the uncontrollable desire to salivate and self-anoint took over.

"What are you doing?" Her diamond eyes flipped wide.

I spread a few more drops of drool over my quills. "Don't you know anything about hedgehogs? I thought you said you were a moron."

"Well, I've only ever seen one other hedgehog. Twenty-seven moons ago. Dead as dead in the garden on the other side. Reeked of dog slobber. The ones next door. Those Boxers have champion pedigree lines dating back to the beginning. Although privately, I see zero IQ in them. All bark, all bite, and no brain. I am, by the way, a ginger tabby. Very rare, you see,

since almost all ginger tabbies are male. In addition, I have a distinct mackerel pattern inherited from a wild *ancestor. I am* sauvage. *Very brave. Very wild. Very rare. Important."*

The way she licked her privates looked fairly pedestrian to me. "I see." I wanted to trundle away. I really did. My head hurt. All that jabbering about IQ and naming things that didn't need names. And all that scent. I retreated to the only topic that was not only safe anywhere and everywhere but also a requirement. "So, what is the history of this place? I've come from across the water."

"Fascccinating," she replied, with a little purring sound. "Then we will have much to discuss." She took three steps closer and again settled her haunches on the ground while gathering her memories. "All was good before the Bonjours took over the earth as all creatures know, great and small—"

"Who are the Bonjours?"

"You're not going to interrupt me are you? Very impolite. Is that a hedgehog trait?"

"Forgive me." I did know the rules regarding imparting history, which required a singsong poetic retelling of our ancestors' experience followed by a more relaxed recounting of the recent past. It was just her aroma that was throwing me off my game.

"The Bonjours are the tall ones, who all look alike. They cover their bodies with lots of different things so they can tell each other apart."

"Right. The Two-Leggeds, that's what hedgehogs call them. Roger."

"*I'll continue.*" She sighed, exasperated. "*All was good before the Bonjours took over the earth. Mice, moles, fish, and fowl were plentiful*"—she crinkled her nose as if deciding if she should explain the species—"*just as foe were plentiful too. Then we made a damned deal with the Bonjours, who gave some of us shelter and food in exchange for our families and freedom. It was a bad bargain. Yes?*"

"*Yes,*" I encouraged. So far it was the same here as over there.

"*Many wars came and went and nothing good came of them other than culling the herd of Bonjours, who caused disease wherever they went.*"

"*Ditto on the land I came from across the water.*" Now was when it would get interesting, I was sure.

"*In the last war here, the Fifty-Two Moons War, there was great destruction. Many creatures big and small were killed. Many Bonjour-made structures were damaged. But many helmeted Guten Tags with Shepards, who were worse than those Boxers, left behind solidly built structures. Those empty, secret places are great hiding places if one needs them. In fact*"—she licked her paw and polished her face—"*there is an enormous one under this house, although you must go over the cliff, and swing behind the hanging vines to find it.*"

"*Good to know. Thank you,*" I replied.

She looked at my little hands and feet and sniffed. "*I wouldn't try it if I were you.*"

"*Any other local history I should know?*"

"*No.*" She groomed her long nose with her paw again,

expertly navigating her long whiskers. "But, the Bonjours have many customs."

"Do tell."

"They like to play where the fish live. A lot. Especially with boards. Bizarre if you ask me. And they take hours to eat and drink in large groups, and sometimes stumble and fall afterward. Their music is terrifyingly bad; they regularly have something called fetes and parades in the village. But they redeem themselves at the Festival of the Sardine. You know what a sardine is, don't you?"

I said nothing.

"A fish. The best fish in the world. Salty, small, perfect in every way. Cats love them as much as the Bonjours love something called foie gras. Don't ask what that is because it will make you cry."

"All right," I replied, "but do they have a Festival of the Slug?" I could barely breathe for hoping. "Or even a Festival of the Snail?" Close enough.

"Mon Dieu, non. Who would like that?"

Again I said nothing.

"Oh, I see," she said softening. "Is that the way of it for you?" She continued without waiting for an answer. "Well, then. Perhaps I should invite you to dine tonight chez moi *after the sun dips. My pet maintains a lovely garden filled with them. And, in fact, I loathe stepping on them and would appreciate you culling the slimy herd."*

"I would be delighted," I said far too quickly. What had come over me? I never spent time with anyone. It just wasn't

natural. I liked being alone. It's the only thing I do extremely well.

"But a caution."

"Do tell."

"In the middle of the night, my pet sometimes meets the old Bonjour living here in the *allée* hidden behind the stone potting shed."

"Allée?"

Her whiskers flickered. "Alley." She looked a bit annoyed. "If you're going to stay here then you should learn French. That is if you want to become a moron."

This obsession with morons and IQs was making me feel very small and very uncomfortable. Then again, at least she wasn't trying to eat me. And in the animal world this was excellent at promoting good fellowship, something mother had never taught in any of her lullabies.

Chapter Six

Every afternoon, the chaos of the acres and acres of gardens surrounding the villa beckoned me. It was a far different place than what I remembered from my childhood. Then, the borders had been manicured, the pea gravel pathways raked, and sharply trimmed boxwoods had framed each flower bed. Now not one gardener in the region was willing to set a trowel here given the legendary nature of Jean's ability to hire but not pay. And since the account at Bank of Kate was in the four digits, and requests to Antoinette, otherwise known as the wildly fun and fickle, yet financially savvy person I called Mother, had been met with a silence as thick as the weeds choking the flowers, I began cleaning up section by section of the enormous garden my mother's almost namesake, Marie Antoinette, would have loved, given the number of low, geometric patterned boxwoods on long terraces—very like those found at Versailles. At least there were very few slugs and snails here now, unlike my teenage years when they'd reigned supreme under every stalk.

Just before the gloaming hours, when memories gathered to wuther the mind, and blame and shame hid tricks in every corner, vulnerability—that lead player in the game—battled assumptions and the what-ifs until a small madness began to swirl in the breeding grounds of my mind. I knew why. It was so obvious. I'd reached the armies of lilies growing helter-skelter in their beds. Early bloomers, late bloomers, every shape and every color invaded the senses. And as the soft, sun-warmed fragrance of the calla lilies—her favorite—enveloped me, a gale of guilt flooded the bloodstream and fear was born.

Would my daughter ever come back to me? Should I want that for her? I blindly groped for something solid to grab onto to stop my mind from being swept away like the leaves swirling in a vortex in the wind. I reached out and gripped the peeling and spotted trunk of a plane tree, and it felt ancient and solid as I stood up.

I missed her with a vengeance bordering on selfishness. It had been too long since I'd seen Lily, and the repeated playing of her old voicemail messages has grown stale and artificial just like the memory of the house in Darien, Connecticut, where she and I had endured the good, the bad, and the ugly in the cavernous, soulless McMansion that was currently listed for sale now that a decorator had finished staging it.

But Lily and I had made a deal. I was not to reach out to her. My duty was banishment to the sidelines of her ruined life. And my punishment was reliving it.

My gaze traveled to the back, less-grand entrance of the ivy-covered villa, and I arched against strained muscles, forcing thoughts of my daughter back into the distant chamber of my mind. Madeleine Marie was like a grande dame, by turns beautiful in her aristocratic old bones and bearing, yet bankrupt from decades of hard living and little thought to the future. She oversaw the haunting beauty of the Bay of Biscay, the cradle and boat of Basque civilization, and the gathering place for what seemed to be a surf-loving league of nations.

She was my temporary holding cell.

Inside, the peeling, gilded wallpaper, leaky plumbing, unreliable electricity, and perpetual scent of mildew were daily reminders of the impermanence of life itself. Loneliness, whose icy fingers burrow into the crevasses of solitude, had taken up residence in this relic, and it seemed the very walls echoed whispers from my ancestors—some gay and some forlorn—but all telling me I didn't belong here.

I didn't belong anywhere, really.

Giving up on the sprawling gardens, I leaned the much battered iron tined rake against a stone potting shed, and forced myself to follow the newfound routine I'd suggested to countless clients: exercise. There was just time for a walk to the sea to swim before dinner.

I darted up the four flights of the spiral staircase that resembled a lady's ringlet of more than a century ago to don a slightly mildewed shorty wetsuit. On the descent, one could spy small brass openings for letters on the wooden wall panels of each landing, dusty from disuse. For centuries, ancestors had dashed off notes and letters, slipped them in the mail shoot to be collected and delivered by liveried servants and horse-drawn post carriages. These remnants would all be gone soon.

Tomorrow the listing agent from Sotheby's was coming, and at the end of the week was an appointment to check out a retirement residence with spacious apartments and a host of activities. Viewing a few small rental cottages dotting the region was also on the agenda.

The shortcut over the cliff to the beach was steep, rocky, and required negotiation with a very long knotted rope near the end. Carrying flippers and a towel didn't help. I rarely won the negotiation and had the skinned knees and elbows to prove it. The only people who used this route were impatient surfers, adventurous adolescents, and, apparently, foolhardy American divorcées. The only good thing about the descent was that it took twenty-two minutes instead of thirty-seven minutes by cliff road to reach sea level. I'd timed it in the era of counting bells. The ascent was another experience altogether, and brought new meaning to the words crazy impossible. I wasn't sure what had come over me in the last few weeks, but I felt like an ugly stubbornness was taking root each day I failed the hand-over-fist routine on the return trip. Or maybe it was just anger. I'd lost all ability to untangle the rare emotions I let out of the cubicles in my head.

This late afternoon, as the sun leisurely slid across a still, azure sky toward the sea, I spied Major Soames clad in trunks and a long-sleeved plaid shirt on a course that would eventually migrate to my path. Convenient. The guy had been as scarce as sleep in a maternity ward.

He fell onto the path two dozen steps behind me. I stopped and turned to wait for him.

"Madame," he said, touching his fingers to his head in a mock salute.

"Major."

He motioned to the path ahead with a sweep of his hand. The hard look in his eyes proved he wanted as little conversation as possible. And if it were not for the kindness of Jean's best friend, I would be happy to oblige.

"Going for a swim?" I finally managed.

"That's the idea," he replied.

"Better than tea and biscuits," I said.

"Indeed."

"How is your uncle?" Man, this guy was closed off.

"Well."

I retrieved a flipper that had slipped from under my arm. "And your family in the UK?"

"Well, too."

We trudged on again in silence a few moments, until I turned around to face him. "Is there something I've said or done that has offended you, major?"

"I don't know what you're talking about," he retorted. "We've barely spoken ten words to each other."

I pursed my lips, but could not hold back the laughter. "True. And whose fault is that?"

"Mine." Not a muscle twitched in his face.

"You know, just because your uncle wants you to talk to me doesn't mean we can't. We're not in kindergarten."

He shaded his brow with his hand. "I don't know. That looks like a fine sandbox down there."

I gazed toward the beach far below and refused to laugh. "Do you always change the subject when confronted? Do you ever let anyone in?"

"Do you always dive into personal questions the moment you meet someone?"

I finally laughed. "Force of habit, I guess. Comes with the job." I waited for a smile but none was forthcoming. "I apologize."

"Accepted."

And then not another word. I refused to push it. The man either wanted to talk, or didn't. I'd done what his relative had asked. Fifteen minutes of silently zigzagging the steep cliff brought us to the rope.

"I'll go down first," he said.

I hung my towel around my neck and was about to sling the ankle straps of the two flippers over my wrist when he grasped them and tossed them down the jagged cliff face. "Okay," I said, dragging out the word. "That's one way to do it."

"The only way," he replied, not looking at me.

He shimmied down the knots as expertly as testosterone mixed with military prowess demanded. And I? Well, as an adolescent, I'd always failed that rope climbing test in gym class.

"Toss me the towel."

"So demanding." It appeared that trying to engage emotionally damaged people was encoded in my DNA. Impossible to avoid. "I'm perfectly able to do this by myself, you know."

"Suit yourself," he said and strode off toward the final stone wall below.

He was already past the breakers and even the paddleboarders when I reached the beach. Struggling with the flippers in waist deep water, the pull of the current knocked me into the next wave and the icy salt water worked its way into the gaps of the wetsuit. I set out to swim to the rock formation I'd always called Mini-Belza, as it rose from the sea across from the Villa Belza.

He was lying on the rock face when, breathless, I struggled to pull myself onto the ledge, which was just a little too high for my underused biceps. "Um," I said. "Could you give me a hand?"

Wordlessly, he reached over, yanked me out of the water, and returned to lie down, his arm thrown over his face.

What person didn't rub your nose in such obvious triumph? He was a man who just didn't give a damn. I was always amazed and a little envious of people who could do that.

I sat dripping on the ocean-pounded smooth rock, arms resting on raised knees as I caught my breath. Looking toward the shore, the backs of the waves undulated and passed under the paddleboarders standing on their boards before moving toward the long and then short boarders all vying for ownership of each wave.

I glanced back at Soames and a sort of eerie calm settled in. I didn't want to help him. That should have scared me but it didn't. I was tired of helping everyone. Tired of rolling out the empathy carpet for people to trample and stain. I'd never been all that good at it in the end. Indeed, I'd failed with the most important person in my life. And all those clients? All those articles? All those awards? Meaningless in the grand scheme.

I awkwardly stood a few minutes later, readjusted the flippers, and dove back into the sea, swimming a long distance underwater before breaking to the surface and catching a wave to the shore.

I was just annoyed enough to decide on the shorter route. And smart enough to find a hiding place for the flippers before grabbing the rope. My hands were rough from trying this almost every day. Hands tight on the rope, I stepped onto the rock face and leaned back to walk perpendicular to the wall. What should have taken fifteen minutes for anyone with any type of arm strength took me twice as long. About the only thing I was becoming proficient in was swearing. Profusely. In English, and bastardized French.

At the top, sweaty and grimy, I fumbled and yanked the wetsuit's long zip strap and peeled down the top half as I noticed Edward Soames, arms crossed, looking up at me from the bottom of the palisade. Of course, he shimmied up the rope in a quarter of the time.

I refused to say a word.

"Well, then," he said, hoisting himself to the top.

"Indeed," I replied.

It only took a few more seconds of awkward silence before he spoke. "Look, I apologize for my rudeness."

Shocker of the century.

"We both know my great-uncle couldn't care less if we became friends. He wants you to fix me. Take my head apart, turn my brain inside out, and return it to its original shape. And, frankly, I'm not interested."

"Got it," I said, standing completely still and locked on his face.

"And besides, you—" He stopped and his hands fisted.

"Besides what?"

"Nothing."

"Look, Ed," I said. "I can call you that, right?" I knew it would annoy him. Push him.

"No."

"Okay, Edward," I continued. "You're right. We're not going to become friends. So you have nothing to lose. You can say anything you want to me in guaranteed confidence and it won't affect me. Remember, I'm a shrink. I'll just analyze anything you say, blame it on mom and dad and how you were raised, and perhaps you'll find a different way forward."

He searched my face and, for a splinter of a second, wistfulness or something tired crossed his features. Then again, he could just be hot and wanting to go coax a tepid shower from clanging French plumbing.

"What were you going to say?" I demanded. "Something . . . 'and besides, you . . .' What?"

His blue eyes looked gray in the half-light. "All right. You want the truth? Unvarnished. I don't think you've got all your ducks in a row. So how can you help anyone? Yeah, it's harsh, but there it is."

I felt the blood rush from my head.

"What? You thought you could hide it? Well, maybe you can hide it from others, Mrs. Hamilton, but you can't hide darkness from someone like me."

"Really? And just who are you, Major Soames?"

"We were talking about you."

"Okay. What do you want to know?"

"All right. I'll bite. What happened to you?"

"I'm sorry?"

"Oh, I know it's something ugly. Just go ahead. Out with it."

"And you just expect me to just spit something out to you?"

"Yes."

"Okay. But only if you admit something about yourself in return."

He almost snorted as he shook his head. "Do we really need to descend to juvenile tit for tat?"

"Yup," I replied. "Quite simply." And I stuck out my grimy, calloused hand.

One side of his mouth raised a quarter inch and he gave my hand one brief shake as he focused his eyes there.

I looked at the panorama of the Bay of Biscay beyond him and wondered how little I could get away with. "So, okay. I used to have a different kind of life than the one I have now. It wasn't a great life, but it was something I knew, something I managed well. And I thought I knew what I was doing. I thought I had it all figured out. I'm a planner. And I thought I could protect the only good thing while I waited for the time I would be able to change the situation," I rushed on. "And then one day, that one good part? The one and only good thing? It was destroyed. Or almost destroyed." I paused to swallow. "I was so sure I knew what I was doing, and I am living, breathing proof that I don't know a damned thing."

"Why?"

Why wasn't he asking me who? "I should have known better. I do know better. I see it every damned day. I'm a fucking psychologist."

A bead of sweat formed a droplet and slid down the side of his face. "Sounds like you're a pretty fucking bad psychologist to me," he said.

A paroxysm of laughter nearly choked me and suddenly I felt lighter. As if I'd lost ten pounds in the space of an instant. I looked down and that jiggle of belly was still there. Sadly.

"Yep. Sounds like you need a refresher course. I think they have those at Oxford. I'd look into it if I were you." The not-so-innocent concern in his expression was marred by a slight smile.

I would not let him off the hook. "Your turn."

"For what?"

"You know exactly what. Tell me what happened to you."

He shook his head. "You don't really think that half-arsed, vague story of yours qualifies you to demand something from me, do you?"

"I do," I retorted. "And you do too."

"Really?"

"Really," I replied. "In fact, you want to tell me."

"You're pushing it, Mrs. Hamilton. Why do Americans always feel the need to force everything? It's a very unattractive quality."

"Kate."

"Kate."

"Is this how you are with your family? With anyone close to you? What are you so afraid of?" I looked at him and waited. I'd wait until the appearance of the mythical *rayon vert*, that flash of green light signaling the sun's retreat on the horizon, before I'd say another word to let him squirrel out of an answer via his British armor of wit, thicker than a Hummer on steroids.

"I understand there is some sort of littoral one can hike along the coast," he said finally. "Do you know it?"

I refused to answer.

"All right, I'll mull it over," he said quietly. "And I'll collect you at zero-six-thirty hours next Tuesday if you'd like to hike a bit. Agreed?"

That was as much of a concession as I was going to get. "Think it over all you like, major. I'm not the one with a family waiting for me to get it together. Wait too long and you'll be just like me." I turned back toward Madeleine Marie and began walking, not waiting for his answer. "See you early Tuesday."

It was a gamble and it took a bit of time for his words to float to me. "Zero six thirty. Sharp."

Well, at least he presented a challenge. It had been a long time since I'd wrangled with an animal of that caliber. He'd so easily manipulated me into doing what he wanted. Gotten me to drop my facade for a few seconds and reveal something personal. Totally unprofessional on every level. Yes, I'd bet my mildewed, rotting wetsuit that it would be a fight to the bitter end to get him to show me an inch of his true self. I had no idea what was inside that shell. Was it an innocent, pure thing losing a war against something dark and fetid and growing? Or just the opposite—something hard, and manipulative, without feeling at its core combined with a practiced facade that rarely, if ever, slipped? And for the first time, I wondered if the only good thing that would ever come from my recent hideous past was a greater understanding of the night inside a person's soul. But facing my festering doubts? Those thoughts that bounced from shame to existential ambivalence in a circle of never-ending pathos? Yeah. It was just too late for a pity party and too early to fade away like the end credits of a movie.

I felt a shadow fall onto my back as I put the key into the heavy ornate door's keyhole to the home of a hundred ancestors' ghosts. The shadow moved over the intricate lace of black wrought iron delicately protecting the two glass panels embedded in the door. I turned. Storm clouds mushroomed over the Pyrenees. There was a hell of a storm stampeding across the vast expanse of sky. Would the villa withstand just a few more of these Atlantic beasts before I could palm off this magnificent, monstrous pile to someone else? And were the ghosts here with me or against me?

I was losing it, clearly, and I was not sure I could blame it on this crazy Gallic atmosphere. Next door, the two boxers' guttural snarls segued to insane barking as an ancient VW bus rattled by, loaded down with a dozen surfboards. The Stones' "Miss You" was drowned out by the atrocious accents of the French surfers singing along. Behind them, a brand-new Bentley glided by, driven by a middle-aged man with slick black hair, Ray-Bans, and a cell phone glued to his ear. The now familiar hoard of German cyclists followed, all cursing as the first raindrops sprayed down like machine-gun fire.

I dashed inside to safety.

A flash of lightning illuminated the long hall before the first boom of thunder shook the villa.

Chapter Seven

*P*ounding. Pounding. Someone—no, Oliver—was pounding his feet as he ran down the long second-floor hallway and down the stairs. He was chasing Lily. Out the door. Up the endless driveway bordered with pink dogwood. And my feet were cemented to the kitchen floor, unable to run after her. Protect her. The pounding started again. Her feet were bare in the snow as she ran away, while her father—

I woke and sat straight up in bed to the echo of Madeleine Marie's brass door knocker striking its matching plate two stories down. Dazed, I clumsily felt for my charging iPhone. One o'clock. In the morning. What?

Outside, the storm bore down with Herculean force. Rain, sounding like gravel, sprayed the shutters. Maybe it was hail.

The pounding restarted. I grabbed the peignoir my grandfather had lent to me from his dead wife—likely the second one—as it featured an embroidered *R* for Rosemary on it.

Two bedraggled men, one tall, the other short and fat, leaned sideways against the gale force. Looking very much like two species of sodden mushrooms in their Basque berets, they tugged the tips in greeting. The smaller one bowed and a stream of rain poured off his beret.

"*Bonsoir, Mme Hamilton! Je suis la maire. Pardonnez-moi mais nous avons un petit problème.*"

The mayor had a little problem? At one in the morning? "*Entrez, messieurs.* It is freezing out there."

The taller one snatched off his sodden black felt beret, revealing a tonsured crown as he nodded a greeting. "Madame."

"*Oui?*"

"*Enchanté,*" he replied, looking not at all enchanted.

The mayor smiled and gripped my hand in a firm shake, looking pleased with himself for adopting an American greeting. "Mme Hamilton, delighted to make your acquaintance."

Water poured off their navy anoraks onto the black-and-white marble of the foyer's floor as they removed them in unison. For some bizarre reason they appeared completely at ease invading Madeleine Marie in the middle of the night.

The mayor continued, glancing at the white marble columns in the hall. "Such a lovely villa, madame. It's been many years since I've been inside."

"Is there something I can do for you, sir? Let me find a towel for you." I prepared to search for one but the mayor stopped me.

"No need! This is but a little sprinkling. Actually, I wanted to introduce you to my good friend, Pierrot Etcheterry. Your neighbor. I was most surprised you have not made each other's acquaintance."

I bit my tongue. "M. le Maire, pardon me for saying this but it is one o'clock in the morning. Can all of this wait until tomorrow?"

"Ah," he said, with a little shrug. "I fear it cannot. You see, here in France, neighbors help one another. Perhaps it is different in *les États-Unis*?"

I gave up, knowing they'd tell me when they were good and ready. "What can I do for you?" I looked at my neighbor.

"Beh, you have flooded my *cave*."

His basement? "I'm sorry. Your *cave*?"

"Yes. It is flooded."

"And how have I caused your basement to be flooded?"

The mayor stepped in. "Why, because of your *puits perdu*."

Lost something. Yes, *perdu* meant "lost." "*Puits*? I'm sorry, my French is not perfect."

The mayor shook his head with a sad expression. "Ah. Such a shame you did not learn French, madame. One can't live in France without speaking the most important language in the world." He actually said it with a straight face. "A *puits* is, ah, a well, I think."

"So I have caused M. Etcheterry's basement to flood because there is a lost well on our family's property? Where is this well?"

"Madame," the mayor said with pity, "it would not be a lost well if it was not lost, now would it?"

"If you were Basque," continued Pierrot Etcheterry, "you would know all about *la légende*. Many centuries ago there was a well, a source really, of the finest water in all of Gaulle. Someone would make a fortune if they could find it and bottle it, I assure you. But you are American, so of course, you do not know this."

Therapists have a saying: When locked in an insane asylum, pretend to understand the inmates. Sort of like "When in Rome . . ." I opened my mouth only to be interrupted by the Basque neighbor.

"Madame," he said, "I would show you my basement now."

I shivered. It had to be forty degrees Fahrenheit outside. "Now?" Another spray of pellets, or rather rain, hit the door and the wind howled. It was time to make a break from the asylum. "M. Etcheterry, while I appreciate the seriousness of your situation, I am not going to go out in the storm at one in the morning to inspect your flooded basement. I will take your word for it. Furthermore, unless you can demonstrate how a mysterious well on our property has been the cause, I can't imagine why you think our family is responsible."

The mayor opened his mouth but I continued.

"And, furthermore, your house is uphill to my villa—"

"Your grandfather's villa, madame," interrupted the mayor, his smile fading. "And one day your uncle's villa."

"It's the du Roque villa, monsieur. My mother is a du Roque and so am I," I said, and was unable to stop my stupid chin from rising in a distinctly Frenchified fashion.

"You are American," the Basque neighbor stated, brushing a few drops of water from a tightly knit gray turtleneck sweater that strained against the bulk of torso.

"And French," I retorted. "And that is beside the point."

"Indeed," said the mayor, rocking back on the heels of his magenta rubber boots, which matched his suspenders.

No American male I knew would have had the nerve to try and pull off that ensemble.

"So, are you here to sell Madeleine Marie or will the house stay in the family?" He fiddled with the black beret in his hands.

"As I was saying, your house is uphill to Madeleine Marie, and I've never ever heard of any lost well. It sounds like what you need is a sump pump."

"A what?" The neighbor stared at me and scratched the back of his head as he turned to the Napoleonic mayor. A brief conversation ensued, in Basque, and was therefore completely incomprehensible. Smiles broke over both men's faces.

The mayor actually showed some of his tobacco stained teeth. "Madame, I see we are on the right course. We count on you to find this pump and have it installed in Pierrot's basement. No later than tomorrow evening. Pierrot doesn't want the water to stand too long." He stuck out his hand. "In America you shake on agreement. Like zee cowboys."

I looked at the outstretched hand and did not grasp it. "Messieurs, do I look like a cowboy? Do you think Americans are fools? You may pretend to misunderstand me all you like, but I'm not going to buy a sump pump, or accept any responsibility—"

A knock interrupted my soapbox speech. What kind of hell was this place that visitors had the nerve to come over any time they wished?

Before I could reach the door, Magdali appeared from the shadowed bend in the staircase and opened it. There stood, or hunched, Mlle Lefebvre in a getup that would make an Alaskan crab fisherman from the reality show *The Deadliest Catch* proud.

In a voice dripping with Alaskan frost, she began, "Jojo Boudin, *qu'est-ce que tu fais là? Et Pierrot? Où est Mäite?*"

What were they doing here? Where was Pierrot's wife? All good questions. Anything to break up this happy gathering.

"Mlle Lefebvre," Jojo the mayor said sadly, "we were just welcoming M. du Roque's granddaughter."

I weighed the pros and cons of the possible alliances I could make. Not really. There was no choice. "How kind of you to come by Mlle Lefebvre. M. le Maire and Pierrot just stopped in with a basket of blueberry muffins to welcome me to the neighborhood." I might have used the French word for lingonberry instead of blueberry. But at least it got the desired response. Blank stares all around.

Mlle Lefebvre harrumphed. I didn't know that people could actually harrumph, as I've only read about it in a two-hundred-year-old story, but this old woman had it down pat. The corners of her mouth hung lower than a pug's.

"We've just finished the muffins," I said, staring down Laurel and Hardy. "They were just leaving."

"*Oui*," said the mayor echoed by Pierrot.

"Tell Maïte I shall visit her tomorrow." The older woman's eyes looked like two black pebbles. "She can tell me all about these muffins I am sure." She shook her head. "Beh, since we're all here, Pierrot, have you arranged for a plumber yet? Lyonnaise des Eaux informed me they require you to divert your rainwater and sewer water properly, like the rest of us. Unless, of course, you want your house to fall off the cliff and collect the insurance."

I squeezed my nails into the pads of my hands to keep from laughing. Life so rarely provided such instant karmic kickback, and all via the Lyonnaise water company.

Pierrot squinted. The mayor raised his eyebrows. There were more wrinkles revealed in those two faces than the day before a Botox convention. "Beh, Mlle Lefebvre, I am aggrieved you would ever suggest such a thing," Jojo said in his heavy accent. "And Mme Hamilton and I were just coming to an agreement about—"

"The joys of fellowship in the Pays Basque," I interrupted, "and his interest in the future of this villa." I paused. "For some odd reason."

"This villa is a national treasure, madame," the mayor insisted. "Of course we are concerned with the future of the villa. And it is collapsing before our eyes. Something must be done."

Mlle Lefebvre, a meager quarter inch taller than the mayor's Napoleonic frame wagged a finger at him. "Not by you. You leave her alone. And you leave Jean du Roque alone too. I remember when you were a boy, bullying all the other children on the street. Your parents might be gone, but I know all your secrets—except why you've got your nose in the du Roques' affairs. I'd wager you're here to measure the house for curtains.

But where you think you'll get the euros to buy this villa you call a national treasure is beyond me."

The mayor, for once, was speechless.

MAX MULRONEY'S THERAPY session and those of my other clients went just as scheduled and as expected that night. Max was in fight mode, duking it out to produce his massively budgeted film. It was wreaking havoc on his nerves. And mine as well.

"Hey, did'ja buy some of that Limerack stock, like I told you?"

"No, Max. You forget I'm stuck in the middle of nowhere and stock trading is the last thing on my mind. Now, let's talk about Heather, your yoga instructor," I replied. "How do you feel about—"

"I knew you wouldn't. We've got some kind of messed up relationship, Katie-girl," he said. "I do some of the things you suggest and yet you do nothing I suggest."

"That's because you're paying me for my expertise. I'm not paying you for anything, Max."

"But I'm giving you these tips for free and you're not even giving me a price cut," he whined.

"Okay, look, I-I'll . . ." What did Max love best? Max, of course. "I'll follow your financial advice when I return to the East Coast and adjust my fees if it is profitable."

"And when is that?" He leaned forward in his chair.

The Malibu beach backdrop behind him was everything gold and blue as the sunlight sparkled on the small murky waves. Why everyone thought California was the surfing Mecca was beyond me. "I'm not sure, Max. Maybe next month. Or possibly another six weeks."

"Maybe? I thought you were coming back sooner. Sounds like you're enjoying yourself." He winked.

"No." But I was. Sort of.

"Running away, then? Hey, know why divorces cost so damn much?"

I shook my head. He was impossible in a ridiculous, obnoxious, and funny way.

"Because they are worth it," he said. "Every damn penny. So live a little."

"Max." I sighed. "While I appreciate your concern, we both agreed you would stop changing the topic. Now, what—" Heather, the yoga teacher, walked in and Max cut short the session when she wrapped her arms around him and whispered something into his ear.

I could not stop myself from thinking about his statement as I got into bed. Seeing my clients brought all the ugliness back. Maybe Mad Max was right. Maybe I was running away from my life, just as my daughter had done not so long ago. It was clear I was not going to wrap up my grandfather's affairs in the six-week time frame I'd planned. And nothing in my world happened without a plan and a goal.

I awoke with none of the expected exhaustion. Missing two nights of sleep a week was becoming the new normal. In fact, it seemed to recalibrate a better sleep the next few days. It was either that or the heretofore undiscovered elixir of salt air, cursing at ropes, church bells, grueling hikes, and hot chocolate.

That morning I followed Magdali and the Sotheby's agent I'd asked for an appraisal, a Mr. Matthieu Smith, as he poked his head into every damp, mildewed corner of Madeleine Marie. We worked our way from the fourth-floor bedrooms, which had once housed hordes of du Roque children and an assortment of ancestors, all the way down to the lowest cave, where rows and rows of wine racks stood empty.

Cracks resembling dark bolts of lightning battled with watermarks for supremacy on the whitewashed stucco walls of every bedroom upstairs. The du Roque family members who had reigned supreme each generation had occupied the wallpapered third-floor bedrooms, in one of which my grandfather now snored. The bathrooms had fixtures that probably looked like those of the *Titanic* in its current resting place. Leaky, cold pipes overlaid white and gray tiles. About the only positive thing was that the bathrooms were palatial and the bathtubs deep. There were no showers. They were apparently too shockingly modern.

Mr. Smith poked and prodded the ceilings, floors, and pipes much like a doctor examining a geriatric patient. He shook his head. "This project is not for the fainthearted."

"Or for those with limited cash." What more could I say?

But the best was in the basement. Pale lichen had bloomed all over the former servants' quarters, appearing very like antique lace yellowed over the centuries. A few stray mushrooms had dared to invade the mildewed environs. Now vacant and cavernous, it was where I'd spent hours playing with Magdali, and where she and her mother had once lived.

"When did you move upstairs?" I whispered to her.

Magdali touched the edge of the only remaining piece of furniture in the main communal living space, a large wooden table scarred by years of hard use. "About fifteen years ago, when my mother died and your grandfather dismissed everyone but me."

I nodded and turned to the real estate agent. "*Alors?* So? What do you think?"

"Madame, it is a beautiful villa. Seventeenth century, I think?"

"I believe so."

"Plumbing and electrical installed likely in the late thirties but never updated. Both should be addressed. The iron on the outside of the house, shutter latches for example, and all grill-work is badly rusted and should be replaced with *inox*. You say, stainless steel, *non?* All rooms and exterior window frames and shutters should be repainted. Wallpaper should be replaced. And most importantly . . ."

"Yes?"

"The roof. I could see from the top-floor balcony that the orange roof tiles are cracked and failing. Plants are sprouting in the shaded, porous spots."

"I know."

It seemed that the banker and the agent and everyone else in the godforsaken place knew about the conditions of the villa. "How much?" Time to cut to the chase.

He raised his eyebrows and rubbed the tips of his fingers

together. "Bien, madame. I cannot begin to
tell you what I think the house will bring. If you
described, I feel confident that five million euros is
price."

That was more than I thought. Far more.

Magdali whispered, "Five million?"

"And if we sell 'as is'?"

"Ah, madame. That is considerably more difficult to say."

"Take a stab at it," I requested.

"Without reinforcing the cliff and the extensive roof damage, it is a gamble few would take."

"Why?"

"Life has changed and families with it, *malheureusement*." Unfortunately indeed. "There was a time when families were larger—extended family and grandparents and cousins all visited or lived in a villa such as this. But in today's world, most want a three- or four-bedroom house with modern kitchens and bathrooms. The clientele of Sotheby's International of course are more privileged"—read multimillionaire rich—"and so, of course, they want larger accommodations, vast gardens, and beautiful vistas, and are very willing to pay for it. But this? While it is magnificent, it is also a magnificent *mal à la tête*. Headache."

"You haven't told me what you think we could get if we sold it as is."

He wrinkled his nose. "One million? One million and a half? The price of the land. Maybe a bit more? If half of it doesn't fall off the cliff. Personally, I would act quickly. Very

imagine. I can only
refurbish all as
a reasonable

understand you are here for
d sell it as is. I have several

dly feeling crawled up my
ine. "Is one of them the

madame, I am not one
...re is a surfing company executive
...ve interest. He has been looking for a house overlooking Parlementia, which so many consider the finest surf
spot on the entire Côte des Basques."

"How would you propose to drum up interest? Start a bidding war, for example?" I couldn't stop myself. "What marketing do you do? Signage? Why are there no for sale signs in France?"

"Ah, madame, it is a bit . . . how do you say? *Gauche*?"

"It's gauche to show too much of a desire to sell a house for the best price?"

"Madame, selling a house is a bit like flirting with a woman. One mustn't be too eager."

"I see." I didn't see at all. Had he never heard of MLS, the Multiple Listing Service? "Magdali?"

"Yes?"

"What do you think?"

She shrugged. "My mother always said that to run is not necessarily to arrive."

I looked first at Magdali and then to the man from Sotheby's and back again. I was clearly a different species. Then again, I'd always been a different species no matter where I'd lived.

Magdali and I hurried the agent out before it was the hour Jean would emerge from his bedroom. We crossed paths at the door with the newest person on the du Roque mythical payroll, a man who would be my grandfather's dartboard for insults.

"*Désolé* to be *en retard*. Late," said a giant of a man. "I am Youssef Tousette. Mr. Soames sent me."

I shook his baseball-mitt-sized hand. "Very nice to meet you, Youssef. Please do not take anything my grandfather says personally."

His laugh was as wide and deep as his happy expression. Youssef certainly appeared physically capable for the job, and I could only hope that the huge white smile that lit up his dark face would still be there after meeting his recalcitrant charge.

"M. du Roque does not like excessive laughter," Magdali said. Her usual shy smile now hidden behind an arch professional demeanor, she escorted the suddenly quiet giant to his quarters, a font of directives flowing behind her tall, slender frame.

I decamped to the kitchen to steep a cup of tea and headed to the front salon on the *premier étage*, or second floor in Americanese. The old French doors opened to the stone balcony where my ancestors had watched three hundred years of events unfold. I imagined rudimentary muddy roads with horse-drawn carriages, stable hands, servants scurrying about with foods, goods, even chamber pots. As the sun emerged from behind the fast-moving clouds, I imagined the first electrical lights illuminating the houses far beyond in Spain, and the first cars driven by stable masters now clad in white, with my ancestors bedecked with furs and diamonds behind. The Great War and all its mustard gas prefaced the gleeful roar of the twenties before the thirties brought back rational thought followed by irrational Nazis.

I rubbed my hand over a chink in this front balcony's railing, and wondered if my relatives had stood here during the last invasion to watch the warplanes and the havoc and detritus of war. Trucks and cranes likely arrived post war to rebuild the coast, along with the first wave of surfers and their wooden boards. It was chilly under the cool glare of the sun and I retreated to the sagging sofa inside.

The faded blue satin cushions had lost their density too many decades ago to count. A flood of unbidden thoughts unleashed themselves.

How many ancestors had been born, married, and died here? The eldest du Roques males had gone through the full cycle of life here, while females had been forced to leave the nest to marry and finish out their lives under other roofs. Unless they became spinsters like the villa's namesakes, Madeleine and Marie, whose father had taken care to make them feel loved and noteworthy by naming the house, a gift to their eldest brother, after the two tiny, unattractive sisters, as legend had it. Legend also had it that they'd given up their dowries to enable their father to build the house since they'd been deemed too ugly to attract husbands. And their brother had reacted with suitable grace by hounding them to death, literally, to give his favorite younger son a larger villa to lord over his elder brother. And so it goes.

I put down my teacup and stretched out, the sofa creaking under duress. My father had taken great delight one summer afternoon, after a round of golf, to tell me about my own history. I'd been ten, sitting on the couch with my legs dangling as I read one of the few English-language stories on the bookshelves. Idly, I'd retrieved the thin gold wedding band he'd left on the silver tray before he'd gone to hit the links.

"Katie, don't you get too comfortable on that old sofa, it's got stories to tell." He was drinking something tall and cold, when I saw his eyes zero in on the wedding band now on my thumb.

"I like stories, Daddy."

He laughed, and the gold crown in the back of his mouth glinted for a brief moment in the sunlight from the window. "This is one of my favorites. Do you know why?"

"Why, Daddy?" It was the rare moment he gave me his full attention.

"You were conceived on that sofa," he said and laughed again.

Bile rose in my throat, and I quickly sat up to swallow it back as I became light-headed. I tried to close the door on the memories but they all came flooding out.

"Oh," I said.

"You know what conception is, right?"

"Of course." Embarrassment rose like a hot air balloon in the pit of my stomach.

"Check out the date," he whispered. "On the inside of the band." A moment later: "It's better I tell you than someone else." The tiny initials and dates inside were already fading. The date inscribed was a mathematical improbability, unless I'd been premature, which instinctively I'd known I wasn't. No one as tall, gangly, and healthy as I was had ever seen the interior of a preemie ward.

He'd laughed again and tousled my brown hair. I never liked when he did that. I might have looked like a girl, but inside I was an adult going on a hundred and three.

"Katie, all the best love affairs are brief and intense," he'd mused with a dazed look. "Your mother was a siren. And I couldn't resist." He winked. "The rest? Well, a gentleman picks up the pieces after their follies. Or at least the important ones." A half dozen deep wrinkles framed his eyes when he smiled. "Especially if their feet are held to the fire. You don't look like her, but then again I also sometimes wonder if there's any of my Hamilton blood in you at all." He'd caught my nose between two knuckles and pretended to steal it. "But don't worry, Antoinette will teach you her tricks. And I don't know any man who can resist her."

My mother, whose scarves were always infused with Eau de Joy, had just dashed, laughing—cigarette between long painted red fingernails—out the door, to supposedly join a group of friends going to San Sebastian for their annual trip to buy leather goods.

We never spoke of this secret again, but the sin of my birth was now exposed, and then covered up by the faded blue satin damask in my mind. It was one of the last summers I would spend under the plane trees, playing with Magdali.

Just how many secrets had unfolded in Madeleine Marie and then been pushed into the dark, damp corners to molder?

And yet . . . it all just didn't really matter. Less than a generation from now, my own secrets would be lacquered and sealed beneath beautiful new sheets of wallpaper and paint. Or perhaps they'd tear down this ivy-covered monstrosity.

Sometimes it was better to start from scratch.

Chapter Eight

From: Anne Berger, Head of School, Miss Chester-
field's School
Sent: Tuesday, May 28, 2016, 11:08 AM
To: Hamilton, Kate A., PhD
Subject: Update Lily Hamilton Auermander

Dear Mrs. Hamilton,

I'm pleased to report this month Lily has made signifi-
cant progress academically and has almost caught up to
her classmates. All her teachers report she has become
less introverted, and participates more frequently.

She has a very nice small circle of friends here. She
is closest to her roommate, Sarah Goodman, according
to the resident teacher on her floor. Indeed, they are both
enrolled in the three-day-a-week after-school photogra-

phy spring module while the other girls play field hockey.

Her arm and shoulder have healed, per the specialist in Boston, who she has seen once a month following your request. He insists there is no need to see her again until six months' time. I shall forward X-ray discs. She continues to see our school counselor twice a week.

During our meeting this morning, Lily finally chose a plan for the summer after reviewing the options. She agreed to spend all or almost all of the summer with you. She understands you are in France presently, but that you may return to Connecticut at some future point. She is willing to go to France, and in fact, I understood she prefers to go there, likely to avoid any physical reminders from last year. She's also been invited by her roommate's parents to spend a week or two with them on the Cape late August. I've taken the liberty of forwarding your email address to the Goodmans.

While Lily has agreed to all of this, she reiterated that she preferred to continue no contact with any member of the family through the end of the term.

Please forward airline ticketing information so we may coordinate appropriate transport to Boston/Logan airport between June 13 and 15.

I strongly urge you to e-sign the reenrollment documents sent last month. Your daughter is quite happy and thriving here.

Best wishes,

Anne Berger

The words on the screen blurred on my laptop sitting on my makeshift desk in the bedroom. Oh God, she was coming. She was coming. She wanted to see me. I mentally counted the days. Fifteen or so.

My head felt heavy in my hands as my fingers dug into my scalp. Pushing back the heartbreak of hope, I was determined not to count on anything ever again. Because she could change her mind. Her father's family could attempt to change her mind. But no matter how hard I tried to stop it, happiness crept in. I didn't want happiness. It would be too painful if something prevented her from coming. I swallowed and opened my eyes to reread the email.

She wanted to come *here*. Not to her roommate's house as had been planned. Not Connecticut. *Not home to her.* The image of the redbrick colonial floated in my mind and my gut froze. That house was not home. It had never been a home. It was a trophy house in the suburbs where the husbands took trains to Manhattan and almost every wife stayed behind to coordinate and implement a complex social life that revolved around country clubs, tennis ladders, horses, manicures, and gourmet cooking by housekeepers in immaculate, open-concept kitchens. Gin and tonics, and whiskey served promptly to guests at seven. False gaiety and posturing throughout dinner. If it was done correctly, husbands and wives and children never had to have serious conversations. All fury and pain boiled under a tightly held veil of secrecy. It was thus, and where, a reign of intermittent, iron-fisted tyranny amid a silent siege had held court, inside that house of brick. There'd been no way out. No choice but to play the court jester and serve the eighteen-year sentence until it was safe to leave with my daughter, whom I'd supervised like a hawk. I'd never guessed Lily would trump my carefully planned move by bolting before everything was ready.

I'd never fit in there. Not in the neighborhood and not with the other wives. I didn't play tennis, didn't do lunch, and I certainly didn't get manicures. After dropping Lily to school, work was my escape just like all the husbands. My only true friends were an eclectic group of fellow doctors and scientists, especially Alice, a vet with a vicious sense of humor who specialized in pigs.

My ex-husband had fit in perfectly. Darien was the pinnacle of success. Soho had been my version of paradise before pregnancy had upended plans. Darien was supposedly a more suitable place to raise a child. Except it wasn't.

I wrote a quick reply to the headmistress, could not stomach the reenrollment forms until I saw Lily, booked her flight, and chucked off espadrilles to get ready for dinner.

Then again, I'd never really fit in anywhere, if I was honest.

My mother, who'd insisted I call her Antoinette the day I turned sixteen, said my father and she had always wondered where I had come from as I was so different from both of them. I'd taken it as yet another personal failure for a long while, and then realized it was the opposite after Psychology 101 at university. I'd never liked golf, country clubs, risky ventures, and the social scene. And they didn't like what I loved: books, stories, animals, hiking, swimming, being alone, and trying to figure out people.

Apparently, I was the only person on both sides of the family who was not born with a golf club in one hand and a tennis racquet in the other. I was neither a Hamilton nor a du Roque.

My uncle was dead set on proving my theory right.

He appeared unannounced half an hour before dinner. Actually, it was his ten-year-old Mercedes that announced his arrival. There was something about the sound of tires on pea gravel that always sent a wave of foreboding.

After a jovial welcome by Jean, and a hurried request to Magdali to set another place at the table, I offered my uncle a Chivas neat, his preferred drink.

Jean-Michel du Roque was every inch a Frenchman. His thinning gray hair slicked back like a bathing cap, his impeccable blue suit, white shirt, and muted Hermès tie and gold Santos de Cartier watch were all perfectly coordinated right down to his polished brown Oxfords. He was the epitome of taste and style. He was a man who oozed charm and knew how to get his way and make others happy to do it. He was a man who children did not like.

Decades ago, I'd been equally fascinated and disgusted by his potent brew of servile flattery and condescending manipulation. His followers in the familial cult had been sucked in like moths to a flame.

Jean-Michel took great pains to come around the oval mahogany table to pull out my chair and properly seat me before assuming the chair opposite his father.

"*Alors*, Kate. How good it is to see you. And how wonderful that you have come to visit us." He held his knife and fork like a skillful surgeon going right for the heart. "I spoke to Antoinette last evening and when she said you were here, well, *naturellement*, I knew I should immediately come down from Paris to see you. And, voilà, here I am."

"Here you are, indeed, Jean-Michel."

"Oh, please, *chérie*, you must call me *Oncle*. I take such great pride and honor in being uncle to such a brilliant and beautiful niece."

See what I mean?

"Well, since *Jean* and Antoinette don't want to be reminded that we're all a hell of a lot older, I figured you might not either. But, forgive me? I apologize for making that assumption, Uncle John-Michael."

He choked on a sliver of baguette.

"*D'accord,*" he acquiesced with a pained look.

Score one for the outnumbered American team.

Magdali served a roast with green beans and potatoes before decamping to the comfort of the kitchen. I wished I could go with her. It's funny how if a child forms a strong opinion of someone, it is very difficult to change that view as an adult. I knew my uncle had some excellent qualities, but my dislike ran so deep, it was almost impossible to see glimmers of them. I tried again.

"How are you faring, Uncle?"

"Happy to see you all grown up actually," Jean-Michel said, sipping a nice little Brouilly I'd bought.

I searched for a polite answer.

"Still shy, I see," he murmured with a smile. "What an interesting coiffure. *Très naturelle.*"

I used my napkin. "Still making unkind comments disguised as polite conversation, I see."

"Kate!" Jean's fork clattered to the plate in a heretofore never-seen clumsiness at the table.

"What?" I stopped eating. "What is the point? I've never seen a reason to beat around the bush. Why are you here, Jean-Michel? What do you want?" Learning how to be direct, the opposite of the last twenty years of my life, was actually becoming a little too much fun.

My uncle laughed. "Not so shy after all. *Chérie,* really, this must wait. We must go around the tree, as you say, because it is never a good idea to ruin a perfectly cooked blanquette de veau with unpleasant conversation." He smiled again, revealing classic subpar French dental work. "Why are *you* here?"

"Antoinette didn't tell you? How keeping in tradition."

"Kate is here to try to convince me that I need another nurse or a retirement home," Jean inserted.

"Papa," Jean-Michel said. "There is no question you will remain here. This is the house you were born in and the house you will die in—like your father and his father before him and so on and so forth. *Naturellement.*"

"*Naturellement,*" I repeated.

"Yes," my uncle said very quietly. "*Naturellement.* Unlike Americans who throw their grandparents in the *poubelle*—the trash."

"Your respect for the blanquette de veau is slipping, Jean-Michel. Pass the salt," I said. "Please."

"Kate!" Jean pleaded.

The silent intermission provided ample time for rearmament.

"*Bon*," Jean continued. "How long are you here, Jean-Mich? Magdali will prepare your room, of course."

"Not long," Jean-Michel replied. "I must return to Paris and then to Chantilly *pour le week-end*. There is a *petit tournoi de golf* and the horses will run."

"Ah," Jean said. "How I wish I could go with you and see it. It's been so long since—" He abruptly stopped after glancing at his son's expression.

Jean-Michel's ascension to the head of the du Roque guild was obvious. I almost pitied Jean until I remembered his own brutal oligarchy and his attempt at a coup to assume control of my parents. Americans always win, thank God.

"And how is my dearest grand-niece? Antoinette hinted Liliane is at a strange pension—boarder school, you say?"

When would I learn to stop expecting anything but betrayal from my mother? The only real question was who was the grand master of the marionettes—brother or sister? I was willing to bet my last *sou* on Antoinette. "Lily is happy, thank you."

Jean-Michel opened his mouth and I interceded. "And she will come here the second week in June and stay until I return to the States." I looked at my grandfather. "If you agree, of course."

"*Mais bien sûr!* Of course. Finally, I shall see this famous great-grandchild of mine!" A smile, rare as a day without three battling weather elements here, lit up his lined face.

Jean-Michel's showed not a hint of emotion. "I shall, of course, come back when she arrives. And I—"

"Please don't," I interrupted. "She requires peace and quiet."

"Why, I'm hurt to think you would—"

"I would, and I will."

"How long will both of you stay?" Jean-Michel carefully placed his fork and knife side by side at an angle on top of the plate.

"Long enough," I replied. "What have you come here to take back to Paris? I noticed a lot of the family paintings are gone."

"Someone has to provide for the family."

I glanced at his gold watch and Hermès tie. "I'm happy to take over the role for the time being."

Jean cleared his throat. "Kate, I don't think you know how much your uncle has—"

"I know exactly how much he has done. He's selling all the silver, and the artwork."

"And why would I be selling my future inheritance unless there was other recourse? I'm the future owner of our familial home after all."

"Technically, Antoinette owns a future half." I stared him down. "So the things you are taking are actually half your sister's."

"The things I am selling are our father's. You should be ashamed of thinking anything else!"

"Kate," my grandfather's voice sounded so old. So tired. "I asked him to sell these things. It's needed to pay our bills."

"Perfect. Let's see the sale receipts."

"Are you suggesting—" Jean-Michel began.

"I am."

"I'll not sit here and listen to—"

"Two of those paintings—the Picasso Biarritz beach scenes—should have brought enough cash to keep the villa going for a decade and maybe even replace the roof. I did the research." Blood was singing in my veins. The same blood as my tiny, feisty, hot-blooded Peruvian great-grandmother who'd ruled the roost during the German occupation. The one who'd protected it when the Nazis had appropriated it. She'd refused to move out, instead squeezing the family into the now lichen-filled basement for eighteen months, and serving the officers vichyssoise tainted with hints of foxglove, watered-down rat poison, arsenic, or anything she could get her little hands on.

Jean-Michel rose and took on a faintly hilarious Napoleonic air of bruised pride. He probably practiced the pose in the long mirrors, which were losing flakes of silver on the backside. He was going to say something boring and clichéd, but for once he did not. Instead, he turned and crossed the long swath of floor toward the gilded French doors without another word.

"Jean-Michel," Jean called out. He tapped his cane but Uncle would not turn around.

He kept walking, straight to the doors, which he exited and slammed shut.

"You must apologize," Jean said.

"I won't. He should apologize to you for not showing you receipts."

"Children and parents rarely live up to one another's expectations, Kate."

Finally a rational answer for how our family functioned.

STILLNESS SHIMMERED THE thin air, broken only by the grateful songs of birds breaking their fast. Palest pink clouds looked like faded patches of ancient wallpaper covering a flat blue early sky. Edward Soames took the lead on the trail toward Santiago de Compostela, a sacred burial site of saints eight hundred kilometers away from the Pyrenees rising from the Bay of Biscay. The littoral had borne the sins and secrets of the millions of pilgrims who had walked or crawled on their knees to finally worship the distant hallowed grounds. It would take a miracle before any secrets were unearthed from Edward Soames, who walked faster than most people jogged. His head was bent forward like a dog on a hunt.

For a military man, he certainly had zero respect for the quality or quantity of the clothes he wore. Today's number was blindingly atrocious—a wooly blue plaid shirt that looked as if it had seen finer days during the Paleolithic period. Apparently, his view of my yoga wear was equally unimpressed.

"You don't have proper hiking gear," he stated, not looking behind.

"Your concern is duly noted."

"You should wear hiking boots next time."

"Next time? Let's see if we can get through this morning before we talk about a next time."

"I didn't realize therapists were so brutal. In my experience they are far more kind initially—luring you in with false empathy and empty promises of a rosy future."

"Yes, we're kind of like spiders. We spin this invisible, inviting web and then, when someone flies into our sticky space, we strap you to our couches and suck you dry."

"About right," he said, and stopped at the top of a rise. His hand shaded his brow as he gazed below. He moved toward an outcropping of rock and lay down. It had been a long, hard slog to the top.

The fingers of a deeply blue lake caressed the feet of the mountains. Toward the sea to the right, a few stunted, gnarled trees struggled to survive the harsh weather; their western profiles bent from the brutal winds. Wildflowers, yellow and violet, blossomed within pockets of bracken and gorse dotted with ferns. I glanced at the major, who had settled into a snooze, his post-traumatic stress at bay. Beyond his crossed arms and feet lay the geography of my childhood.

It had been my mooring in the cyclone of George and Antoinette's ever-changing lives. During the year at Miss Chesterfield's and their divorce, a period of abject silence ensued on both sides. My roommate, Elle, had often commented on it.

"They're always so busy," she had said.

I had watched her put aside a small stack of letters from her parents and two brothers and then reach for a geometry textbook. "Yup."

"Look at the bright side. They're so oblivious, you could get away with murder here."

"Yup," I had replied.

"I don't know why you study so hard," she had said, using her protractor to draw a geometric figure. "You okay with them getting divorced?"

"Yup." An economy of words had never hurt me in my life. Then and now.

Major Soames's snoring was impressive, and I allowed my mind to drift back to more than two decades ago when my own brand of post-traumatic stress had taken root.

It appeared neither of my parents had thought enough to ask the other who would be in possession of their (or at least my mother's) mixed gene pool the following year. Yes, that fifteenth summer, no parental unit appeared at LAX after the flight from Boston, post Miss Chesterfield's. Evidently, I'd been cast off the merry-go-round of perpetual movements. There was just only so much parenting Antoinette, George, or I could handle.

Very graciously, in all their weed-stoked generosity, the three UCLA graduate students, who had apparently sublet our rental house at some point during the divorce, offered me the cot in the garage, which had been converted into a dance studio complete with incense, mini fridge, hot tub, and a spare bike or two on the walls. It was silently understood in this pre–cell phone era that Mom or Dad would collect me in time.

Or maybe not.

Liberty was sweet. Hell, it was far better than boarding school. What girl could resist foggy mornings hitching rides to SaMo High before sunlit afternoons on the back of a surfer friend's Yamaha? Darwin's Theory became my religion—adapt or die, my motto. And surely, surely one of them was coming if only to curb my use of their credit cards. By the ninth week, assimilation was complete; emotions blurred under a circle of friends and the rotation of subletting tenants, who adopted me like a beloved pet, retrieved from the garage to sit at my parent's dining table on the rare night someone made dinner.

It was heaven for a teenager.

It was supposed to feel like repressed sadness and insecurity to a trained psychotherapist, but it didn't. Just seemed normal. It was—

"This is a pleasant surprise," Edward said, sitting up and looking again at the vista.

I exhaled, unaware I'd been holding my breath. "The best part is that the views are always changing, along with the weather."

"True," he replied. "But I was referring to your silence."

I did not reply. Instead, I moved past him and took the lead down the other side of the hill.

"Is this how all your sessions go?" He called after me. "You just let silence do your work until the patient ties themselves up with curiosity?"

"Is that what you are? Curious?"

He must have gotten up and followed as his voice was close

behind me. "Yep. Like wondering why you looked like petrified wood. Not one iota of emotion just now."

"Well, since talking to you last time was like having a conversation with the pyramids, I thought you might enjoy silence."

"Huh," he grunted. "Are your eyes good, Doctor?"

"What?"

"Eyes. Good?"

"Yes. Why?"

"I've got a pricker I can't get out."

I stopped, indicated a boulder to sit on, and bent over his hand. It was long and thin, and it looked like it hurt like hell, but he said not a word. I knew he wouldn't.

"So what's the précis of therapy under Kate Hamilton? And can you prescribe drugs?"

"Précis?"

He shook his head. "Crib notes. Short version of a long story. Come on, Kate, keep up."

"In the *colonies*, they're called CliffsNotes, major."

For the first time that day I saw his teeth. His version of a smile needed work.

"CliffsNotes. Roger. We have them too." He took off his sunglasses, wiped his eyes, and replaced the glasses. "So?"

"What do you want to know?"

"How you purportedly cure people."

"Purportedly?" I said. "Your confidence is staggering. Is this how you inspired those under your command?"

His eyes became focused. "What's the cure? The short version, Doctor."

"It's like I told you before. Revisit your childhood. Or in your case, revisit your war experiences. Maybe both."

"And?"

"You asked for the short version. I gave it to you."

"A bit longer," he said. "Please." Such an effort for so little a word.

"All right," I relented. "We revisit the past horrors of war you've experienced. You did five tours, correct?"

"Yep."

"Where?"

"Iraq, Afghanistan three times, and Bosnia before that," he clipped out.

God, that seemed like a lot. "Well, oftentimes, just talking about what happened and finally feeling repressed emotions can make a huge difference. Or . . ."

He was shaking his head. "Or what? I've heard all that before. Doesn't work."

"Or, if there is a childhood wound, perhaps reopened by the trauma of war, with time and work, there's discovery of unmet needs, resulting belief systems and fears, an attempt to take off false armor or identity, and with any luck, and a lot more time, much of it gut-wrenching"—*why sugarcoat it?*—"the person ends up deciding if they want to be courageous and make different choices, or sink back into the mire of the tried and not so true. Is that short or long enough for you?" I took a step closer to him.

"What if I already know my past, know what happened, and have no false armor? What if it's too late to make different choices? Damage done. Talking just doesn't change facts."

"Don't you realize almost anyone can say that? Talking, having the guts to hash out old events, doesn't change the past, but it can make a huge difference for the future."

"Has it made a difference for you?"

"We're talking about you."

He raised his brows. "Now there's a no."

"It's more complicated for someone like me. I know too much."

"Sounds like an excuse to me, Hamilton."

"Therapy is just one way of getting to the cause of a client's pain, anxiety, depression, and a host of other issues."

"That's when drugs are thrown into the mix."

"Sometimes. Sometimes not. It all depends on the condition presented. And . . ."

"And what?"

"Someone's natural resilience."

He unfolded himself and stood, picking down to select a rock, which he threw into the valley below. His eyes on the horizon, he said, "Well, at least you're not talking about mindfulness. What the fuck does that mean anyway? The Ministry of Defense therapist I was forced to see after the last deployment kept talking about mindfulness. Total bollocks if you ask me."

I had to laugh. "It's essentially living life in the present moment, about—"

"For fuck's sake, is there any other way to live? Do we have a choice? We live each moment as it comes."

"You like to say *fuck* a lot."

"What? Now you're going to try to take away one of my few present joys?" His smile deepened. "Pretty fucking unmindful to my way of thinking."

"A lot of people live in the past," I said. "Or live for the future."

"Nothing all that wrong with doing both, don't you think?" He picked off a piece of grass from the plaid monstrosity he called a shirt. "I say learn from your mistakes and build a better future."

"I see." I pressed my fingernails into my palms. I wasn't going to sell him on anything. He'd have to come to a decision to seek help on his own, no matter what his great-uncle wanted.

"Look, no man in his right mind believes in therapy. At least in England they don't. It's for the weak. Okay, maybe we'll go for a little marriage counseling upon threat of divorce, but that's it. Americans, as I understand, have an affinity for talking about feelings, but not us. Not me."

"No surprise there."

"Brits have far less suicides than Americans," he continued.

"You've examined military suicide rates, have you?"

"Twenty a day in America, the land of the free." The striated muscles in the hollow of his cheek tensed and then relaxed. "The way I see it, Doctor, I might be willing to start this experiment if only to get my family off my back, but I'll only do it if you are willing to do the same. And absolutely no drugs. Got it?"

What? "I'm sorry?"

"Yeah. I'll go through that examination of my past and other moronic crap, if you do the same."

"That's not how it works. I must become a pseudo person to you—a mother, father, brother, commander, whatever. There is no tit for tat."

He blinked. "Take it or leave it. Trust is a two-way street."

He was a master manipulator and controller. And that off-kilter look in his wide gray eyes tinged with ashen darkness hinted at zero emotion, indeed, possibly a borderline psychopath, albeit a good psychopath, the newest favorite animal under the microscope of many psychology texts now. "You were diagnosed with post-traumatic stress disorder, correct?"

"Such a dry, pretty little phrase." He laughed. "I don't know a soldier who spent any amount of time in a war zone who hasn't suffered some form of PTSD."

"Understood." I pulled off the long-sleeved cover I wore over a T-shirt now that the sun had emerged from the clouds.

"You said you couldn't protect someone last time," he began.

"And you said you'd tell me what happened to make you the person your wife and children left behind when they returned to England."

"Brutal," he said and smiled. "You want to know what's wrong with the military?"

I waited. Denial via a change in subject was just so last Freud.

"When you go into a war zone, you see the worst things you never imagined. And you see men in all their glory. The best and the worst. The real and the unvarnished. You learn about love and hate on a whole new level. What is love between a man and a woman when you compare it to the bond between soldiers? I've seen eighteen-year-old boys throw themselves in front of certain death to protect their mates. Soldiers don't talk about feelings. They show and live their truths. In a marriage, it's all about words, and petty emotions, and the mundane. To-do lists. 'Clean the garage, water the garden, buy crisps and bin liners at Tesco' lists. All part of the ultimate goal of a man going out into the world to provide. And it's mostly a one-way street. To be fair, I'm a dick, but I get it."

"I see."

"You don't see it at all. You have to live it to get it. And you're missing some key anatomy to get it."

"Keep going. Explain it to me."

"I just did. I thought therapists were good listeners."

Unresolved anger—such a polite word for a pressure cooker of merde.

"Anyway." He stopped abruptly.

"Let's keep walking. There's room to walk side by side up ahead. Why is your marriage a one-way street?"

"It's not really. She ran the household when I was away for months at a time and I owe her for that. But, really? We have nothing in common except our children. We made the mistake of marrying far too young by reason of raging hormones."

"And now?"

"We have nothing in common and the hormones have gone dormant."

"Common in a long-term marriage. How do you feel about that?"

"Really? Come on, Kate, you must know how most men feel about that."

"Yup." I stopped abruptly.

"What was your marriage like?"

I forced myself to reply. "Not the best."

"You're divorced."

"I am."

"Why not the best?"

"We didn't suit each other." Understatement of the century. "My father said he was shocked we actually married. He said he'd have put his money on Oliver marrying a nubile, young secretary, and I a rich, old man."

"When did he say that?"

"On my wedding day." *Why was I telling him this?*

"Any other little gems he told you?"

I swallowed. What did I have to lose? He wasn't a patient. I wasn't his friend. He was someone I'd never see again after I left here. "He said that I should never ever deny my husband his rights."

"Never?" Edward raised his eyebrows. He looked ten years younger in his shock. "An intriguing view. But, seriously? I'd never tell my daughter that. Your father sounds like a worse dick than I. And I should know. Sorry. But not really. He sounds like a fucking sad excuse for a father. You know that, right?"

"He was impossible, but everyone loved him. He was the most charming, funny, intelligent man I ever knew."

"And meaner than a snake. What father says that to a daughter?"

I hadn't remembered those things for years. I looked at the ground. What was bringing up all these putrid, bone-sucking memories?

"Okay. No need to go on," he said. "Next question."

It looked like I was going to be a sister figure to him. More realistically, if I was honest, he was going to be a brother figure to me. "Do you have any siblings? Mother and father still living?"

He looked at me as if I'd grown five heads.

"I realize I'm jumping around here, but I sense, ahem, that your patience is limited. Just trying to move ahead at breakneck speed."

"How very untherapeutic."

"Indeed," I agreed. "So?"

"Three older brothers. All dead. In Northern Ireland, Bosnia, and the last in Afghanistan. One sister, living in Wales, where my parents moved to be near her new family."

"Why didn't they stay in England, to be near you, your wife, and children?"

"I was not their favorite."

"They told you this?"

"They did."

"When?"

"Who the fuck cares, Hamilton? There are always favorites in families. My sister is the light of their lives. Bingo on Thursdays, pub night quizzes on Wednesdays, and lunch after church on Sundays. It's all good."

"Do you have a favorite between your two children?"

Incredulity and disgust marred his features. "They're like chalk and cheese."

"And which do you prefer? Chalk or cheese?"

"Winnie loves animals, constantly has a smile plastered on her face and has a social life that rivals the royal family's. She never stops talking, orders me around—a real ballbuster, which I love. My son wants to murder her half the time but is too busy playing some bloody vampire video game to actually do it. He is far too smart and stupid for his own good, and has a way with words that makes me laugh like no one else can whilst he's doing everything he can to infuriate me."

"So you love them equally but differently."

He stopped in his tracks. "Don't you dare say my parents should have loved us all equally."

"Okay."

"Do you love your children equally, Kate?"

"I only have one child."

He waited, refusing to keep walking.

"A daughter. Lily."

"The one you didn't protect."

He was getting too close. I started walking and he had no choice but to keep up.

"Why didn't you protect her, Kate? That's your job, for fuck's sake."

"It's complicated." God, I sounded pathetic. "So when did your marriage begin to fail?"

"Answer me," he barked. "Why didn't you protect her? There's no excuse. None."

There was a look of such darkness and disgust in his eyes that finally reason and the doctor in me returned. Or perhaps it was just my way—my favorite way to deflect someone. We were two of a kind, Soames and I. Two solitary creatures of the wild who didn't know how to get along with the rest of the people in the world. And I had tried. There was a reason I'd chosen psychology as a profession. At least he was finally showing me he cared too much to be a psychopath. Or else he was a hell of a good actor, and I'd seen a lot of those. "You're too intelligent for me to play games. Such an extreme reaction is really a reflection of yourself. Who did you fail to protect?"

He stopped again along the path. A complete and total blank slate replaced the tumult of emotion in his expression. It froze the marrow in my bones.

I'd taken a chance. Pushed him too hard. "I apologize. You asked me a question. We agreed—or at least you commanded—that we each share our lives with each other. And I get why. It's to build trust. And really? You are doing me a favor. I could use a booster class on trust along with you. And hey, you're not paying me."

"Do you have many clients, Kate?"

"Of course I . . . Why do you ask?"

"You talk too much."

I bit my mouth to keep from laughing.

"And you never ever laugh," he continued.

"Me? Why, I've attended funerals with more laughter than spending an hour with you. And stop changing the subject."

"I laugh all the damn time," he replied. "Inside."

"Okay. Live a little and try laughing on the outside from time to time."

"When didn't you protect Lily?"

I paused. "Last year. And, to be honest, I'd failed her a number of times before then. But last year was the ultimate betrayal."

"What happened?"

I just couldn't open my mouth. My throat constricted and it was so damn predictable and clichéd, I felt sick to my stomach. I reached toward an enormous, wild, white parasol-like flower just emerging from its veined envelope of protection. How could something so delicate survive the harsh winds of the Pyrenees? "May I not answer that just yet?"

"Kate, I've sent so many men to their deaths. Tried to deny my part in it. And that's just the tip of my mountain of lies and irresponsibility. How can anything you might have done compare?"

"Because she is my child. Because if there is one absolute in life it is the duty of a mother to love and protect her children, like you said. I should know. Every day I see the walking carcasses of humanity whose mothers and fathers betrayed them. It's just inexcusable. It's what causes depression, unfulfilled lives, divorce, suicide, crime, even war."

"Let's turn around."

"Why?"

"We're at a stalemate," he said. "We're not going anywhere."

"I know. We've already established a pattern."

"And what pattern is that, Doctor?"

"The one where you try and control the situation by deflecting all my questions by turning them on me."

"Really?"

"Yes, it's kind of like psychological hot potato."

"I like potatoes."

"Or you try to be witty and you're not."

"Americans. No sense of humor at all."

"Well, at least I'm not French."

"You're half French," he said dryly.

"Lucky for you."

"You're good at deflecting too, Kate. I can tell we're going to be good friends. The best really."

"Men and women can't be good friends unless they're related." I reaffixed the scrunchie holding my ponytail.

He raised his eyebrows. "Says who?"

"World history."

"I think you're referring to the problem of sexual desire."

I rolled my eyes. "It's the reason why therapists meet their clients in controlled circumstances, where the session is all about the client and I am but a pseudo figure or mirror."

"Don't worry, Katie. I'm not remotely attracted to you."

"Well, thank God for that."

"I'm married and, to be fair? I'm not attracted to anyone. What's the point? It all ends badly. We've nothing more than a living, breathing death sentence at the end."

"Are you on *any* medication?"

Chapter Nine

Whispers from the Garden . . .

Delicious darkness fell upon the land, and I waddled from the little cove of leaves near the stone potting shed that had become my favored resting place. A cooling wind swept from the sea, up over the cliffs, and down the alleys around the stone villa to the drift of white flowers swirling and releasing their delicate scent. The annoying whine of tiny Buzzers crisscrossed over-head, ever looking for a warm body from which to extract their next red-hot meal. One of the Barkers erupted in a paroxysm of mania, my perfume obviously sending him over the edge. My world is ruled by scents and sometimes sounds; sight being the least important sense.

Those bloody clanging noises began again for no reason—sort of like those massive metal monsters connected to each other, wending their way through the countryside in the distance with billows of smoke erupting at the place where they always seemed to pause before chugging on. Like those clanging sounds, there was no apparent schedule to the metal monsters. Unfortunate.

I wondered what that cat called the metal monsters. She had a different name for everything. I didn't like that I had begun to use some of her words. I was me and I liked me and I didn't want to be like anyone else.

I didn't need anyone, and didn't want to start now. But uncertainty about everything was creeping in at an alarming rate, and spending time with Yowler calmed my frayed nerves. Then again, I was almost getting used to the uncertainty of it all. Uncertainty should have been my name—not what she called me.

But, it felt good to live on the lam, take up with wilderness. The dry food from my former little keeper was a thing of the past. And no more twice monthly baths with a toothbrush, and running on a wheel to nowhere—sort of like the clocks in the old house and how the hands kept going around with different Two-Leggeds coming and going at certain points on the clock face. Yowler had given me the name for clocks but they still didn't make sense. And neither of us, even if she wouldn't admit it, understood why the Two-Leggeds had them. Everything for us was about the location of the sun and the moon, day and night, high tide and low. And for me, the Call of the Slug.

The thrill of the hunt was a maddening, beautiful thing.

It was just the Barkers who could drive one to distraction. And Yowler. Yes, I liked that name for her better than cat. She was beyond annoying in her fickleness. Not at all a lass with regular hours nor a desire to plan ahead. I shouldn't care, really I shouldn't. As I said, I am a solitary creature through and through.

But that scent.

I should be over it by now—obsessed with a new perfume— yet I was not. Even the thought of that strange scent made the saliva rise in my throat.

The Barkers snarled on the other side of the fence, and exploded, furious by . . . her. I should have known it was she. Obviously, my subconscious was ahead of my mind, sort of like how my nose was ahead of my brain.

She leapt down from a tree in a less than elegant fashion, but the arrogant tilt of her head suggested that she was deter- mined to pretend she had meant to take down a rash of leaves on her descent.

She dropped to her haunches and began licking her front legs from shoulder to paw in long, fast strokes. I couldn't un- derstand why any creature would want to lick themselves. So unattractive. And all that hair in your mouth. Prickles were ever so much more convenient, just shake and go, and a fabu- lous defense system compared to animals who thought their IQ was superior to mine. I really could not be bothered to think about these things. Then again, her garden was a veritable Slugfest of delight.

She wrinkled her nose and made a strange sound. "I see you there. Are you mocking me?"

"No," I lied. Maybe I was mocking her, then again, I didn't know what mocking was, but I did know I didn't want to give her another reason to think I was an idiot. And that infuriated me. I just shouldn't care. This is why I liked to be alone. But that scent! I would give up a hundred Slugs a week all for a whiff of it.

"The Boxers are getting completely out of hand. They have no respect for the hierarchy here. No idea how to accept their lot below me," she said.

"To be fair," I said, "their sheer size might give them the advantage."

She curled a paw, exposed those vicious claws and gave a quick swipe. "They don't like these. They're just bullies, putting on a show to exert the canine ego. I might be willing to let them sort of think they had some kind of advantage, if they were nicer, but then again . . . No. I'm a cat, and that's just not me."

"Figured out that claw thing the first time we met."

"Are you ever going to let that go?" She ran a paw over her face and paused. "Alors, but you've got that quilly ball maneuver. Course that's just a defense. Got any offense?"

"I don't do offense," I said. "Don't need to. And why would I want to? Too much work. I'm not a fighter."

She flicked her tail. "Obviously. But sometimes in life you just have to stand your ground. Or go down trying. Otherwise *you're just a pathetic weakling and your self-esteem suffers, something a cat would never allow. I think—"*

The high whines from across the fence had risen to a fevered pitch, and one of the Barkers took a running leap, jumped off the back of his mate, and high kicked it over the metal-spiked fence. A ball of wildly slobbering, barking, terrifying energy careened toward us. Shockingly, beautiful Yowler stood there; the fur on her back expanded to make her look twice as big. Me? Well, I think you know exactly what I did. I shut my eyes tight. Who wants to watch a bloodbath?

A high-pitched yip nipped the air and I opened my eyes. She was glorious. I had to admit it. There she was, hissing and swiping. Standing her ground. The Barker lunged and retreated, rendered berserk as he circled her in cowardice.

Well. He was smarter than he looked. Oh, he tried to hold on to his pride whilst cutting her a wide birth, pretending to ignore her on his way to me.

I flexed my drawstring tighter. Only my little snout poked out of my soft underbelly fur, curled in a ball as I was.

"Va-t'en! Go away, you idiot," she hissed and crossed to stand in front of me. A sardine would not melt in her mouth.

Oh, the Barker kept up the racket for a few minutes, until Yowler gave an insipid swipe that had no real force to it as she sauntered a step closer to him. He clearly knew her from past experience, and with his dignity in complete tatters, he hightailed it to the pea gravel and slunk beyond the gate, now unable to even go back over the fence from whence he came. His brother whined his frustration.

I felt rather small and unimportant as I relaxed and un-folded my thin little legs.

Yowler coughed. "Pas mal, *Quilly. Not bad at all.*"

"*I'm sorry?*"

"*Your defenses.*"

"*What is Quilly?*"

"*My name for you.*"

"*I thought it was hedgehog.*"

"*No, that is your kind. Your species. It's better we have an individual name too.*"

My brain hurt. But I couldn't disappoint her after every-thing she had just done to protect me. "*Okay. What's your individual name?*"

"*Charlotte Edwina Leglise Jacqueline La Chatte. The old Bonjour named me.*"

"*I don't know if I can remember all that,*" *I said quietly.* "*May I just call you Yowler?*"

"D'accord." *Okay.*

Then I said something I've never heard my kind say. "*Thank you . . . Yowler.*"

She looked me over, her gold and black eyes giving me the up and down. "*Of course. Friends help their own.*"

"*Friends?*" *Oh, this was too much for someone like me. I desperately needed to find my comfortable, shaded bed of leaves and curl up for a long spring nap all by myself. I forced myself to stay.*

"*Yes. You and me. I don't usually form relationships, but I kind of like you. Must be because you smell just like me.*"

She inched closer and sat next to me, her fur touching my relaxed spines. I sighed deeply. "So how does this friends thing work?"

"We look out for each other," she purred.

"Okay," I replied. My brain was expanding just by knowing her. Yowler. My friend. Who knew? "May I go take a lie-down now?"

She snickered and her whiskers trembled. "D'accord. Come on. I'll walk you over there. And perhaps later, you can investigate la poubelle, *the trash can here, to see if there are any delicacies tonight."*

"Do you want me to save a Slug for you?" It was the nicest thing I could offer. Sharing was a hard business.

She made a yakking noise.

I don't think it signaled sheer delight. This relationship was going to be more complicated than I thought.

How is Youssef doing? My grandfather still insulting the poor man?" Rain battered the windshield of the ancient Peugeot I navigated down the narrow country lane in Arcangues, a sleepy village about fifteen kilometers from the coast.

"Not yet," Magdali replied. "Youssef refuses to take offence at anything he says."

"Excellent," I said, glancing at the small house up ahead. "Tell me again why For Sale or Rent signs are gauche?"

"It's just not done," she replied. "Unless the property is uninhabitable or someone is completely desperate."

"Right. Do you think it's the one up ahead?"

Magdali leaned forward and peered through the windshield. "Yes. But I still don't know why we're going."

"You can stay in the car if you want," I replied. "I'm going in. It's perfect. Four bedrooms, two baths, a living room, and study, kitchen, and no maintenance. Rent with option to buy."

I could feel Magdali's gaze, but refused to meet her eyes.

"Enough room for Jean, you, your daughter, and Youssef, or whoever replaces him one day. And Jean's pension will cover it. The sale of Madeleine Marie will cover living expenses for many, many years. And it's even near the golf course and the château." We passed the beautiful ruin of the Château d'Arcangues. "Unless you'd like to, perhaps, find another position with better benefits, Magdali. We haven't spoken of this, but have you considered it?"

"No." She said it so quickly and softly I barely heard it.

"Why not? You could make three times as much, I am sure. And you deserve it."

"Madeleine Marie is my home and my family is in it."

"So you are not willing to help me help you and my grandfather?"

"It is not my place."

"Dammit, Magdali. It is your place. Tell me what you think is best. Or how we can afford to keep it?"

I pulled onto the gravel drive, parked under a massive oak tree, and turned off the engine.

"No, Kate. It is your place. You must make the decisions. My mother always said that a family is like a forest. When you see outside it is dense, when you are inside, you see that each tree has its place."

"Well, I am trying to move the forest, but no one is willing to uproot themselves. Even you."

"Perhaps it's not necessary then."

The windows were beginning to fog. I wanted to grab Magdali's shoulders and shake her. "Of course, it's necessary. It's better to sell before every last painting and stick of furniture is sold. Before the damn house falls off the cliff or the walls collapse. Sometimes I think the only thing keeping those walls standing is the ivy intertwined and glued to every square inch."

"My mother always said—"

"Magdali, my family, and especially my father, loved Africa too. I've heard all the proverbs. I have. But they are not going to help in this situation. Something's got to give," I said, trying to keep exasperation at bay. "No one is willing to be practical. Pragmatic. Do you think I enjoy being the person herding everyone else to the only solution?"

"Of course not. Why did you agree to come?"

That stopped me. "You're changing the subject."

"So are you," she replied quietly.

"I came because I used to love this place and the people here too. And I wanted to make sure everything was taken care of properly."

"Of course you do. That's because you've always taken care of everyone and everything—even though no one ever looked out for you." Magdali looked away.

I couldn't think of a single thing to say.

"*Alors*, if no one else says it, I will. Thank you, Kate."

I stared straight ahead.

"But you haven't considered other solutions," she said slowly.

"I am all ears. What are you suggesting?"

"It is not my place."

"If you say that one more—"

"Don't sell it," she interrupted. It was the first time I'd ever heard her interrupt anyone.

I breathed slowly in and out, resisting the urge to speak. What the hell was the point? I didn't want to hear any more platitudes. The du Roques, the Hamiltons, and apparently Magdali's ancestors were all about fairy tales and proverbs. "Are you coming?"

She stared straight in front of her and briefly shook her head to say no.

"Suit yourself. I'm going in." And I did.

The owner, a middle-aged man who lived in a much larger house on the hill, was delighted to show me the cottage.

"Mme Hamilton, it is a pleasure," he said. "My father used to play golf with your grandfather at Arcangues and Le Phare. But may I ask why you are interested in this house? Is this for you?"

His faintly condescending and disapproving air was getting on my last nerve. "No. We are selling Madeleine Marie and I am looking for a place to either rent or buy for my grandfather."

He made a tsk-tsk sound that I thought was something found only in children's tales. "But you cannot sell Madeleine Marie. It would be a tragedy."

"May I take a look at the house, then?"

He appeared to consider it and I could swear he almost said no. But his avaricious nature took hold and he motioned me to follow him.

And it was perfect.

Perfect for any normal family in our circumstances, and we would be perfect tenants for the owner.

But *normal* was not a word ever used to describe my family or, apparently, this owner's. If I didn't know that now, I would soon.

Chapter Ten

The second week of June swept in on a painfully bright blue day with a chill to chase away any hope of putting away sweaters. A few long days later, when the bulls of nearby Pamplona were being examined, selected, and prepared for the annual wine-infused and frenzied festival next month, my daughter was due to arrive at BIQ.

I'd prepared my somber, old bedchamber at the end of the hall to give her more privacy. A small bookcase of children's books covered one wall. I'd read every single one of them, from *Aesop's Fables* to *Auntie Mame*. The toys in the chest at the foot of the bed were a jumble of board games and a collection of Madame Alexander dolls on top. They lay like a row of corpses from the League of Nations, their eyes closed, their traditional foreign country dresses perfectly pressed, albeit their aprons yellowed with age. Why hadn't someone cleaned out this room? Keen pain hit my solar plexus when I spied my ancient Tiny

Tears doll under an unfamiliar blue blanket. I thought it had been lost during one of the many moves of my childhood. I shut the top of the chest.

The room looked out over the side garden of Pierrot and Maïte Etcheterry's traditional Basque house next door. Ever since one of their boxers had disappeared, the barking had been considerably reduced only to be replaced by a small troupe of workers from Lyonnaise des Eaux, the regional water service. Mlle Lefebvre had appointed herself chief of traffic and street parking, performing her task like a drill sergeant on steroids.

Conflicting thoughts ricocheted in my mind as I drove to the small airport, which buzzed with an international mix of people. A group of airport employees loitered in the small café as the passengers from the Hop! Air France flight from Paris descended the escalator. Harried Parisians in their wrinkled suits interspersed with surfers wearing Ray-Bans, and all the while I sweated next to a column, waiting for Lily to appear.

And all at once, she was there. Taller, chestnut hair longer, and just so achingly beautiful to me that my sight became blurred. I gripped my hands until the pain of my nails digging into my palms forced my emotions to retreat.

She gave a small side wave when her eyes met mine, and finally a shy, small smile lit her beautiful angular features. Stepping off the escalator, she slipped past the throngs. Dropping her backpack, she melted into my arms and suddenly I couldn't stop the wave of tears flooding my face, dripping onto her navy blue school fleece. She smelled the same—the sweet scent of her favorite shampoo infused her hair, and the indefinable essence with which she had been born assaulted my senses. She was my daughter. My every last thing of importance.

"Mom . . . it's freezing here! I didn't pack the right stuff. I know it. I—"

I couldn't let her go. "It doesn't matter." She started to break away but I pulled her tight. She gave in to it and hugged me back, allowing me to rock back and forth for a moment or two. I could feel that she was now taller than me. "We'll go shopping." She pulled away and retrieved her backpack and I quickly wiped my tears away with the back of my hand.

"I can't believe I finally get to see France. I want to try surfing. We can walk to the beach from the house, right?"

I pushed back my immediate thought of her damaged arm. "Yes. Of course. You must be tired. Are you hungry?"

Lily laughed, and the blue of her eyes was so bright. "I don't even know." She rolled her eyes. "I think I've had two breakfasts. So, how far away is the house? Wow . . . I never thought I'd ever see this place."

I pointed toward the baggage carousel, and we began walking. "About fifteen minutes from here. Everyone's there. They all can't wait to meet you."

"Is Antoinette there? What about your grandfather? And Magdali? I've heard so many stories about her, I can't wait to meet her. Does she still speak the click language you told me about?"

I'd forgotten all about the language of Magdali's mother. I

could even feel the clicks in the back of my throat. The secret, funny language of my shared youth with Magdali. "You'll have to ask her."

"You haven't tried it with her?" Lily frowned. "Why not?"

"I-I don't know," I replied. "I guess I forgot about it."

She reached for a massive navy blue duffel bag on the carousel and I rushed to grab it, to save her arm.

She wrestled it off, nudging me away. "I'm fine, Mom. I can do it."

"I'll get a cart."

"I don't need it." Defiance brewed in her expression.

"Got it. Okay, then," I said. "Let's go. The car's right out those doors." I just didn't have it in me to Mom her.

"Wow. Palm trees," she said, exiting. "You never mentioned palm trees."

"Hmmm. Never thought about it. But there's all kinds of trees in the area. Doesn't really freeze here."

"I can smell the ocean."

"Yup. It's low tide in about two hours."

"Why does that matter?"

"Well, everyone kind of has the tide schedule in the back of their minds," I said. "Many beaches completely disappear at high tide."

"What about the beach at our house?"

Our house . . . A trickle of anxiety slid down my spine. I didn't want her to get too attached to something we wouldn't have all that much longer. "Madeleine Marie overlooks the Côte des

Basques. Best beach here. But, yes, the waves crash onto the rocks at high tide.

"How far is it from Madeleine Marie?"

It was the first time I'd heard her use the name of the villa. "Depends if you take the long or the short way." What was I thinking? She couldn't do the rope. "But the long way is more fun. Um, about twenty to thirty minutes either way."

She was laughing and pointing at things as we drove to the villa. "Why are all the roofs made of orange tile? I saw that from the plane as we were landing. And the houses are almost all white."

"You won't find many brick houses here, or if you do they're usually ancient, patterned, and crumbling."

"It's about as far away from Connecticut as I can imagine." She said the last into the wind of the open window.

"I know." And for the first time, I wasn't eager to return to America. No place felt like home without my daughter.

"I think I like it here," Lily said. Her profile was so even and beautiful, so very unlike my own.

When the old Peugeot's tires crunched the gravel of the drive, the wood and iron door swung open and Magdali came rushing out. Gone were the smooth, graceful movements I knew.

"You must be Magdali," Lily said, exiting the car.

"*Oui.*"

"Oh, do you speak English or should I speak French?"

"Either," Magdali said, nodding. "Your mother said you attended a lycée and speak fluently."

"Well, one of us had better," I muttered.

"I'm Lily." And my daughter immediately gave a huge hug to a woman who matched her height. "Is your daughter here?"

"You are, indeed," Magdali said, with the smallest degree of embarrassment from the hug. "No, Solange is . . . still at school."

"Well, when will she be here?"

I suddenly felt terrible for not having asked Magdali this same question.

"Soon. Next week, if it suits the family."

Lily looked at me with uncertainty and then shook her head as she turned back to Magdali. "Well, of course it would suit the family. Why wouldn't it?"

I rushed forward, "Magdali, I don't know what you're talking about, but please arrange for Solange to take the train as soon as her school lets out. When is that?"

"The end of the week. But they have a summer term she may attend."

"Let's buy the train ticket today."

Magdali smiled at Lily. "Your great-grandfather is very eager to meet you. He's been waiting in the front salon all morning."

"Is he still as grumpy as my mother said he was when she was a little girl?"

"Lily!"

"Well, is he?"

"Yes," I answered, saving Magdali from embarrassment. "And now he prefers being called Jean. You are forewarned."

Lily giggled then yanked the duffle from the open trunk.

There were freshly cut blue irises and white peonies in several old silver golf trophies on the mantle. Lily, in the unaffected way of youth, ran to Jean, who was sitting in a chair, and he crushed her to him with his gnarled hands, burying his face in her long, dark chestnut hair. She sank into the sofa next to him and smiled. My grandfather appeared a decade younger in that moment; all wrinkles seemed to fade from the force of pure joy.

"Nice to meet you," she said. "So am I supposed to call you Jean or . . ." Her inflection ended on a question.

"What do you think?"

"I kind of like Granddaddy," she said. "Maybe because I've never been able to call someone that."

It was a sad fact that all of her grandparents were deceased save Antoinette, who would outlast all of us, I was sure.

"Granddaddy it is, then."

"Yay," she said and ran a finger over the mottled horn handle of his cane. "So, can you walk? Or are you in a wheelchair?"

"I try to walk from time to time, but mostly the wheelchair. Do you want to see the garden? Perhaps you could wheel me there. I think the—"

The small bell rigged to the main door sounded, and a few moments later Mr. Soames appeared. His white mustache was immaculately trimmed as always and he appeared quite natty in his herringbone jacket and tan trousers.

"Is this the great-granddaughter I've heard so much about? Forgive my intrusion, but I felt it absolutely necessary to welcome you to the neighborhood."

Magdali magically appeared with Mr. Soames's favored biscuits and a tea tray. Clearly, she had known all about the impromptu visit.

As Lily shook hands with the elegant gentleman, Mlle Lefebvre's petite frame appeared at the doorway. She did not break a smile upon introduction. Instead, she gave a sour look toward Jean, who ignored her.

I glanced at the tea service. Nine cups and saucers. Youssef entered bearing another large silver service. And completely ignoring all French rules of social seniority, Lily shook hands with this incredibly strong man, in personality and strength, who had withstood the withering blasts of my grandfather and earned his place in the household. Lily then kissed both cheeks of Mlle Lefebvre, who almost smiled before remembering herself.

When the mayor and Pierrot and Maïte arrived a quarter hour later, I finally understood.

It was to be a party. A surprise welcome party. By the people who were determined to embrace, like, and eventually love my daughter whether she or I liked it or not. I wasn't even sure if they did it for Jean. I think they arrived not out of curiosity, but rather out of the ancient tradition of welcoming a member of the tribe into the fold.

Amid the raucous chattering and booming laughter that I knew would go on for quite awhile—for let's face it, the French like a good party—I slipped out the door and searched out Magdali in the kitchen. She wasn't there. Instead, she was outside the kitchen side door, staring at the tiers of gardens, now awash with summer blooms. The scent of freesias perfumed the air.

"You did this, didn't you?"

"No, not really."

"Yes, you did."

"You forget, Kate. Everyone knows what's going on in everyone else's life here. There's no such thing as privacy. And when something good happens everyone wants to celebrate. When something bad happens everyone cares or mourns on some level."

"And you knew and so bought the pastries and arranged the tea and everything."

She nodded. "Of course. And you'd best send Lily for the croissants and the journal tomorrow morning early because the baker and *bar-tabac* owner are not to be put off."

I stared at her. And then she folded me into her thin arms. "Oh, Magdali. She's here. She came back to me."

"She did," she whispered. "I knew she would. No matter what happened, I knew she would. You're a great mother, Kate. I'm certain." I felt Magdali's slim hand run over the curve of my head.

"It's the opposite." My hands heavily hung from my arms like cement blocks and I could barely breathe. "She jumped out her bedroom window." The words felt like hot bricks of sin and shame. "Oliver wouldn't leave her alone. He was screaming and beyond reason. Tormenting her. Again. Banging on her door. Refusing to be deterred. He had that horrible look in his eyes—that Dr. Jekyll turned Mr. Hyde look. And, and . . .

"I had just come back from the grocery store . . . and couldn't get him away from her door. Couldn't make him calm down. I still don't know what set him off." I closed my eyes and imagined for the millionth time what Lily had done. "And at some point, she silently jumped. From the second story. And when he got into her room, she was gone . . . without a trace. Except for a few strands of her hair . . . which I still have.

"I found her six months, two weeks, and three days later. In a homeless shelter clear on the other side of the country." I choked on a half sob, half laugh. "At least she chose a nice place. She hitchhiked to Monterey, California. And all with a broken arm and collarbone." The words were sluicing out of me like the rare rains flooding the immense creek beds of Southern California.

Magdali stroked my head.

"And don't say it wasn't my fault. It was. I wanted to divorce the son of a bitch the year she was born. But I was terrified a judge wouldn't grant me full custody because it would've been my word against Oliver's, and he'd have argued I'd had a bout of postpartum depression. I just couldn't take the risk of him ever having any sort of custody. I was idiotic enough to think I could control the situation. He sometimes would go a year or two without losing it."

"Did he ever harm you or Lily?"

"Forgive me, Magdali, but I hate to talk about it. It was more verbal and emotional abuse. He just could not control his fury. No matter how much anger management he tried. And, for good reason, Lily blamed me for not leaving. For not protecting her. She will never understand why I chose what I chose."

"Then tell her," Magdali said quietly. "At the right time. But don't leave it too long. Don't be afraid of conflict, Kate. Never expect perfection in an imperfect world. Storms make you defend your borders, make you speak up for what you believe, and truths become self-evident."

I nodded. "Thank you, Magdali. For listening. For your wise words."

She raised one brow. "I think you really want to thank me for not sharing another proverb from Namibia."

I finally smiled. "Let's get that rail ticket for your daughter as soon as the guests leave. Yes?"

As we linked arms and walked back to the celebration, I had an idea. A way to truly honor the first friend in my life for her goodness.

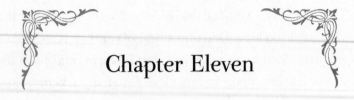

Chapter Eleven

M om, I can't hear you well. You're breaking up," I said, speaking into the iPhone microphone an inch from my mouth. I kicked myself for even hoping for help. Hope, in the face of history, was a futile effort. It would have been more fruitful and far more amusing to consult the psychic home network. Instead, I was in Bayonne, post interviews with two different notaries who handled real estate transactions of all kinds. A half-eaten strawberry tart sat mocking me from its plate on the petite outdoor café table. Sadly, I was becoming immune to the previously excellent numbing effects of *crème chantilly*.

Antoinette's voice crackled. ". . . I wish you were here. I'm having so much fun. We went to a clambake hosted by friends of the Kennedys last night, along with dear Paolo's daughter and her husband. They are very nice. You would really like them. I told them all about you and your consulting business.

You should bring Lily here. She would love it. It's so beautiful. The weather is amazing. And we could practice Spanish. Paolo would love to teach Lily."

What was the point of even trying? Words never deterred her. And I was over her embarrassment regarding my profession eons ago.

"Mom, did you hear what I said? Jean won't agree to sell. Your brother is selling anything not nailed down and doing God knows what with the money. The villa is a disaster. I might be able to get one to one point five million euros if we don't fix anything. I found a great little house near Arcangues that we could rent but I can't get anyone to agree to move. It's a complete bust. I've spent over six thousand euros paying all the bills that have been in arrears for months. What should I do now? Any advice?" I downed a forkful of strawberry tart with gusto and hope.

"Um . . . What? Couldn't understand half of that," she said. "Oh, here, Paolo wants to say hello to you."

"No," I shouted, mouth full of cream. "I don't want to talk to Paolo. I—"

"Of course you want to talk to me, *chica*. Hey, have you sold the villa yet?"

"No, Paolo. May I please speak to Antoinette?"

"Oh, poor baby. Sounds awful. You poor thing, having to go all the way to the South of France to vacation in the sun and sea. Well, I hope you get busy and sell that place. Antoinette is counting on you."

I refused to answer by reason of sanity. "My mother—may I speak to her?" I signaled the young, swarthy waiter via an air signature to bring the check.

"Of course, *chica*. Here she is."

I could hear the lizard hissing at Antoinette, "She's such an unpleasant, impolite thing, isn't she?"

My mother's response was muffled as if she had placed her hand over the receiver. And then she was talking to me again. "So, could you and Lily fly here next month? I'd arrange the tickets, of course. Could put the two of you in a hotel down the street. Very chic. There are just not enough bedrooms in the house, you understand, with all of Paolo's family visiting. You would like them so much. Especially his son, Manuel. In fact, I might have to play a bit matchmaker with you. You've had long enough to sulk over this entire affair with your stupid ex-husband. And look, even he is getting on with his life. Rita Shepard called me last week to tell me Oliver's engaged. How amusing is that?"

I pulled the cell phone from my ear and looked at it. Who was the woman talking to me? Why was I even bothering? Why was I still trying? Wasn't the definition of insanity attempting the same thing over and over and expecting a different result?

"That's just great, Mom. So. Again. Any advice about the situation here?"

The waiter, carrying an immense platter of dirty dishes, expertly slid a small silver saucer in front of me with *l'addition*.

"Merci," I mouthed.

"Well," Antoinette continued, in that hard to define accent

that was uniquely her own—perfect English with hints of British nanny and American fast food. "I can send a bit of money, if needed, to repay you, of course. I can't send a huge amount as Paolo and I are considering a new venture—a joint one for the first time. Then we're off to Italy in two months. That's why you and Lily should come here before we go. Martha's Vineyard is just heaven, I tell you."

"Got it," I said, with zero intent to visit. I wouldn't get within one thousand miles of Paolo and his brand of snake oil. Thank God Antoinette knew well the delicate balancing act of holding on to the vast majority of her assets while placating a man's ego. "But, again, is there anything I can say to Jean to make him budge from his position?"

"Well, he does like his whiskey in the evening."

"Yes? And so?"

"It always puts him in a better mood."

"Not enough to make him sell the house."

"Perhaps you should arrange for a buyer first."

"You are not suggesting I find a buyer and then get him drunk to get him to sign the papers?"

"Absolutely not! I would never suggest that."

A seventy-four-year-old woman giggling is never amusing. "Mom. Antoinette, I need—"

"Okay, darling. Must run. We're all leaving for lunch in Edgartown and then a bit of shopping. Do you or Lily need anything? What is your size now? Have you gained any weight? Are you following that Mediterranean diet I told you about? And you never drink as much water as you should."

"Got it. More water. And olives." I hated olives and would never put one of those slimy, briny things in my mouth.

"Is my darling granddaughter still a size six?"

"We don't need anything, really. I just need—"

"Nonsense. Every woman likes and needs pretty things once in a while. And I love spoiling you. And Lily. How is she liking Biarritz after two weeks? Oh, is she as pretty as when I last saw her?" She laughed again. "Does she still look like me? It's amusing how she looks more like me than you. You don't really look like anyone in the family. Except perhaps your nose."

She would never change. And my role was not to even try. "Yes. She's beautiful, Mom. Just like you."

Her voice became faint. "Oh, Paolo. Tell everyone I'm coming. Okay, darling. Do take care. Lots of exercise is always a good idea. Stay away from the foie gras and *les frites*. It's not on the diet."

"Right. French fries and goose liver, no. Exercise, yes. Got it. Have fun."

She was gone. Had probably hung up ten seconds ago. And I was right back to square one. Day one.

Me against everyone else in the family.

Indeed, against everyone in southwest France.

Except perhaps the short mayor, whose perpetual bad mood was likely due to a stomachache from puffing out his chest and holding in his abdomen all day long to exude authority. It became patently clear that evening that Jojo, despite his puffery, would be delighted to take the villa off my hands. Indeed, he was vying for the position of my new BFF, a term that deliciously embodied the ingredients of our budding relationship: juvenile brevity, tempestuous deceit, and absolute temerity.

"Mme Hamilton," he said during the gloaming hour in the village square with an unusually small traditional Basque building, *la mairie* in the background. We stood on the long fronton court, where that ancient game known as jai alai in the States was played by the local teams several times a week under the orange glow of a harvest moon in late summer. "As you can see, our extraordinary *marché* has grown and grown. You do know that *Paris Match* magazine named our village 'The Crown Jewel of the Pays Basque'?"

"Yes, M. le Maire." It was the fifth time he'd imparted this little gem of information in the last month.

He glanced toward the village butcher, who was taking great pains to display an impressive haunch of Serrano ham just next to us. The mayor escorted me to the privacy of the World War II memorial inscribed with all the townspeople who had lost their lives during the occupation.

"Well, it's just a little idea of mine that we need *un plus grand espace* for our *mairie*, for the fronton, for everything needed to make sure the jewel is properly displayed. Don't you agree?" He didn't wait for an answer. "I would be happy to talk to your grandfather about this as I think the time is ripe, *non*?" Again, no pause. "I spoke to my dear friend in Arcangues, who tells me you toured his cottage last week. I feel sure we can all come to a mutually satisfying agreement about the future of Madeleine

Marie. And your family would become known as *les anges*—the angels—of the Pays Basque for providing a better setting for our pearl."

Finally an ally was presenting himself, albeit with overblown prose. The only problem was I didn't trust a word he said. We were completely different species. This smacked of a Nazi-Vichy collaboration and I was afraid I was feeling like the traitor and my poor grandfather represented old France.

"Ah, and who do we have 'ere?" The mayor smiled broadly. "Why, it's Mr. Smith from Sotheby's and M. Landuran from Barclays. Bonsoir, *mes amis!*"

"How convenient," I commented without any surprise. I looked at the two men who at least had the decency to appear embarrassed. "Good to see you both."

The banker kissed my cheeks very correctly. The man from Sotheby's didn't dare. He nodded instead.

"Antoinette rang me earlier," M. Landuran informed.

"Not surprised," I replied.

"She's wiring money to your account."

"I know."

"She rang me too," the man from Sotheby's added to me.

Now there was a surprise. "What did she expect you to do, Mr. Smith?"

"Find a buyer."

"Oh. I thought I asked you to do that a while ago. And since that day, I've not heard a peep from you."

"Yes, but I didn't fully understand the dire situation."

"Really? I thought your description of the plumbing, roof, and cliff quite inspiring."

He had the audacity to feign innocence. "Madame, *pardonnez-moi.* It's just that we are in a strong growth cycle now. And we have the full support of so many people at present. I feel certain we can arrange for the sale." He looked at the mayor, clearly the head of the village mafia.

"May I remind you that I have not signed a contract with Sotheby's yet?" I glanced at the inscriptions on the memorial. "So far, I've been unimpressed with your service. I'd expect a reduction in commission if I use you."

He blanched, his face almost pale blue in the darkening hour. He looked like a soldier caught consorting with the enemy.

"And furthermore," I added, "I'm employing a notary in Bayonne instead of here to complete any sale."

It was the mayor's turn to take on the mien of a sardine's belly.

"But, please," I said, "don't misunderstand. I'm delighted by the prospect of a swift resolution regarding the future of our family's villa."

"*Naturellement,*" the banker inserted. "Jojo, or rather, M. le Maire, would coordinate a long-term loan by the French government to purchase Madeleine Marie."

"Really? How much would *la République* offer for Madeleine Marie? And Mr. Smith, I would like to see the list of potential buyers you have contacted since last we spoke."

The mayor stepped in. "Oh, well, we mustn't talk about such

things right now. We must enjoy the beauty of the evening. The festivities. And I must accept the microphone to begin the Festival of the Sardine properly. The grillers are in position. Then the Strong Man competition. They will be climbing and sawing logs tonight, and then the crowd favorite tug-of-war. And we will have *une boum*—a dance—for the young and old here tonight."

I plastered a smile on my face. The mayor was immensely fond of the microphone if recent history was any indication. It was going to be a long evening, with the sardines and rosé counteracting the microphone and music with any luck. "Of course," I said. "Please give me a call in the morning, Mr. Smith. And when you have—" I felt a tap on my shoulder and turned to find Edward Soames with a quizzical look on his face. "Yes?"

"Your daughter requires your attention." His eyes gave nothing away.

"Oh. *Excusez-moi, messieurs.*" A round of advanced French leave-taking could not get me away fast enough. Major Soames's arm-pulling did. "What's going on? You were just trying to save me from those bureaucrats, right?"

"Mostly yes. But I did just see Lily around the corner at the little port. She was helping unload the last of the sardines off the boats." He leaned in. "Uh, there was a young man who appeared more than ready to improve French-American relations with her. Not too concerned. She had him by two inches. But—"

"Hey, should I be worried or not?" I picked up the pace.

"No, but walk faster, please," he said, leading the way.

I had to run to keep up. "You would have stepped in if you were worried."

He didn't reply.

"I *know* you would have stepped in." I sounded pathetic.

"Yep. I'm not worried. Just thought we should check on her again."

A quarter hour later and she was still not to be found. We stopped near the stand-up paddleboards chained to the rusting rings of a port that had probably protected fishing boats since before the Roman Inquisition, if the thickness of the port walls was any indication.

"Are you sure the girl you saw was Lily? This is ridiculous. I refuse to panic." I started to panic.

"She's hard to miss," he said. "She's the tallest girl in this village and I could hear her voice."

"What about the guy? How old was he?"

"Never seen him before. Maybe early twenties. Looked like a typical young recruit."

Bile rose in my throat. This was the last place in the world I could envision a problem. And she wouldn't run away again. She just wouldn't. But perhaps she would. I just didn't know her anymore. My nerves were dancing on the thin wire of fear and losing ground. Really, I needed to get a grip.

"Hey," the major said softly, "you're really worried, aren't you? She didn't run away if that's what you're thinking. Just thought you wouldn't want some Gitanes-smoking young Frenchy flirting with Lily."

I felt like a miserable mother.

"She's probably back at the villa," he insisted. "Why don't you go there and I'll keep looking here? I'll call you or Magdali for an update in twenty."

I nodded, and left without a word, negotiating the patterned cobblestones of the tiny port in my striped espadrilles. It was nine in the evening and still the sun had not set. The crowd was becoming more raucous by the minute as the scent of sardines and olive oil tinged the salt air and a large orange tabby cat darted behind a fishing boat.

Past Madeleine Marie's heavy front door, I took the red-carpeted winding stairs two at a time toward the bedroom floor. Heart pounding, I edged open her door to find Jean, reading glasses low on his nose, a book propped high, in a chair next to her bed, my old bed of youth. A small lamp cast a yellow glow in the room.

And Lily was asleep—a wild spray of dark chestnut locks spread over the pillow, her mouth slightly open, and her arms thrown carelessly over her head.

It was the most beautiful tableau I'd ever seen.

Jean brought a finger to his lips.

I silently choked back a sound, and tears began to fall. My grandfather opened one arm and I went to him, kneeling between him and my daughter. And for the first time in forever I felt something warm in my chest. He rested a hand on my shoulder.

This was what safety, security felt like. Perhaps. It was, of course, just an illusion. Everything changes. Nothing is secure from the havoc of time.

"Stop thinking," Jean whispered.

He'd always been a mind reader. I remembered that from my youth.

"Really," he insisted quietly. "Just stop thinking."

I nodded, unable to speak.

"She's exhausted," he said. "We had a lovely little talk, and I read to her one of my favorite poems—'Le dormeur du val.' Your daughter had brilliant observations. She has far more wisdom than most her age."

"She does. She's seen too much and she loves to read anything and everything."

"Just like you, my darling. Just like you."

"No. She experienced hell. More than she ever should have." I paused. "'The Sleeper of the Valley.' You read that one to me too."

"I think it captures that horrible sight after a battle when young lives are cut short in war."

"Did you see that?"

"*Oui, chérie*," he said simply. "It's something you can never ever forget no matter how many years pass. May I show you something?"

It was such a tender moment and I was desperate to hang on to it. It felt as fragile as a bubble caught on a summer breeze. "Of course."

I helped him to his feet and handed him his cane. We slowly navigated the distance to his bedchamber, which I hadn't really had a good look at since my childhood. Instead of appearing smaller as most things do in adulthood, the room seemed even larger than I remembered. Its walls were covered with a few of the remaining exquisite portraits of ancestors, some of whom I knew by name, others were strangers frozen in time, looking back at me, through fine spiderwebs of cracked paint. Golden toile wallpaper relieved the darkness of the portraits, and a marble bust of a lady with a single long curl resting on her elegant shoulder stood coyly on a pedestal in the corner.

Jean said nothing as he stood by the long doors leading to the balcony, and I went from object to object, remembering almost all of them. The slight scent of peppermint permeated the air, and the poignant memories of cajoling one from my grandfather flooded into this chamber. A jungle of golf trophies littered the room. The largest one, a magnificent, enormous, tarnished, and dusty bowl stood proudly in the corner behind the door. The shadow of something at the bottom of it piqued my curiosity and I fished out a red beribboned medal.

"What's this?"

"What's what, *chérie*?"

I moved toward him and showed him the medal.

He made a disparaging sound and waved a hand. "An elegant symbol of something quite the opposite."

"What did you do?"

"What thousands of Frenchmen and women did during the war," he said.

"Which was?"

His eyes were watery and very pale, almost silver blue in the low light. He appeared very frail, very old. And the warmth I had held within grew cold and numb.

"The Germans appropriated houses up and down the coast. Madeleine Marie was one of them, as you know." He looked toward a painting of his mother, Marguerite, in her youth, the tiny Peruvian powerhouse, so opposite from her tall son, my grandfather. Her shrewd black eyes stared back at me. "Well, while my mother tainted their food to make them ill or sleepy from time to time, we copied their communiqués and transmitted them." His eyes took on a dreamy quality, lost in thought. "We tried to sabotage them at every turn—charming them with the daughters of our friends, with gambling, with wine, and even with golf."

"Where was Antoinette?"

He smiled. "Why, here of course. Did she never tell you?"

"I remember her talking about stuffing newspapers under the doors and how cold it was. And also how she hated her governess. She said she used to give her own rationed butter and chocolate squares to the gardener only to annoy her governess."

Jean smiled. "Sadly, she didn't take to her stepmothers or any other woman in the house except her grandmother."

"Antoinette must have been too young to play any part in the sabotage."

He shook his head slightly. "She might have been very young, but at eight she was already adept at capturing and holding attention. One of the *Kommandanten*, the one who slept in this bedroom in fact, was completely under her spell. He had a daughter of the same age, waiting for him in Berlin. Antoinette did what we asked. She charmed and delighted him, holding his hand in the garden, giving him bouquets, kissing his stern face in the morning, littering him with false compliments to distract him when we needed. She deserved this medal more than I."

"Did she know how dangerous it was?"

"Of course she did. Anyone who watched the Nazis arrive in Biarritz with guns and dogs understood. They marched right past the glittering splendor of the Hôtel du Palais. Napoleon was surely spinning in his grave. Antoinette saw it all. Jean-Michel was sickly and in bed, and petit Nicolas was far too young. But I wanted Antoinette to understand, and her grand-mother insisted she go too."

"Nicolas died," I said. "On the balcony here."

"Yes, along with my second wife."

"His mother. Rosemary."

"Yes. You know, I suppose, the story. She was English. And killed by her own countrymen, bombardiers from England who missed the railway target behind us and dropped a bomb on the balcony just a week after the Kommandant and his regiment had departed for Paris."

I looked closer at the medal and brushed away the layer of dust with my thumb. The white enamel points of the star framed twin French flags in the center with the gold words *Honneur et Patrie*—Honor and Country—embedded in the dark blue enamel. The French Legion of Honor . . .

"Come, Kate. I told you I wanted to show you something."

He depressed the brass door lever, and I preceded him outside to the cement, crisscrossed railing. He joined me and we both gazed at the stars just emerging in the darkening night sky. There appeared to be thousands of them all around us, falling down the edges of our vision until they met the tall trees edging the vast gardens. We stood there for long minutes, and for the first time, I imagined the pain my grandfather endured each time he stood here, where his bonny English lass and their only child, Nicolas, both blond in the pictures he had by his bedside table, had died.

I felt his hand cover mine on the cold railing.

"Watch," he whispered.

At first I couldn't see anything. Then, out of the evergreens rose fireflies—a living, breathing chimera of sparkling iridescence gusting across the gardens, reaching ever skyward until they mingled with the lowest stars on the horizon, blending heaven and earth in a symphony of natural beauty.

"What do you think?"

I swallowed against something hard in the back of my throat.

"It's hard to feel sad," he said quietly, "with such magnificence, *non*?"

"How did you cope?"

He understood perfectly. "It was easier in those days. Everyone was mourning someone lost. I was no different than anyone else. But, of course, Antoinette and Jean-Michel suffered the most, because they probably felt like they lost their adorable brother and two parents, not just one. I disappeared for the rest of the war, joining the resistance in Paris, and following the allies to push the Germans all the way back to Berlin—finally returning to Paris to help rebuild the government. I just couldn't bear to be here, without my wife. She was the one I loved with all my heart." He paused. "My mother, despite her advanced years, raised Antoinette and Jean-Michel, until I returned seven years later. By then your mother was fifteen and Jean-Michel two years younger."

"Jean . . . I—"

"Granddaddy," he said.

"Granddaddy," I swallowed. "I've made such a mess of it. And my life was so much easier than yours."

"Not from what Antoinette tells me. And you've raised an extraordinary daughter."

"I just don't know how to live a good life. I've lost my sense of purpose. I always said I wouldn't let the past affect me when I could escape, but I was a fool to think it wouldn't mark me."

He picked up my hand and examined it. "You've got the long fingers and hands of your great-grandmother, my mother, Marguerite. She believed there was only one goal in life: To love and be loved. And it doesn't matter if it's romantic, fraternal, parental, neighborly, or for one's country even. But I think there's one other thing."

"Yes?"

"Happiness is a risk and it's also a choice. It's very easy to play it safe. Live alone in the privacy of your mind, never sharing, never showing vulnerability, and never risking your heart, all in an effort to protect it from pain." He paused and studied my face. "But it never works."

"But I do love. My love for my daughter is almost painful in its intensity. And, of course, I love our family. I wouldn't be here if I didn't. And my friends and job—I love too."

"Do you, really? Do you love them all properly?"

"What do you mean? Of course I do."

"Just promise me you'll think about it, Kate. I know you and I have been hiding behind bickering, but I'm asking you to think about how you want to go on."

"I will," I said. "But I must also ask you to think about how you want to go on. I refuse to try and force you to do something against your will anymore. And I don't know what to do."

"Kate, my darling, I am too old to find a solution. I'm smart enough to know that progress has surpassed me. So the only thing I can do is trust you. Up until now I have not had faith in you. After seeing Lily, I have faith. And so, I will promise you now that I will follow your lead. If you want me to go to the nuns, I won't be happy about it, but I will. If you want to arrange another house for all of us, I will go. If you want to sell this bag of stones and ivy so Jojo and the rest of the village have a new *mairie*, I will sign. And yes, I know all about Jojo. He's a complete *idiot* even if he does have a good heart. But I ask you to not forget your uncle—my only remaining son. And also to remember the legacy of Madeleine Marie and the people who loved you without ever knowing you—all because you are a du Roque."

I breathed deeply for the first time in a very long time. Fear of disappointing him was to become my constant new bedfellow. It was just my luck that Major Edward Soames had the perfect anecdote or distraction from that fear. It was called constant chastisement and brutal honesty. In large doses.

Chapter Twelve

The earth trembled the next day. Ever so slightly.

"What in bloody hell was that?" The major reflexively crouched and braced his hands on a large boulder, flanking one side of the littoral.

"Just a little quake," I replied, walking past him. "It happens all the time here. Nothing to be alarmed about. Nothing like the San Andreas Fault on the West Coast of the United States. Trust me."

"There's just about nothing I like about this country," he muttered. "Or your gun-loving nascent nation across the pond."

"What about French wine?"

"I'm not a fool," he said, shaking his head. "I put up with a lot for the wine."

"So I understand. But . . ."

"Yes?" He resumed walking behind me along the narrow, orange clay path.

"But how is your intake? Moderate? More than that?"

"I see my relative has been telling tales."

"Are you comfortable with the amount you drink? Do you drink alone? Are you trying to numb the pain?"

"I drink all the damn time. It's relaxing and one of the few pleasures in this Gallic wasteland. What are you suggesting?"

I felt his hand on my shoulder tugging me. I turned and stood my ground.

"I'm not an alcoholic if that's what you think," he said. "I can stop anytime I choose. In fact, I stopped for a few months just to make sure. It's just that I don't choose to live like a monk the rest of my life. Moderation in all things. I like a glass or two of a good red in the evening like most people."

"That was a long answer."

"Bloody hell," he said. "This is never going to work if you can't trust me."

"Okay. All right," I replied, giving up traditional therapy in lieu of getting something through this ox-brained Brit. "How about if you ease off the sauce for a bit if only to calm everyone in your family. Can you do that? How about trying six months this time?"

"Roger. Now, did you bring water for yourself?" He paused. "And by the way, now it's my turn."

"Does that mean you'll actually stop drinking for at least six months?"

"Stop doubting me. Do you have water or not?"

"Answer my question."

He smiled. "How about if I give it up for a year?"

"Well, that would be something I think your wife and relatives would appreciate," I said, searching my backpack for water. I fished it out and drank seven-eighths of it.

"Water is life," he said.

"Exactly."

"So," he began, "this no-drinking business doesn't include cider, yeah?"

"What?"

"Cider."

"Is it alcoholic?"

"Somewhat."

"Then that would be a no," I said. "A hell no."

"Fine. Have it your way. Honestly," he added, "you should have been a teacher. I've never met someone so exacting. No one likes a hard-ass, you know."

"Maybe, but everyone's relatives will thank a hard-ass."

He rubbed his hands together. "Now it's my turn."

I ground my teeth and sped ahead to walk up a set of log steps single file. I could hear him right behind me, and I had the feeling he could mow me down and keep on going if he wanted.

"Move your feet, Hamilton." I could barely breathe but I was determined to keep up the pace.

"So," he said, right behind me. "We talked about the necessity of voicing our fears. Are you ready to tell me yours?"

"Sure." I was panting so hard I could barely speak. "My fears are my oldest friends. They're not very original. Fear of harm re my daughter or family and friends, fear of failure, of conflict, and of death. And there's always the old standby."

"What's that?" he asked, his breathing even.

I stopped abruptly at the top of the steps and he rammed into me.

"For the love of God, woman. Move your arse well ahead if you're going to stop like that without any indication."

"Yes, major." I added a mock salute. "Are you always this charming with everyone?"

He gave me a disgusted look. "No, Hamilton. I make a special effort with you since you, according to Uncle Phillip, are a walking saint. Okay, don't tease me with that melodramatic crap about an old standby fear."

"Do you have *any* friends? Any at all?"

"Not in France."

"Except me," I said, trying not to sound annoyed. He just brought out the worst in me.

He finally laughed. "You've got me there. I forgot the wine merchant. He's a nice, old chap. Has even started to import Guinness for me. He's not going to be happy about the sudden absence of my business. Bloody hell, stop sidestepping. Your. Fear. Now."

I gazed at the profile of the mythical lady, crowning the mountain up ahead. "That I'm unlovable." I turned to look at him in all his untidy, sweaty glory. He'd let his old standby two-day growth of beard grow wild for an extra week. "I think most people worry at least a little about that. Do you?"

"Absolutely not. I'm one of the most loyal and lovable people on earth," he stated, "but I can also be incredibly stupid. Sort of like a Labrador retriever."

It was impossible to tell if he was joking or not. "I see."

"You asked the wrong question, as usual," he continued.

"Okay. I'll play along. What should I have asked?"

"If other people think I'm lovable."

"And?"

"The answer to that would be a, uh, resounding no."

"Why do you think they think you're unlovable?"

"Because I'm a pain in the arse, Hamilton. A complete dick. Haven't you figured that out yet? Keep the bloody hell up."

"Today you seem to really like the word *bloody*. Are you giving *fuck* the day off?"

He looked at me and then burst out laughing. "Keep that up and I might warm to you."

I rolled my eyes. "Will wonders ever cease?"

"I'm not a fan of clichés. Try harder." He tipped back his hat and looked toward the peak of the mountain. "Have you noticed that the mountain peaks sort of look like a person's profile?"

I gazed toward the mountaintops. "Of course. Local lore has it that it's a beautiful woman who lies asleep on top of the mountain. It's known as Les Trois Couronnes—the three crowns."

"Pity she's got no tits."

He wanted a reaction and so I didn't give him one. Instead, I began walking.

"Fight, damn you," he muttered behind me.

I stopped dead in my tracks. "What did you just say?"

"I said, fight. I've seen dental floss that has more life to it than you."

I turned to face him. For the first time in my life I wished I knew how to make a fist and smash it in the smug face in front of me. Instead, my hands lay limply by my sides. "What? You think inappropriate comments are going to make me open up? It's just the reverse, major."

"I want proof that you know how to stand up and say what you want to say. Call me a misogynist pig. You know you want to."

"I don't have to prove a damn thing to you. You don't know me at all."

"I know a coward when I see one."

I ran at him without even knowing I was doing it. My fists rammed his abdomen and he barely moved. He grabbed my wrists, placed both of them in one of his ugly mitts, and continued, "Um, we'll have to work on that. If you really want to do some damage, aim for the bollocks. Okay, settle down. Let's sit on those rocks ahead. Americans are always so hotheaded. Always resorting to violence. All guns, no humor. You being the prime example."

I wasn't sure if I was angrier at him or myself for losing it. Heretofore, I could say I'd never attacked a patient. Then again, he wasn't technically a patient.

He took his time wiping off the large rock with a rag from his pocket. He indicated a seat and I took it. His face inches from mine, he began. "What the hell happened to you in this lifetime? When did you stop fighting? How did you fail your daughter?"

And so I told him. Told him the same things I told Magdali. Of Lily breaking her arm and collarbone when she'd jumped out the window to get away from her father.

"It could not have been an isolated event," he said calmly. "Had he ever physically harmed your daughter before this? Or you?"

I hated telling him. He just wouldn't understand that I was different from other people. That I could handle anything and everything. That I understood that it was my ex-husband's problem, not mine. That I could compartmentalize, analyze, and file away serious stuff and never ever let it affect me. It was obvious Oliver was just caught in the cycle of repeating childhood abuse and would never change. His problems were not my fault. I never took anything personally.

"Where the hell are you? Answer me. What did that fucker do to you?" Soames barked out every syllable of the question with a voice I'd never heard him use. It demanded response.

"I was married to Oliver for well over a decade and a half. In all that time, he did only one thing to me, aside from the endless stream of verbal abuse, which was easy to tune out."

"For Christ's sake. And that thing was?"

"He pushed me down a flight of stairs. Right after Lily was born."

"What?"

Suddenly, Soames's voice faded away. Blood was pounding in

my ears. And I shifted focus to the profile in the mountains. "I was holding Lily at the top of the stairs, and he was screaming at me in the middle of the night, telling me I had to get her to stop crying because he had to go to work in the morning. And his mother was behind him, watching the whole thing, begging me to give Lily to her." I stopped to catch my breath. It felt like I had run a marathon. For so long I'd kept this hidden away in the depths of the darkness of my mind and now it was oozing uncontrollably. "I couldn't go outside because it was the dead of winter. Snow on the ground. I told Oliver to go back to bed. That's when he lost it—went nose-to-nose with me and started stabbing my shoulder with his finger . . . and I fell all the way to the bottom." I moved my gaze from the deep-blue, calm sea to his face. "I had a hand on the banister, which helped break part of the fall and protected the baby. I just overstretched the ligaments in one of my legs." I finally shifted my eyes to his.

Edward Soames was stone cold calm. "And?"

"And I looked up from the bottom of the stairs and told him I wanted a divorce, and ordered him to get out by the morning and take his mother too. I locked myself in Lily's room with her. All night long I sorted through the possible courses of action."

"There was only one possible course of action. Take the bastard to court and sue for divorce," he said with the authority of a military man.

"As I was saying"—I shook my head—"by the morning, I realized I was in trouble. I had no viable solution that would keep Lily out of harm's way. No one I could depend on to keep her in hiding. And I feared no judge would grant me sole custody as it would be my word against his and his mother's. And his father was president of the country club, chairman of the bank board, and the head of the richest, most respected family in Darien. People knew Oliver was a conventional, churchgoing, mild-mannered, successful man. They never saw the fury that lurked just under the surface. I didn't see it until Lily was born. It was just a horrible Catch-22 situation all the way around. But there was no way on earth I would ever have risked allowing Oliver any custody. And so I didn't divorce. I waited for Lily to grow up instead."

Soames shook his head. "And that's where you are dead wrong. Not that I blame you. It's a common mistake. You're just not thinking the way a man would think. You've just got to attack a bastard until you break him."

The sting of insult battled with curiosity and the latter won. "Really? How would you have handled it?"

"I would have looked him in the eye and told him that if he ever dared lay a finger on me or the child again I would inform every person in our acquaintance, his father, including everyone at his work that he was a fucking lunatic who abused women and children."

"I see. You think that would've worked." My voice was too high. I could hear it.

"Yep. I guarantee he would have never ever touched you or your daughter again."

"You have no proof of that. He was a narcissistic, tortured man. And no matter what I said or did, it didn't make a difference. Lily and I just went along for the wildly out-of-control ride. It was simple. His fits of rage always wiped clean by confession on Sunday. But you were right that Lily and I were held hostage by my own fault. I was the idiot who married him. And the idiot who didn't protect my daughter."

"What happened when you found her at that homeless shelter?"

Fingers curled into fists, I couldn't feel my hands. I forced myself to release them.

"Tell me what happened then," he commanded again.

"By then, I'd filed for divorce, during which I allowed my attorney to subpoena Lily's best friend, who spent one summer with us and who testified against Oliver since Lily was gone. I was lucky, the judge assigned to the trial had no ties to Oliver's father and he believed us instead of Oliver and his mother."

"Of course he did," he said. "What happened after?"

"When I found Lily in California, we met with a social worker. Lily refused to live with me even though her father was gone. She would not agree to go with me. She said she hated both of us," I said. Guilt dripped from every word. "As she should. Sure she was underage, but I knew it was futile to force her to go with me as she would have just run away again."

He sighed heavily.

"Don't look at me like that. The only way she would agree to leave was if I sent her to Miss Chesterfield's."

"Maybe you shouldn't have offered a choice. Maybe she just needed you to insist that the two of you start anew somewhere *you* wanted to live. Begin a new life somewhere other than Connecticut. Maybe New York. That's where you work, right? Your daughter just needed you to be the parent and set the ground rules. She just needed you to be strong, firm, and love her."

I could feel my blood now churning in my chest. I hated him. "I could say almost the exact same thing to you, major. Your wife, daughter, and son would like nothing more than for you to go back, be a great father and husband, restart your life, and move your heart and head onto a new, healthier path by dealing with your issues. Why aren't you doing it? That's how to love your family."

"Don't change the subject," he barked. "We're talking about you."

"Look, Lily and I are going to be just fine now. She's back, Oliver and I are divorced, Lily won't see him, and I have a great job." *Most of the time*, I thought. "I've won the trifecta of life: happy child, great job, secure future."

He shook his head. "Well you don't look happy if you ask me. You've isolated yourself and you're just going through the motions of living. Have you started dating yet?"

"Absolutely not! I have my child and I have no reason to tie a dance card around my wrist ever again. Not in this lifetime or the next. I'll be happy the rest of my damn life alone. I don't need or want anyone. I've got everything I need."

"So your idea of a life after your daughter leaves for college in several years is to do what?" he asked. "Listen to the lives of bored housewives and the wolves of Wall Street? Punish yourself? Live your life for your daughter when she visits on vacations? Run away from all messy entanglements? Keep on living for others instead of for yourself?"

"I've served my sentence. I'm done pleasing everyone."

"Doesn't seem like it to me. Here you are again—wasting your life trying to solve everyone else's problems instead of going after what you, Kate Hamilton, want."

"And what do I want?"

"Exactly. The. Problem! You can't even say what you want because you don't know! How sad is that?"

"You know what I hate most about you?" I whispered.

"Don't know. Don't care."

"Exactly," I replied.

"Okay, then. I'll play your game. What don't you like?"

"That you think you have all the answers when you haven't a clue. You have a family who loves you, a great-uncle, a wife, children . . . all of whom are pulling for you," I said. "You'll never understand what it's like to not have one person you can count on. Ever."

"I think the real problem, Kate, is that you don't trust yourself. And that's a serious problem."

"Just shut up," I whispered. "I've never met anyone so condescending or with so little empathy." He had the hallmark of every personality disorder in the guidelines for mental health.

"Just look at what empathy got you, Kate. You probably felt sorry for your poor excuse of a husband. You worried about him instead of yourself or Lily," he said quietly. "You're not who I thought you were." His eyes, rimmed in dark memories, were more gray than blue in the half-light.

"Well, you're not who I thought you were either," I said.

His stark eyes pierced me; his jaw clenched.

"What?" I pushed a strand of hair behind my ear. "No retort?"

"I have nothing more to say to you."

"I see. So we revert back to silence, your favored way to show disapproval." I paused. When he did not respond, I continued, "You might know what to do in a war zone, but you are the one who is the coward when it concerns everyday life. You refuse to face down your demons and rejoin the rest of us mere mortals. Instead, you tell everyone how to live their lives all the while not moving forward with your own."

He fingered the edge of his hat as the blank, faraway look returned to his eyes. "Tell yourself whatever you like, Kate. Just figure out how to do the right thing—for your daughter and for yourself. Stand your ground. Figure out what you want. Maybe it's okay to ride out a storm, floating on your back for a little while as you did all those years to avoid drowning in conflict. But if you adopt that position the rest of your life, you'll never be true to yourself or be happy."

A thread of fury was taking root in my belly, and I could not hold back any longer. "Really? You're advising me on how to be happy? Less empathy, less caring for others, and more conflict and selfishness. Sounds like quite a recipe for hurting everyone around you. Something you appear to do well. Right now being a prime example."

"Hmm," he said. "First time I've ever heard a therapist tell me exactly what they truly thought instead of asking me how I feel. I might have to start trusting you. A little. A very little. Don't get a big head about it, okay?"

Whispers from the Garden . . .

I couldn't exactly put my quill on it, but something was making me edgy. Oh, the heavenly Slug gods had seen fit to provide enough of the lovely creatures to make me drunk on happiness. But the earth under my feet just didn't feel safe. Sometimes I found myself endlessly trotting around the borders of the garden in the middle of the night, if only to feel like I was escaping something ominous. Even Yowler was not acting herself. I watched the last inch of her long orange tail flicker in the moonlight. The long-stemmed white flowers looked blue in the shadows of the night. I loitered in the perfume of the blooms and then looked longingly toward the protection of the potting house. My mother had never warned me about this sensation in our lessons and it left me feeling very exposed.

"I see what you're thinking, Quilly. You know, you can't just spend your life always looking for a hiding place. What are you afraid of? There's nothing amiss here."

"It's the exact right thing to do. Hiding is underrated. Sometimes you just have to hide until you feel ready to come out into the light."

"It's night time," she snickered.

"Don't be rude," I replied.

"I'm a cat. We're supposed to be rude. How do you not know these things?"

"Well, I'm not rude. No one ever told me to be rude. I'm very polite. I'm so polite I prefer to be by myself than annoy others."

She stretched both her orange paws out in front of her and lay down in front of the hydrangeas.

I tried again. "Is it just me or do you feel like something is just not quite right in the air?"

She tilted her head and sniffed. "Maybe a storm? It's hard to say since it rains so much."

"No," I insisted. "It's something else."

She tried to pretend that I didn't know what I was talking about by simply staring at me with those big round black eyes of hers that turned golden in daylight.

"The ground . . ."

"Ohhh," she said elongating the sound. "That? Well, that's normal. It's always trying to settle itself into a more comfortable position. It's not comfortable in its own skin. Haven't you ever heard that expression? Of course you haven't," she answered her own question with exasperation. "You're hiding within your skin."

I ignored her provoking comment. "So it's always like this?"

"Well," she admitted, "it seems a bit more active the last few months."

"So you're not bothered by it at all?" I refused to leave it alone.

"*Not really.*"

"*Why do you feel like you have to act like it doesn't bother you? It's pretty obvious to me by the way you flick your tail that you're as nervous as I am.*"

"*Am not.*"

"*Are too.*"

"*Oh, are we having our first little spat? How very* drôle. *I like airing differences regularly. Sometimes I even start them to have a little excitement when things get boring. I'm at risk of that with you, I fear. You are just going to have to try to amuse me a bit harder.*"

"*Why am I not surprised?*"

She snickered.

"*I told you, I don't fight,*" *I insisted.* "*Nothing good ever comes out of fighting.*"

She stood up and strolled toward me. I edged toward the stone potting shed.

"*If you like me,*" *she said,* "*you'll fight with me. Just a little. Just drop the polite attitude and let's have* une petite dispute *for fun.*"

I shuddered. "*Why? A row doesn't sound amusing at all.*"

"*Come on. Sometimes I can't figure out the real you. I need to see a little passion. A little anger.*"

"*I don't do passion,*" *I said.* "*I don't like anger. I like hiding.*"

"*Oh, you have passion,*" *she insisted.* "*I see how you look at those little slimy things hiding under the leaves and the*

Boxer on the other side of the fence. And see? Bad things do happen when you hide. Those Slugs are hiding. I feel sorry for them."

"How ridiculous," I said. "You don't feel sorry for them at all. If you want to feel sorry about something, then just consider those Wing Beaters you're always pouncing on, and those little gray Scramblers with the long tails. It's a bloodbath out here every night, I tell you."

She licked one paw and groomed her face. "Finally. You do have a personality."

The air around me was getting very hot. I didn't like it. Not one bit. Made me squirm.

"Now," she purred for some stupid reason, "you know what it feels like to be angry. That's better than always running away and trying to hide when something doesn't feel right."

"Well, that's not always the correct thing to do," I said as calmly as I could manage. "Sometimes it's brilliant to just hole up, think, and plan, before we act. Everything has a proper place and a proper time."

"I like things that are more messy. More genuine," Yowler said. "Must be my Latin blood. My grandmother was Spanish. Was the best mouser in the stable of a picador from San Sebastian."

There was no way I was going to waste time asking what a picador was. I backed into the leaves of my favorite hiding hole and settled myself into a perfect position with only my snout peeking from under a mulberry leaf. Electricity was threading the air—a sure sign that a storm was on its way from Yowler's Latin roots. It felt big and messy. Well, at least Yowler would like it.

"I'm going to sleep," I said.

"Of course you are." She meowed and swatted at a lightning bug. "But it's okay. You are who you are and I'm not going to change you. I heard one of the geese say to its mate that he liked her just the way she was—goose shit on her tail feathers and all. Unbelievable. And they mate for life. How utterly ridiculous. No one is monogamous here. You know that, right?"

"Sounds rather nice if you ask me." I yawned. Maybe that would make her understand how much I longed for sleep. I was so ready for hibernation after these endless exhilarating but nerve-racking days. But I feared it was a long time before the days would begin to get shorter and the leaves would start to fall and I would finally get my long autumn's journey into sleep.

She padded over to me. "Well, don't start stepping in goose droppings. I'm not sure I could put up with that smell if you started anointing it. And don't worry, Quilly, I was just teasing you. I love you just the way you are. I don't know why, but there it is."

I felt her strange tongue gently lick my head and I pulled away.

"Owww," she howled.

"Quills," I deadpanned. "Tough love at its finest. I'm so glad you love me just the way I am."

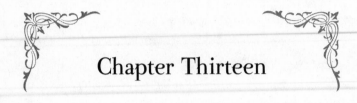

Chapter Thirteen

Her eyes large with shock, Lily flew through the front door just as I descended the stairs to go to *les halles* to buy vegetables. She came to an abrupt stop when she saw me—her chest heaving, her eyes accusing.

"What's going on?" I reached for two baskets at the door.

"Why didn't you tell me?" Her anger pulsed in waves.

"Tell you what?"

"That you're selling Madeleine Marie. Why didn't you tell me?" Lily paused. "Why? You never tell me anything. You never do anything! And now you are. Why this? Why now? Why haven't you mentioned this to me?"

"I honestly thought you wouldn't care, Lily," I said softly and tried to stroke her cheek.

She pulled back out of reach. "Well maybe I do care. Did you ever think of that? You've told me about this place my whole life," she said.

I carefully replaced the baskets to their spot near the door. "I'm sorry. More sorry than I can say. But we can come back to visit anytime we want. I found a nice cottage for Jean and—"

"What is wrong with you? Of course I care. This place is the coolest ever."

I could see the storm of emotions roiling within her, and I prepared for the blast. The curtains were closing on my reactions and a sense of calm washed over me. At a certain point, I've learned, you can withstand everything with a smile.

"You should have divorced Dad a long time ago and made a real home for us like this one. But you didn't. You just made us live there in that house of hell."

I swallowed. "I made a huge mistake, a very bad judgment call, and I'll regret it for the rest of my life. I wish I could rewrite what happened, but I can't."

"It was awful, Mom," she said slowly.

"Lily, I stayed because I wanted to protect you. I wasn't sure I'd get full custody. I didn't want to take that risk."

"That's the problem with you, Mom. You never ever take risks."

"I won't take a risk when the potential loss is too great."

"Yeah, well, you lost me."

"I almost did," I said quietly. "I made a nearly fatal mistake that will always haunt me."

"And now you're doing it again. You're refusing to take a risk. You're refusing to try to save Madeleine Marie."

"Who told you this?"

"Your uncle Jean-Michel. He's in the garden. I met him

when he drove up. He said he's come to take one long last look around. When I asked why, he said you were selling the villa and I ran inside to ask you if it was true."

"Lily, you have no idea the impossibility of keeping a villa going like this. There's no money to do it. If I could, I would."

"Really? You can't figure out a way? Well, I think you can, but you just don't want to be bothered. You just want to tuck everyone into their neat little boxes, including me, and go back to the States."

A small part of me was thrilled that she was challenging me. She was finally becoming a teenager—rebelling, not staying silent, or running away. But, sadly, I couldn't do what she wanted; I could only do what was financially possible. "Lily, we're going back, yes, but I was thinking we could move to Manhattan. Soho even. Or would you prefer to be with your friends in Darien if you came back? I suppose I could find a small bungalow there if you insisted. What do you think?"

"You don't get it," she said. "I'm not going to New York, and I'm not going back to Connecticut. That is for sure. I'll go back to Miss Chesterfield's if that's the only other choice. But I want to stay here. And, yes, I hate Dad for what he did. But most of all I hate you for not figuring out what to do. For not getting us out. I had to get myself out."

"Lily—"

Her beautiful face turned into a wildly contorted vision of fury and hatred and she ran out of the room without one telltale sound of sadness.

I couldn't feel my arms. And I couldn't move my feet. It felt like cement coated every part of me. I could barely turn my head to look toward the open door. How could it be sunny? Nothing made sense in my world.

"*Ma pauvre chérie.*" My uncle's figure, black against the brightness of the day, filled the doorway. His voice pierced the buzzing in my ears.

I still couldn't move. A dull roar began in my head, and my heart turned over with each hard beat in my chest, clogging my throat. I would have given anything for a chair. "Please, leave."

"*Mais, non. Absolument pas!* You are very white. Like a ghost, *chérie.*"

"Stop calling me *chérie.*"

He tsk-tsked. "But of course you are my *chérie.* My darling niece from America. And now my darling great-niece is here too. I just met her. Adorable child. Looks just like Antoinette when she was that age. And she's in top physical shape."

If one more person discussed our physical forms I would stuff their face with a dozen croissants. No. Really. "What are you doing here?"

"I could ask the same of you, Kate."

"What. Are You. Doing. Here?" My voice rose in pitch with each word. The exotic fumes of hate were filling the deepest part of my sinuses.

"Why, I rang my father. Your grandfather."

"Condescension is so unoriginal, Jean-Michel. I don't need you to clarify who Jean du Roque is."

"*Oh là là,*" he said. "You had better learn to insult with a bit more flair while you're here. The ideal is to do it in a way that leaves the person unsure if you've insulted them or not. You Americans are so blunt and brusque. No finesse at all."

A sound echoed off the high ceiling. We both turned to see Jean with his raised cane in hand seated in his wheelchair pushed by Youssef. He was about to dash the cane again against the parquet floor of the long hall. "Enough. I'm tired of you both being at each other's throats."

I nodded toward the salon door in response to Youssef's silent questioning expression.

Youssef pushed Jean's chair into the room with Magdali bringing up the rear carrying a magnificent silver tea tray. It was silent except for the low squeal of the wheels on the wood veneers. Youssef parked the wheelchair on one side of the long low table as Jean-Michel and I sat on opposite ends of the famous blue sofa.

"Merci, Youssef," Magdali said. "You may take your lunch now."

The flash of Youssef's wide white grin against the black of his face did not disarm Magdali. She showed not an inch of emotion as he bowed and departed.

"How lovely, Magdali," Jean-Michel said. "You've got yourself an underling to order around. Finally!"

Magdali, her face impassive, placed the tea tray on the long low table and began pouring tea for everyone without a word.

"What is going on here? I can smell something is very off," Jean said.

"Nothing at all, Papa," Jean-Michel continued. "Other than

the issue of the magnificent Kate, with her PhD in meddling with other people's lives, and whatever else. Yes, well, she has no control of her own daughter. A daughter who detests her and doesn't trust her. And this is the person Antoinette has sent here to fix our problems. A woman who has so far done nothing but interfere in our affairs and bring strife wherever she goes. Do you know she's concocting to sell Madeleine Marie to Jojo, that imbecile of a mayor? She'll probably ask for money under the table and keep it for herself. Why can't you—"

"You're just annoyed that you're about to be cut out of the deal you planned the minute you inherited," I said coolly.

"How can you tolerate her, Papa? She's got that tainted Hamilton blood. You can't trust her."

"Jean-Michel, enough!"

"No, Papa. I'm tired of doing everything to help you without a word of thanks. Indeed, I'm now subjected to questions and insinuations. Where was Antoinette when we needed her? Not here. And she could well afford to help. Instead, she sends her daughter, who has no sense of tradition. No sense of birthright. Indeed, our dear Magdali would have been a better branch on our tree. And she is in a strange way, after all. Somehow the Hamilton blood did not take in her though, but by—"

"Jean-Michel," Jean said with bite. "*Tais-toi.*" Shut up.

"Magdali knows her place," Jean-Michel continued. "She's a devoted member of the family. And would never suggest this beautiful family treasure be sold. And certainly wouldn't do it behind our backs."

Magdali moved toward the door.

"No," I said without thought. "Don't you dare leave, Magdali."

She stopped and parked herself near the door with her head bowed.

I felt as if I were in some sort of strange tale about Cheshire cats and going through a looking glass. Just couldn't figure out what my uncle was saying. Something was lost in translation.

"It's such a pity your father couldn't seem to produce males to carry on his line," Jean-Michel continued. "But he liked to spread his seed, so perhaps there are sons we know nothing about. Yes, I vaguely recall—"

The cane descended with such force that the sound echoed for long moments in the room. "I said, *tais-toi*, Jean-Michel," Jean demanded.

Finally, blessed silence.

"What the hell is he talking about?" My voice was hoarse.

"Kate, Magdali. Leave us," Grandfather demanded.

"No," I said. "I will not. Magdali, I said don't leave."

Magdali took her hand off of the brass door lever.

"What does my father have to do with Magdali?"

Both men began speaking at once. The son's sharp tones cut through his father's. "Why are you protecting her from the truth? She has the right to know. Magdali does."

A dozen insane ideas battled in my brain. "Granddaddy. Tell me. Please."

Jean looked first at me, then toward Magdali, and finally

his gaze rested on his son. "I've overlooked your deficiencies in character for too long. I'd hoped you would change. But you haven't. I want you out of Madeleine Marie by tonight."

"Wait a minute," I said. "He doesn't go until he tells me what he's insinuating."

Again, Jean tried to speak but Jean-Michel won out. "Magdali is your half sister, you little fool."

"Pack your affairs and go," Grandfather said, quiet fury building. "And don't return. I don't want you at my funeral or anywhere near my grave. Get out. You might be one of my legal heirs, but you are not my son. And I shall redo my will to leave the full twenty-five percent the law allows me at my discretion in Kate's name."

Jean-Michel disregarded his father and instead focused on me, his eyes small and bright with hate. "When your father, the ugly American, arrived in Biarritz, he stayed at the Hôtel du Palais. Had his way with Magdali's mother, who was a maid there at the time. He then met Antoinette, and managed to impregnate both of them within the same month. And you take after him. Your character is proof. You've tainted my father's mind, which everyone knows is questionable due to your psychological influence."

"You're lying about my father," I said. "Jean. Tell me he's lying. Magdali?" I looked at her standing by the door ten feet away and the parquet floor seemed to contract half the distance. "Magdali?" I repeated.

She shook her head.

"My father did not—"

"Oh, but he did," Jean-Michel said with a cool smile. "Repeatedly."

My grandfather's hoarse voice rose and the two men began shouting at each other in French, while my thoughts darted in every direction.

It felt like we were all players in an off-off-Broadway tragicomedy. As if on cue, Lily appeared at the doorway. She was holding Solange's hand. My gaze fell to the doll dangling from Solange's other hand. Tiny Tears. My . . . I strode over to the girls and dropped to my knees to look at my old doll. My first and only doll. The one who had listened to all my fears for so many years and then had been put in a chest to hold all my secrets.

But the ancient doll had strange striped overalls, not the white lace gown she'd had when I'd seen her in the chest in Lily's bedroom. "Who gave you that doll, Solange?"

Solange, eight, looked at her mother. "Maman."

I rose up on my feet and looked at Magdali. "Where did that doll come from?"

"Leave it, Kate," she said slowly.

"That is not my doll. The one my father gave me has a crack at the hairline."

And once again, as usual, reality was tipping past the point of understanding. There was no ground beneath my feet, nothing genuine or real to stand on.

North was south and east was west. Beyond the windows the leaves of the plane trees threshed the turbulent hot July air as the winds collided from every direction. The church bells rang, and the monstrous orange tabby cat streaked across the pea gravel drive. Air flowed from an open window and it smelled of rain and earth. People were speaking, loudly then softly, none to me. It was hard to care. The only thing that made sense was what I could see, and smell, not hear.

And all of a sudden I realized I was standing all alone by the window, looking out. I must have walked there. I felt so calm, all alone. It was my favorite way to be. By myself. The only time I could relax.

I wasn't meant to be with other people. I've always known that. I told you that at the beginning of the story, remember? I've never had that resilience my profession insisted was the key to life. I just know how to plod on without emotion.

"Kate, are you listening to me?" Jean's words finally registered.

I turned to face him. All the others had departed. "Is it true?"

"Yes."

"Why . . . why didn't anyone tell me? Or did everyone just forget? Or were too embarrassed?"

"I don't know. It was just understood. There was never a reason to discuss it. It was obvious we should keep it a secret."

"Obvious? So I would have gone to my grave not knowing I have a sister? A sister I didn't see for years and years. And she knows."

"Your father decided you were too close to one another. And none of us thought it wise for anyone outside the family to guess the truth. But it's why I took in Nadine before Magdali was born. The Hôtel du Palais showed Nadine the door when it became obvious she was pregnant, and she came to the villa in search of your father. By then, Antoinette was pregnant as well, and I'd given my consent as there was no other option. I would have never agreed if I had known about Nadine. It was your mother who insisted we employ Nadine. Magdali's mother told her all the sordid details just before she died."

I could barely breathe. "Did he know Nadine was pregnant when he married my mother?"

"Yes, I believe he did."

"Well, at least now I know why you hated him so much."

"Kate, I watched helplessly as he choreographed the most confounding life for you and Antoinette. Constantly moving, always restless, always new ideas, far too smart, and far too charming."

"No one is perfect," I said dryly. "And by the way, to her credit, my mother loved our life, until it became too much even for her. And I didn't mind the life we had. At least it was exciting."

"You've got it wrong, Kate," Jean said. "You were the adult and they were the children. You raised yourself. But I can't blame Antoinette. Her childhood was nonexistent."

A sudden peace washed over me. "We all do the best we can."

"But sometimes life requires more than that."

"Granddaddy—"

The door to the salon opened, and Jean-Michel strode in. "I'm leaving. Here is the key to the house. I've packed my affairs and taken one last look around to say adieu to the house that was supposed to be my legacy."

"Half your legacy," I said. "You keep forgetting about your sister."

He pretended I wasn't in the room and finally a great ball of recklessness took root in my belly.

He dangled the key right beyond the reach of my grand-father, who was leaning forward to take it. Slowly, he lowered his arm.

I jerked the key out of my uncle's hands.

"And, Kate," he said, "take care in how you spend my fam-ily's money, for I shall have a lawyer review everything when all this is said and done and then monitor every last *sou* spent going forward. Because that's French family law, in case you don't know. You can't disinherit your children like the *bestioles* in America."

"Oh," I said. "How *drôle*. Now I'm a beast from America, am I? Perfect. Well, from one beast to another, how much more money do you want to bilk from the family? How much money will it take to buy you out of your legacy—so you will be per-manently out of all our lives?" I didn't know what I was think-ing. It was pure emotion.

He scrunched his face, bemused, but barely hesitated. "One million."

I turned to look at Jean. His face was ashen and he said noth-ing as he stared at the turbulent, darkening sky out the window.

"Come now, Jean-Michel," I continued, "the Sotheby's agent

said the most that could be expected was one point five million euros. And if my grandfather can lawfully give *my daughter or me*"—I sent a glance to my grandfather—"twenty-five percent, then your share would be . . ." Math had never been my forte.

"Five hundred sixty-two thousand five hundred," my uncle said far too quickly.

"This is ridiculous," Jean finally whispered. "Jean-Michel, you will not hold anyone ransom by your—"

"Half a million will do," Jean-Michel interrupted, sensing an immediate windfall in the offing.

A thousand voices told me to keep my mouth shut. "Done," I said. "I will have a lawyer draw up documents for you to sign relinquishing any claim and you shall receive the money in return. Within the next six weeks."

He smirked. "You think you can sell it that fast."

"That is none of your business," I said. "Now get out of our house."

"You have no right to tell me to leave my—"

"I do. And I will. Get the hell out of here."

He looked at his father, who refused to turn his face to his son. Instead, Jean du Roque looked at me.

Jean-Michel bent to kiss his father's cheek only to have his father turn his head away. "*Mon Dieu*," Jean-Michel muttered, shaking his head. He slowly crossed the floor to reach the door and left, slamming it behind him.

I closed my eyes against the unbearable sadness. "Grand-daddy?"

"Yes, my darling."

"I don't want you to worry. I will figure out a way to keep this damn mold-ridden villa even if I have to sell my soul. I don't want you to move. And if I understood it, and it's not some childish whim, which I don't think it is, knowing Lily, then it appears we will both be living here with you, if you allow it."

His old hand, rich with history, reached toward mine, shaking. I met it halfway with my own. I finally dropped to the sofa beside his wheelchair.

"There's only one thing," I said.

"What's that, dearest?"

"Either this sofa goes, or I do."

A smile finally broke over his features. He scratched his head. "Never let it be said that a du Roque doesn't have a sense of humor. You get that from me by the way. And you're the only one who got it."

Tomorrow I would wonder what on earth I had just done. Today, I would simply luxuriate in—for the first time in forever—the feeling of doing instead of enduring.

"Kate?"

"Yes?"

"Forget me. Forget Magdali—all of us."

"What—"

"No," he said softly. "Let me have my say. I just want to know one thing. Do you want to live in this house or are you doing this for me or Lily? Because I won't have it. I will sell it myself if that's the case. Our ancestors Madeleine and Marie wouldn't have ever wanted anyone here who didn't want to be."

"I know it's hard to understand my change of heart, Granddaddy, but you see, I think I never felt like I was part of the family. Not the du Roques nor the Hamiltons. Here I was the American, and in the US I was French. So, I didn't feel the right to live here. But you know what? My daughter is right, and you are right. This is more a home than anywhere else could ever be. And I think I always have known it but didn't want to hope because I've never really had a home. Seeing Lily here, and you, and Magdali—there's nowhere I'd rather be."

Peace, that old-dog-with-a-bone emotion, washed over me as I gazed into my grandfather's old, wise eyes.

And worry, that slippery-rope emotion, soon followed.

How I was going to finance this grand scheme so quickly cobbled together and so poorly thought through was beyond me. But I would rather fail at this than succeed at anything else.

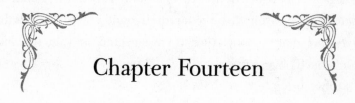

Chapter Fourteen

M r. Soames," I said, sitting at his opulent dining table that following midday. "Your house is just lovely. The mix of Basque artifacts and modern everything else is stunning."

"Why, thank you," Phillip replied. "But I know you did not come here to discuss this house. I am guessing you've come to pick my brain on how to raise money to pay off that uncle of yours."

"You know the one good thing about living in a village? It's that it saves all kinds of time and embarrassment coming to the point," I said dryly.

"Please help yourself to the asparagus and the duck. We eat very informally. The servants can't stand it as it limits their access to gossip." He winked. "And by the by, I am honored you've come to me. No one bothers any more. But I've got a few more tricks up my sleeve. So what are your options?"

"Well, the house in Connecticut will be sold. But it has a huge mortgage. I bought out my ex. I can only expect two hundred thousand. I have another one hundred grand in retirement after taxes, but that's it other than a college fund for Lily, which I won't touch obviously."

"Obviously."

"And I've tossed around some crazy ideas such as renting out bedrooms. I think the surfers wouldn't mind the state of disrepair. They just want access to lodging close to the best waves."

"And?"

"Or we could turn it into a luxury bed-and-breakfast."

"Or?"

"I could take out a loan here. I will have to open a practice too. Eventually. But God knows it will probably take years to be licensed here at a guess. Until then I have a few clients via Skype, who I'm not sure will continue on."

"I see."

"But there are problems with every idea. I couldn't turn it into a bed-and-breakfast without spending quite a bit of money renovating. Several issues must be corrected immediately."

"I know." His mouth twisted. "Any other options?"

"I could ask Antoinette to kick in something, but she has her own expenses and expanding businesses."

He tilted his head and pursed his lips. "Jean told me the same thing."

I carefully placed a few spears of asparagus on my plate and spooned a duck breast beside them. "Of course, I could also consider the rantings of one of my clients who keeps insisting I invest in a movie. But I only mention that for comedic relief."

Phillip Soames smiled. "How very American. Okay, then. You have gotten yourself into quite a financial bind. But let me think on it a bit. One option that immediately comes to mind is renting Madeleine Marie to someone and all of you renting another house for half Madeleine Marie's income. At least you would still own the property. I know this might not be appealing."

"I thought of that, but I fear the insurance to rent it out in its condition would be impossibly high, and combined with the rent of another place, well, the idea of renting out rooms while we stay put is a better financial risk."

"Kate, I will think about it. But I do hope you'll consider one last thing."

"Yes?"

"My own personal offer of a loan, and if not a loan then an outright gift. I have no immediate heirs other than Edward and his sister. And I am embarrassed to admit that I have more than enough to share. Your grandfather has been my best friend for over fifty years. I would only ask you not to ever tell him about the loan or gift."

I immediately shook my head.

"Wait," he insisted, and raised one hand. "You know, Kate, sometimes it's important in life to know when and how to accept a gift. You cannot imagine how much joy I will receive knowing

I might have helped put your entire family's minds at ease. This would be as much for me as for you and your grandfather."

"I could never accept a gift or even a loan that large. But you are very, very kind to offer."

He appeared gravely disappointed.

I cleared my throat and changed the subject. "How are you feeling, Phillip? My grandfather mentioned that you were a bit under the weather. Magdali has a wonderful cough medicine she makes. I'll ask Lily to drop some off later today."

"Actually, I'm feeling much better, thank you. But I was just going to ask you how my nephew is faring."

I put my fork down and used my napkin. "I'm sorry, but I cannot discuss it. It's unethical."

"I knew you would say that. But, as I understand it, you and Edward do not have a traditional doctor-patient relationship."

"Nevertheless, I prefer not to discuss anything. I am sorry, Mr. Soames."

"Phillip, please."

"Phillip."

"I ask because his children are coming for a visit at the end of the week. Without their mother."

"How nice," I said. "I'd love to invite all of you to dinner the day they arrive. Will you come?"

"I'd be delighted. It would be most welcomed."

"How long will they visit?"

"It's undetermined," he continued. "Edward doesn't know, but I received a letter from his wife asking for news."

"May I ask you your opinion regarding the marriage?"

"So I'm to tell you things, but you will not tell me anything?"
He smiled.

"Exactly. I'm so sorry."

"It's all right. I understand." He paused and used his napkin.
"His wife, Claire, is very cordial with me. You must understand
that she had to raise the children on her own when Edward was
called for duty. And that happened repeatedly."

"Of course."

"She is a good mother." He looked like he wanted to say
more but instead he stopped.

"But?"

"They married very young."

"And?" I felt we had reversed roles. Me pushing and him
halting in response.

"They barely tolerate each other."

"Why? Is this since he returned from his last posting or has
this been long-standing?"

"I don't think their marriage was ever a spectacular pairing.
But this last return, it unraveled more so than ever before, as I
understand it. And he won't talk to me or anyone. These moods
take over and he becomes as silent as sin. And he's drinking
more than he used to, as I told you. It's made it all worse."

"Was your great-nephew a happy child?" I leaned forward.
This was important.

"He was."

"His father, your brother's son, was of good character?"

"Yes, but . . ."

"Yes?"

He looked uncomfortable. "Kate, I've always blamed myself for not stepping in. I think he battered his boys a bit, maybe, but not his daughter. And he drank himself to oblivion, especially after his sons died in the war."

"And his mother?"

"A bit batty and kept to herself. Always knitting, but never saw the end result of all that needlework for some odd reason." He pushed his plate away. "Those children raised themselves. Never a good thing."

"Hmmm." I sighed deeply.

"What?"

"There are no serious problems with Edward's children, are there?"

"Lord, no. They are delightful. And in the past, he was an outstanding father. I've never seen a man more devoted to his children, when he wasn't serving the Queen. He is the opposite of his own parents."

"And he's never hinted at any event that caused him to fall into this current state?"

He shook his head. "He won't talk about any of it, and I've tried."

"All right then," I said. "That's all I need to know for now."

"Is he talking to you? Can you tell me that at least?"

I took a last bite of the duck confit—so tender it almost melted in my mouth. And I smiled. "Oh, he's talking to me all right. Not about himself, of course. But he has a lot to say about me. Suffice it to say, I don't impress him. At all."

"Kate, may I say something at the risk of sounding a mite patronizing?"

"I think we're beyond formalities, Phillip."

"Excellent." He paused. And I saw the almost imperceptible movement of his body as he pressed the servant buzzer that most likely rested under his foot.

"So?"

"I'm proud of you."

I swallowed.

"You didn't have to come to France. No one else stepped in. I was worried, of course. I would have invited Jean to live with me if it had come to that. Indeed, we are both two old bachelors now who enjoy each other's company immensely. But he would have never accepted. His pride would have gotten in the way just like your pride is not allowing you to accept my offer of a loan or gift. But, you see, ever since you've come here, everything and everyone has improved. Your grandfather. Even my nephew a tad. Everyone. And no one has thanked you. So thank you for coming. Thank you for coming when you had your own problems to sort and you could have easily looked the other way."

I'd never been good at praise. Never knew what to say. Nothing ever sounded right. I opened my mouth but then closed it again when I couldn't form a sentence.

He reached across the table, covered my hand, and gave it a squeeze. "You don't have to say anything, my dear."

I nodded and mashed my lips together.

"Edward should be here any minute to whisk you away for another one of those marches he's forcing on you. So I just have two last questions."

"Yes?" I managed.

"Please wait."

A cadre of servants entered to clear the table, brush the crumbs from the place settings, and place dessert and cheese plates in front of us. A platter of fruit tempted, alongside wedges of Comté and Brebis served with the traditional cherry jam. A golden Gâteau Basque à la crème awaited in the center of the table. The servants departed from whence they came.

"So, Kate," he said, all efforts of holding back a smile removed. "I admit I'm a wily old goat who doesn't accept defeat all that graciously. Have you figured out a way to stave off Jojo's relentless effort to turn Madeleine Marie into the new *mairie*? And what about Pierrot, your friendly Basque terrorist neighbor?"

I sighed and shook my head.

"My offer remains extant," Phillip said.

I REGRETTED THAT second slice of Gâteau Basque during the third mile. I'd agreed to a very long trek from Bidart to Saint-Jean-de-Luz and back. Edward wanted to explore the old Nazi bunkers that dotted the coastline. Right now, I wanted to explore the possibility of Uber in France. God, it was hot today.

A storm had been brewing and threatening to break for the last week. The barometer was all over the place and so were the winds. The moon was full, and the tides at their lowest points for the year.

And I wondered, once again, the same thing I wondered each time I saw Edward. What was it going to take to get him to open up? Would he ever trust me enough to say what was going on in that massively large hard head of his?

"Come on, Kate. Keep up. It'll be dark before we get back at this pace."

"Yes, *sir*," I said, bringing up the rear in pathetic fashion.

"How are you faring anyway?"

I laughed.

"What?"

"That's the first time you've ever asked me that question. Are you warming to me?"

"Uh, that'd be a no," he replied, in a tone that spoke the opposite.

"You are. Definitely. Now, don't get all soppy on me. I'm not sure I would know what to do."

"You really don't have a comical bone in your body, Hamilton. Americans are just so bloody emotional. No sense of irony or understatement at all."

"Got it. Next observation."

"And you never say please. So rude."

"Next observation, *please*," I said. "Although it does seem a bit ridiculous to be asking for yet another insult."

"You're always prodding me. Please try another tactic. If only to keep me interested. I'll never pour my guts out to you if this is the best you can do."

"So why don't we stop wasting each other's time and you just tell me?"

"Roger."

I stopped dead. "Roger, what?"

He turned around. "Come on, keep walking for Christ's sake."

I kept walking. I wasn't sure when I'd started obeying him blindly, but it was annoying. I'd decided I'd never take orders from anyone ever again the day I'd paid for the privilege of a divorce. "Roger, what? Um, please."

He stopped abruptly and started laughing.

I caught up only to see he had tears in his eyes from laughing so hard. "What? What's so funny?"

He stretched. "You. You've got some wit in you after all. Never thought I'd see the day."

"Me neither."

He started laughing all the harder.

"What's wrong with you?"

He wiped his eyes and replaced his hat. "Nothing. Nothing at all. Okay, then. Listen up. I'm only going to speak about this once. And don't ask any of your bloody stupid questions. Don't ask me about feelings. Don't interrupt me. Just pay attention. And don't rush me."

"Can we sit down?"

"No! Already a question. An interruption."

"I am not under your command, major."

"Come on. Let's go." He began to walk ahead of me. Again. "I assume you've heard of Op Herrick?"

He had picked up the pace, and I dug in and prepared for a hike long on exhaustion and short on water. I'd forgotten my supply. "Um, sounds familiar, but better explain all."

I saw his head shaking in probable disgust. "Well, then. It's the name for a British operation in Afghanistan. Okay, then. I'll skip educating you more otherwise we'll be here all day. Suffice it to say that I was based at Camp Bastion, a fortification built by Royal Engineers—you know that's what I am, Roger?" He glanced over his shoulder.

"Roger."

"Okay, then. It's what we built in the Helmand province. It's a lovely little spot if you like the Taliban and sand in all your orifices. Local pastimes included grenade fishing and detonating Russian mines. Ten million of them. Not being nicknamed Stumpy was considered a win."

I studied his shoulders. They were becoming more hunched as he spoke.

"Excellent," he said, and then was silent for so long I wasn't sure he'd say another word.

"I was deployed there three times for six months at a go. I was CO of a Specialist Team Royal Engineers—a squadron— talented in civil, structural, electrical, and mechanical engineering. Essentially, we built infrastructure—everything from roads, bridges, repairing airfields, ports, and more. You need something built or repaired? That's our job. Sappers—that's our nickname—have their hands in just about everything. Got it?"

"Roger." My hamstrings were going to be tighter than a new clutch if he kept up this bruising pace.

"Good."

Again silence. I could almost hear his brain humming and sorting.

"So. I was assigned an Afghan interpreter the first tour. His name was Abdul Aarash Abdullah. I dubbed him Triple A when we first met six years ago. He was loyal, dedicated, took grave risks to help the allies, and spoke Pashto, Russian, French, and English with equal flare. He had wanted to be a writer or a teacher. I could not have done my job without him. He was twenty-two on the first tour and twenty-six the last one. I watched him grow from a young man to a young father. I remember how innocent he was despite growing up in a war zone. He . . ." Edward stopped in his tracks and turned to look at me.

I stopped in front of him, grateful for a moment's rest.

"I remember listening to him talk about the beauty of his bride's hands with a wonder and reverence I'd never encountered. Anyway." He resumed marching and I had to follow.

"I was sort of a big brother figure to him. I saw a photograph of his father, his two younger brothers, his bride of the beautiful hands, and his mother." He paused. "He took grave risks for us, which only became more dangerous with each tour. The Taliban killed Afghans working with us, and Triple A knew it but never spoke of it. At the beginning of the last deployment, he came to me and asked for asylum for himself and his entire family. Eight in all, for he had two children by then—a two-year-old and a newborn. He wanted to live in Kent, where my family lived at one point. He dreamed of owning an oast house, and kept yammering on about planting mulberry trees and pomegranates. Questions?"

"Not yet," I replied. I wanted water, but didn't dare side-track him.

"Excellent," he barked, his voice a bit high. "So, it's a simple thing really. He's dead. His family too. All of them were wiped out by the Taliban when they finally learned his identity. I put in the asylum requests too late. Anyway, that was one of the issues on the last tour."

His gait had become narrow and ever faster, and he was avoiding every blade of grass for some odd reason. Every muscle in his back was visible through his sweat-soaked drab green shirt.

"Major, could we stop for a moment? I—"

"Sodding hell! No. We don't have time to . . ." He stopped in his tracks. "What do you need?" He barked but did not turn around.

I closed part of the distance between us and touched the side of his arm. His elbow automatically rammed back in stunning response and I was lucky he missed me.

"Sorry. What do you want?" His voice was unnaturally calm, like the sea before a storm.

"Water. I forgot mine."

He slowly turned around and his expression made me suddenly realize I was all alone in the middle of nowhere. It wasn't the chilling Mr. Hyde face I'd seen too many times on my ex-husband in my past life. It was something far worse. It was black death come to call in all his random nothingness draped in no meaning. For some odd reason I wasn't afraid for me. I was afraid for Edward.

His voice was a low rasp in the heat of the day. "How could you be so stupid? Water is life. Without it you'll die out here." His mind was not in the lushness of the Pays Basque. He was in some desert three and a half thousand miles away.

"Got it," I said. "Won't forget."

He watched as I looked around for a place to sit and, seeing nothing, lowered myself onto a grassy knoll with wild primroses next to a gorse-like hedge overlooking the deep blue sea. Goose-stepping over patches of wild grass, he removed his water bottle from his shoulder string and offered it to me.

"Thank you." I gulped down a third of it and held it up to him.

He was still standing, surveying the area. He finally leaned against a shelf of rock face. "Okay, Hamilton. I remember your fondness for questions. Try to keep it to under a dozen. Please." His expression was halfway to normal.

"Abdul and his family's deaths are so tragic. That must have been terrible for you."

"It's just part of war. You can't be deployed and not see death and suffer from some form of PTSD. You can ask, Hamilton. Just say it. You know you want to. Am I fucked up from too many deployments or just fucked up because of a handful of Afghan deaths?"

"Okay. Which is it?"

"All of it. The last one was probably just the proverbial cherry on top. And I hate clichés."

"How did Abdul die?" The hair on my neck was tingling—always bad news.

"Ah, that is the wrong question."

"Okay." I tilted my head questioningly. "What should I ask?"

"How did his family die?"

"Okay, then. How did his family die?"

He took a long swallow of water and carefully screwed the top back on. "One at a time." He replaced the neck of the bottle in the elastic loop of the shoulder string and focused on my eyes. "We were on the move. Part of the transport convoy of a two-hundred-twenty-ton turbine to the Kajaki Dam. Op Eagle's Summit comprised three miles of more than one hundred vehicles. We had a lot of security, of course, to protect the billions in equipment during the transport through territory heavy with insurgents." He rearranged his shoulder strap. "Just before rejoining Highway 611, near known areas of recent active Taliban insurgency, the convoy was forced to stop so NATO could bomb the hell out of the insurgents to allow safe passage to the final destination. Abdul and two other members of the squadron and I were in the third vehicle, chewing the fat, when we heard someone shout, 'Stand to.' You know what that means?"

"No."

"It means stand ready for attack because something is amiss. In this case, we could see a goatherd and a handful of goats heading toward the road to probably cross it. Something you see all the time. The man had a staff and something slung across his body. Abdul and I got out and walked to the front of the convoy in case Abdul needed to translate, yeah?"

"Got it."

"The goatherd was terrified. You could see it in his eyes as he held his hands up and begged for them not to shoot. Abdul was translating, explaining the man had been sent on a proxy mission for the Taliban. The man's wife was being held hostage until he delivered something to us along with a note he kept waving in the air. Of course, that made everyone very twitchy and the bomb team moved forward. The goatherd finally said the note and package were for Abdul, using his full name. The goatherd was told to retreat into the dunes until the bomb blast area was secure and finally he was ordered to remove the canvas bag slung over his body. Blood was seeping through in several places. He was ordered to open it, and when he looked inside he made an unholy sound, a sort of raspy scream. He dropped the bag and note and ran. We didn't go after him. Rules of engagement. Oddly, the goats didn't follow him." Soames's throat convulsed in a swallow. It was the only part of him that moved.

"Abdul elbowed through the bomb squad before anyone could stop him and ran into the dunes beyond the roadway—a completely unprotected area likely filled with improvised exploding devices. I followed in his footsteps. And there, in the bag, which was a British Army canvas laundry bag—were his parents' heads. I didn't move fast enough to grab it from him. And you know what I did?"

I shook my head.

"I arrested him. Zip tied him to stop him from leaving. How's that for compassion?"

"You did it to stop him from getting killed."

"Nope. You're far too sentimental. I did it to protect the people on mission and myself. The insurgents would have tortured him for information." He examined his hands. "Every day, for the next three days and nights, the Taliban sent proxies to deliver more bits of Abdul's family, of which I took possession. The note had promised more of the same unless he left the convoy. Yes, we all knew he was a dead man if he left and that the Taliban would kill his entire family no matter what—as a warning to any Afghan working with us." Soames finally swung his eyes to mine. "The last day, his wife's hands and his two children were delivered. His babies' heads. I never showed him or told him any part of it. But it was as if . . ."

"Yes?" I whispered.

"As if the insurgents knew he loved his wife's hands. And they probably tortured her to find this out. And they also probably knew it would drive him insane, wondering if she was still alive."

"It tortures you," I said slowly.

"*He* never faltered," he continued. "He didn't ask about his family. He knew they were all dead. Instead of grieving, instead of seeking comfort, his only concern was for me. He told me it was all part of Allah's plan." He paused. "Whilst I was putting zip ties on him and escorting him back to a secure area of the convoy."

"He saw it was torturing you."

He shook his head. "You don't get it."

"Tell me, then."

"You probably think he committed suicide."

"That was my first guess."

A magpie, in his tuxedo of black-and-white feathers, landed on a nearby bush.

"He died in our mess hall ten days later, when we arrived at the dam. He choked on corn beef, according to witnesses. I wasn't there. The irony of it. I was busy trading British ration packs for American-made cots."

"You weren't there," I echoed.

"No. I was more concerned with securing a good night's sleep."

"For all the men serving under you."

"Don't try to pretty it up," he barked. "You just don't get it. Abdul was the most selfless person I've ever known. He was innocence in a land of hatred. The Western world failed him. I failed him."

"Because you couldn't protect him."

"Yes, goddammit. That's my job. Protect the innocent. Protect all that is good and right from evil."

And there it was. My reflection staring back at me. "So you're going to punish yourself by destroying your family—and your life—as atonement for not saving Abdul and his family?" I was the worst psychologist on the planet. What part of "it's more powerful and healing to let them put the pieces together and figure it out for themselves" did I not learn?

"No," he said.

"Then what the hell are you doing? Trying to figure out the meaning of life? Don't you think a better penance—if you can't get it out of your thick head that you're not responsible—would be to lead a productive life, in memory of Abdul? Wouldn't he want you to love and honor your family as he did? If he was as selfless as you said, wouldn't he be ashamed of the way you are conducting yourself?" Yup, I should be in the Psychology 101 dog pound, and on the list to be euthanized.

"Pathetic attempt to insult me into action." He shook his head. "Kate, there is no meaning to any of this. Life is an oxymoron. A random chain of events that will soon be forgotten by the generations who follow us. What is the point?"

"The point? Of life?" I pushed my hair behind my ears. "Are you asking my philosophy?"

He shook his head no, and his words matched. "Not if it's a load of sentimental psychobabble."

"Edward, you're not going to adopt my viewpoint. And lately, very lately actually, the last twenty-four hours in fact, I might just have formed a new view, and yes, it's far too saccharin for your taste. But I'm just going to ask you one last question."

"Yes?"

"Picture your son or your daughter. Picture him or her exactly in your situation. Late thirties, multiple deployments, a spouse, two young children. Charles or Winnie experienced too many years of war and saw death and destruction on a daily basis. They are blaming themselves for the death of someone like Abdul and his entire family, for failing to secure asylum for them in time. What would you tell Winnie to help her live a meaningful life? What would you advise your son?"

"I'd tell them . . ." He paused and looked toward the distant sea of churning currents. "I'd tell them that war fucks up everyone. That it wasn't their fault. That they should rest. That I will protect and take care of them until they're well again. That I'll help them find their feet. I'd tell them to stay strong, and good things will come. And then I'd speak to their families and ask them to be loyal, to stick by them, to give them a break, to help them heal."

"To love them," I said quietly.

"Yes. To love them as I do."

"Because they're lovable," I whispered.

He refused to respond.

"So you wouldn't tell your children to tough it out. Or numb themselves with alcohol or drugs. Or keep their thoughts to themselves and handle it on their own? You would hate the idea of them suffering all alone, wouldn't you?"

He looked at me and his eyes narrowed. I could see the striated muscles in the hollow of his cheek working.

"Then why are you shutting everyone out? How are you different—less deserving? You are worthy of being loved, don't you see that?"

He pushed himself away from the rock and brushed himself off. "Kate?"

"Yes?"

He removed his water bottle and walked over to hand it to me. "I'm going on ahead. Alone. To Saint-Jean-de-Luz as planned."

"But—"

"Look, that's about as much as I can stand."

I clenched my hands until the nails bit into the skin, to keep myself from forcing it. "Okay. See you at dinner at the end of the week. I'm looking forward to meeting your children. You're bringing them, correct?"

"Yes."

"Okay, then." I turned and headed back down the sandy path toward Bidart.

A few moments later I heard his voice call my name. I turned.

Thank you floated on a wisp of wind back to me.

I nodded once and returned to the path.

A colleague once described the emotional equivalent to a runner's high while working. It was not just when you felt like you made a difference in someone's life. It was when you also made a difference in your own life at the same moment and discovered we are all connected by our shared humanity. Edward Soames might be my complete opposite, but, eerily, we were just the same.

I knew he would never agree.

Chapter Fifteen

The days were growing ever longer and the waves ever larger, much to the delight of the surfing population, which had swelled in the last week due to the annual European Surf Festival in Biarritz. Even Jean was willing to adapt to Spanish dining hours this time of year. Dinner was at ten o'clock on the balcony tonight. Lily and Magdali and her daughter joined us *á table,* and we enjoyed Magdali's culinary genius of *Merlu Beurre Citronné et Belle de Fontenay pomme de terres avec Piments d'Espelete*—grilled hake fish with butter and lemon and very elegant potatoes with a dab of Basque peppers. I'd recently been informed by the *patron* of the Panier de Luz vegetable and fruit market in Saint-Jean-de-Luz that of course there were more than thirty types of potatoes. Who knew? It was just too bad the meal ended with my less than elegant strawberry shortcake. I'd never figure out French ovens and centigrade conversions.

We moved into the salon when the evening grew cool.

Youssef joined the group for an epic game of gin rummy and poker, taught by Lily. I watched the happy group as I sat at an ancient desk, writing emails, running numbers, and trying to figure out ideas on how to raise funds.

The idea of the bed-and-breakfast I'd all but given up. Tonight's attempt at strawberry shortcake, followed by plumbing problems in the main-floor bathroom, were all the proof I needed that it was a bad idea. At least the realtor in Darien had said the open house had gone well and there was a potential buyer. I'd go back to the States to sell everything in the house worth anything, haul the rest to the dump, and ship Lily's and my personal effects.

Leaving behind my practice would be another matter altogether. It had been one thing to be absent for six weeks; it was another to shut it down. And I'd face the challenge of opening a new practice here. How many French men and women were going to want to unload their burdens to an American with poor vocabulary and no French license, and no way to collect government health insurance? The mayor would probably shut me down in less than a week. And did I want to practice anymore? Did I even have a choice? As far as I could see, the only things I could do were become an English tutor, a nanny, or a really bad gardener. And I was willing to do it all now. I couldn't afford to wait on repairing Madeleine Marie. Worse, I was still short two hundred thousand to pay off my uncle and get him out of all our lives.

I looked at Lily, her eyes shining above the cards she held in her hands. And none of it mattered. I would learn how to plaster, install plumbing, and put down a new roof myself if that's what it would take to keep our new old family together.

A sort of peace had invaded without fanfare or notice. I'd always thought during the struggle of my marriage that after the long-dreamed plan to divorce was realized and Lily settled in college, I'd finally float about my days filled with happiness. It had taken a lot longer to accept that emptiness would be the new normal post divorce and post Lily's departure to boarding school. And as life does, just when I'd accepted—no, embraced—emptiness, peace and contentment had swooped in. It was just all so surprising. And yet, I feared there was no way to sustain it. I was going to disappoint her and my grandfather unless I worked day and night, and even then there was a good chance I'd fail.

There was no way around it if I couldn't raise enough money. And I couldn't invest a euro in the villa without paying off my uncle first, for he would drag us to court the minute Jean died, to protect his share, probably suggesting my grandfather hadn't been in his right mind when he'd decided to leave me or Lily the lawful 25 percent. Having to sell the villa would devastate Lily. There was just no way out. No immediate failsafe solution. But I knew the next steps. It was time to live paycheck to paycheck as I'd done in my twenties.

I chose a book from the shelves and strolled to the French doors leading to the balcony to take in the beauty of the waning light on the water. Orange and gold melded with black sea, and the ever-present surfers ebbed and flowed just like the tide.

It still hadn't rained. It had now been more than two weeks, and there was a stillness to the air that was almost eerie. The hydrangeas were wilting, and the villagers' moods were elevated just like the old barometer on the mantle. I spied a little round creature speeding along the perimeter of the flower beds bordering the pea gravel below.

It was probably a rat. An oddly fat one at that. *Lovely.* One more thing to add to the list: check for signs of rats in the house. Well, it certainly was a noisy, bumbling thing.

It was ten thirty and there was another half hour before the weekly Skype sessions would begin. At least I'd gotten Max to agree on an earlier time frame. Apparently, I had the yoga teacher, Heather, who was now his fiancée, to thank. My East Coast Skype clients were dropping appointments left and right. Apparently, only Californians embraced therapy on a screen. But life was chugging on for all of them—sometimes for the better and sometimes for the worse.

Gillian St. James had decided to stop therapy as she was now wedded to liar and cheat number three. She just wasn't ready to change, and I understood and had seen it hundreds of times before. Anne Bishop had found a job and was taking online courses toward an MBA. She had not flamed out. Now I was down two weekly clients from the original eight. Something more to worry about.

Tomorrow I'd arranged to meet with the banker at Barclays to discuss a loan, something impossibly difficult to obtain per Phillip. Then there was a meeting with Jojo to put a lid on his dream. Sotheby's would have to wait. There was a dinner party to plan for tomorrow. And I was determined that everyone have an extraordinary time.

Settling into the chaise longue under the stars on the terrace, I opened the book, turned on the mini book light, and, despite all my worries, truly relaxed and tuned out for the first time in almost twenty years.

A short while later, I glanced at my watch and jumped out of the cozy chair. I was late. For Max. Oh God! I ran past the card players to take the stairs to my bedroom.

And there was Lily. Sitting at my desk in the corner, Skyping with . . . Max. And Heather, the infamous yoga instructor.

"Lily!"

"Yes, Mom?"

"Um, what are you doing?"

"Hey, she's great, Katie-girl," Max said. "Maybe I should hire her instead of you. She knows a good deal when she hears it, isn't that right, Lily?"

"You're funny," she replied with a giggle.

"Max," I said, walking toward my desk and indicating silently to Lily that I'd like my chair. "You are not allowed to talk to my daughter. Got it?"

"Mom! How rude."

"Max? Got it?" I repeated.

"That overprotective-mom thing you've got going, Kate, is something else. I've never seen this side of you."

"I see it all the time," Lily inserted.

"Indeed," I replied. "Lily, I need some privacy."

"Mom, I want to see what you do," she said. "Can I stay if he allows it?"

"No," I said.

"Come on, Katie-girl," Max whined. "It's two against one. Actually, Heather, would you back me up here?"

Of course she would.

"So, Lily here was just telling me that you've decided to stay in France permanently. That's a real kick in the pants.

"What else did she say?" I glared at my daughter, who giggled.

"Lily also told me that the place is falling apart and that you don't know how you're going to come up with the funds to fix it."

"I'm surprised she didn't tell you about all our other family problems." I shot her a glance and she smiled.

"She did. Nasty piece of work that uncle of yours. Sounds like a narcissistic prick, if you ask me. Pardon my language, Lily."

It took one to know one.

"So," Max interrupted, "how you going to raise that million you need?"

"What?" I glanced at Lily.

She shrugged her shoulders with as much innocence as a second grader during First Communion.

"I'm sorry, Max, but there must be some sort of misunderstanding. First, I don't need to raise a million dollars. And second—"

"Of course you need a million. A half million to pay off that viper of an uncle. And another half million to fix the roof and a hell of a lot more, if Lily's calculations are right."

And suddenly, déjà vu entered the room like a ghost on a mission. It was Antoinette all over again in the form of Lily. Wheedling and cajoling to have others do her bidding. I guessed I'd have to wait a generation for my more reserved genes to kick in with her children.

Who would be born here?

"I give up," I said, laughing. "What's the difference—half a million to a million. It's like Monopoly money at this point."

"Okay, then. How much do you have to invest?"

Lily was whispering, "Do it, Mom. Do it."

I gave her the evil eye. "Max, I can't afford to lose a penny. And the payout would probably be too late anyway."

"Limerack is a guaranteed win."

"There are no guarantees in life, Max."

"Sure there are," he insisted. "Why don't you ask Heather's advice. She has a stock portfolio rivaling mine."

That woke me up.

"The studios pay me a fortune to get their stars in shape each season," she said with a giggle.

"Heather?" What did I have to lose at this point?

"Yes, Kate?"

"Do you have any advice for me?"

"Absolutely. Invest in Limerack. Oh, and, um . . ."

"Yes?"

"Your daughter and I think you should find a boyfriend."

I looked at Lily and she smiled.

"Well, that's just a great idea," I said in a tone that suggested I thought the exact opposite.

"Mom," Lily said, "you're not getting any younger. And I saw the way that hot surfer looked at you at the beach today. I think you should date Russ."

"I am not going out with a half-Aussie, half-Danish vaga-bond half my age," I retorted. "And what daughter wants their mother dating anyway? Stepparents are evil. Haven't you seen enough Disney stories to have that burned in your brain?"

"I didn't say anything about a stepfather," she replied.

Max's hand was back where it didn't belong. "Katie-girl, live a little. Your daughter just gave you permission to get laid."

"Okay, that's it," I said. "Session over. I'll see you, Max, and you alone, next week, same time." My finger was poised over the mouse.

Three people howled *nooooo* in unison.

"Okay, look," Max began again, "just give me twenty-five grand. Fifty if you can, and I'll run it up as far and as fast as I can."

I looked at the three inmates in this loony bin and capitu-lated. Sort of. "Twenty. And that's as far as I'll go. And if you lose it, I might ask you to double your payments for a while."

His eyes widened with a deal on the table. "Make it twenty-five and I'll match it. But you gotta give me free therapy for . . . well, let's say for five years."

"Three."

It was if I'd agreed to finance his latest film. "Thatta girl. I'm so proud of you that I'll do what you've always suggested."

"And what is that, Max?"

"Why, show a little empathy." He looked at Heather with an expression I'd never ever seen in his jaded eyes. "My darling Heather, what can I do to make you happy, sweetheart? Wanna go shopping on Rodeo?"

"Nope," she said. "Let's go take Bobo for a run on the beach. Say bye-bye, Kate, honey bear."

"Bye-bye, Kate, honey bear."

The couple nuzzled, and then froze as the call ended.

Maybe I'd been wrong about Max. Maybe he wasn't the misogynistic narcissist I'd always pegged him to be. Maybe he just hadn't met the right person—the right fit. Then again, Heather would be most men's dream come true. She could be a chameleon. And I was getting too jaded.

"You know, Mom," Lily said. "This is a pretty cool job. Way more fun than I thought. I think I could be pretty good at it if I decided to make this a career. How much do you charge an hour?"

The fun house just kept moving deeper into crazy town.

And I loved it.

Whispers from the Garden . . .

Yowler had disappeared. It had been three nights, and panic was setting in. Panic was not an emotion I was used to having more than a minute or two when in danger. It was definitely something I didn't like. Even Yowler's pet, that old

Two-Legged, was tired of calling for her. Her voice had grown thready and sad. Then again, it took forever for her to call Yowler, what with that ridiculous string of names she had given her.

Still. A thousand disasters could have befallen Yowler. Maybe that horrible Barker she called a Boxer had got her next door. Or, more likely, the other Boxer, still on the loose, had eaten her. I shivered. Maybe she'd gotten stuck in a tree. She had said that had happened once before. I told her that no matter how tasty the Wing Beaters were, she should just stay out of the trees. But she never listened to me.

I could feel the saliva rising on my tongue, only I couldn't exactly remember her scent anymore.

Oh, I didn't like this feeling.

What was this feeling?

"Miss me?"

I turned to find her big, round golden eyes watching me from under the pink blooms that were drooping from the dry spell.

"Oh, Yowler, where did you go?"

"Miss me?" she repeated.

"What do you mean?"

"I mean, did you wish I was here while I was gone?"

"Yes, exactly that," I said, and breathed in her lovely, poignant scent. "I thought you might be dead."

Her whiskers fluttered, and she stretched out a back leg and started to lick herself in a most undignified manner as usual.

But I didn't say anything because I was just so happy to see her. Yes, this was happiness. Almost—no—better than a slew of little Slugs gleaming in the moonlight.

"I went on a little adventure," she said. "You might call it a retreat. Or a semester abroad. Whatever. You know what I mean, right? Hedgehogs do that, don't they?"

"You mean hibernate? Yes. I live to hibernate."

"No!" She sounded annoyed. "It's the complete opposite. It's when you succumb to the call of wildness. You explore. Find new hunting grounds, meet others of your species to, ahem, well, mate, although I must admit that I've never, ever enjoyed it. I mean, really? Who likes to have some idiot sinking their claws and teeth into your neck and doing something completely embarrassing? Not me, I tell you. And then, ten weeks later, your figure is gone, and a litter of demanding kittens appear and they almost never look like me."

"So where did you go?" I asked again, desperate to change the subject.

"Just over a few hills and valleys. Saw a horse or two. You know the horses are a little different in the mountains—much shorter, and sturdier."

I was so happy to see her, but I wanted to understand. "Why didn't you tell me you were going away for a while?"

"You're not going to start that, are you? Trying to keep a collar on me? If you do, it's going to get tedious fast," she said. "Besides, you should never give up your power like that."

"Power? I don't have any power. I don't think I even want any power."

"Don't I know it," she continued. "But, Quilly, you need to know that now that you're out in the world, relationships between creatures are always under the control of those who care the least."

"Well, I don't want to care the least. I've been alone so long that I like the idea of caring the most. And where I come from everyone pretends not to care at all."

She made a strange tsk-tsking noise. "You've got to get your game on."

"Why?"

"Well, what are you going to do if I die or leave and never come back?"

"Go into hibernation early. Probably. Or just focus on Slugs and hiding. It's who I am."

"Forget I said a thing," she muttered. "It's almost impossible to explain things to you sometimes."

"That's okay. I don't need you to explain things. I just don't like it when you leave for a long time and not tell me you're going."

"Where did you think I'd gone?"

"I thought the Barkers had got you. Or maybe one of those big, smelly, loud things the Two-Leggeds ride around in."

"You should never assume anything, Quilly."

"Why not?"

"It's a waste of time and energy. You'll never know what's going on in someone else's mind unless you find the courage to ask them. And you can't afford to waste any time or energy given your average life span."

"What!? How long am I going to live?" I was afraid I'd started to whimper.

"Forget I said anything."

Yowler got a little closer and I felt her lovely, long orange tail curl around me.

"Could you please come a little closer, Yowler? I guess you're right. It was that missing thing that was happening."

"All right," she said inching closer. "But don't expect me to lick you or anything. I'm not a fool. I don't make mistakes twice. I only have six and a half lives left and I don't intend to lose one with you."

"Oh," I said, wondering how many lives I had. A dark sense of time and space enveloped me.

"Now, don't take it personally," Yowler said with a meow. "Never take anything personally."

"Is that a waste of time too?"

"Exactly," she said. "You might not follow directions well, but you're a fast learner."

I heard a funny sound emanating from her throat. It was sort of like the drone of the scary machine that clipped the grass—only much softer. "What's that sound?"

"Oh, nothing," she said, and sounded a trifle embarrassed. I knew that feeling well.

"It's okay, Yowler. I won't take it personally and I won't assume anything. So I guess I just have to be courageous and ask you again. What's that sound?"

"I'm purring, Quilly. I can't really control it. It just means

I sort of, kind of, like you." She coughed. "For now, at least. I might change my mind. You never know."

It took a while for all of this to sink in. But finally I understood. "Whose got the power now? I'll tell you who. I do!"

"Oh, shut up," she said.

"But you like me."

"Don't get your quills in a twist, will you? I knew I shouldn't have said a thing."

I could see a sudden wild swirl of the plane tree branches silhouetted in the moonlight. "Yowler?"

"Yes, Quilly?"

"I like you too. You can have the power back. I don't need it."

A crack of sound and light rolled down to earth from the night sky, and Yowler's lovely purring stopped.

"Come on, you," she said. "Time to go into hiding. I knew this was coming and it's going to be the worst one in many, many moons."

I didn't need her to tell me that. I could smell it and feel it in my bones. I ran as fast as my legs would go.

"Can't you go any faster?"

"No," I moaned.

She dashed to an ancient boxwood at the front near the gate and waited for me to catch up. "Okay, we've got to get to that cave on the cliff face. But I found a shortcut for you. Just please tell me you're not claustrophobic."

"I don't know what that is, but I promise not to be if that's the only way."

She crouched on her hindquarters and began madly digging. Yowler stopped and walked behind me. "Okay, then. Down the hatch."

"What?"

"Go down that hole. I promise you'll be safe."

"You just told me not to make any assumptions."

"I also said not to take anything personally. So don't take this the wrong way." With that she shoved me with a swipe of her paw. And we both yowled. She then sang out, "Meet you on the dark side!"

I fell and fell and fell some more.

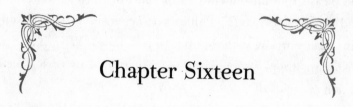

Chapter Sixteen

It was a good thing we'd laid up enough provisions for ten days or so since the beginning of July. Everyone in the village had been talking about the coming storm. All the restaurants on the beach had battened down for a flood rivaling the days of arks and plagues. Even the BBC weatherman, usually as cool and emotionless as a coma ward, had broken a sweat when issuing a warning for the southwest coast of France this morning.

"The storm, expected to commence late tonight, has now been upgraded on the Beaufort Wind Scale from nine to ten. Gale-force winds predicted. Flooding in low-lying areas, major damage to structures near shore due to waves predicted to exceed twelve feet. Residents advised to secure property and stay indoors."

In the way of all storms, it was due the exact night and hour most inconvenient—the evening of the dinner with the Soameses.

"You don't think we'd let a spot of rain keep us away from the pleasure of introducing all of you to my great-great-niece and -nephew, do you?" Phillip Soames insisted when I rang him that morning with an offer to postpone. "Why, if an Englishman stopped socializing when it rained then we'd be a nation of recluses!"

By the time the four members of the Soames household appeared, the wind had picked up and the trees were bending with each large gust. Lily took on the role of hostess as if she'd been born to it as I'd relegated myself to the kitchen with Magdali, following her orders. No amount of the Food Network had prepared me for the wildly creative flare of a French-American-Namibian in the final throes of preparation for the first dinner party in over a decade.

I'd never seen this side of my half sister. Who knew clarified butter and onions could elicit such passion? Then again, after sniffing her *Poulet Basquaise à la Magdali*, a traditional stew of tomatoes, onions, sweet peppers with chicken, and Magdali's twist of a dark African spice she refused to name, I felt like dancing. And, indeed, I did. Right outside the kitchen door—all by myself.

"You look very happy, Kate," she said with a rare laugh.

"I am happy." A smattering of raindrops hit my upturned face and I reached out to her.

She joined me in her apron, tapping her two wooden spoons in a tribal beat. We collapsed in each other's arms a few moments later.

"*Allez, allez!*" she ordered. "Back to work. Find the Cointreau for the *soufflé à l'orange.*"

The mood at the dinner table improved with each course.

"Mrs. Hamilton?" Edward's seven-year-old son was dressed like a seventy-year-old man, complete with a bow tie and enough plaid to give an instant headache.

"Yes, Charles?"

"Father said you are a head doctor."

I shifted my feet under the formal dining table and cleared my throat. "I am."

"How do you fix people's heads? Do you know how to do the Vulcan mind meld like Spock on *Star Trek*?"

I glanced surreptitiously toward Edward for help. The laughter in his usually somber eyes proved he was going to enjoy watching me flounder my way out of this.

"Shhh, Charles," his sister, Winnie, interrupted. "You're not supposed to ask such things. Honestly. Don't you know anything?"

"Father said only the weak don't ask questions. Idiots just pretend to know when they don't."

His sister sighed and just shook her head.

I pursed my mouth to keep from laughing. "Charles, you are exactly right. You can't learn without asking questions. No, I haven't mastered mind melding, although I wish I could. It would make my job much easier. What else do you want to know?"

"What's psychopeppery?"

Lily leaned forward and grinned at Charles. "Ohhh, I like that term."

"Psychotherapy," I replied, "is what courageous people do to examine their lives and make better choices."

Edward shook his head. Phillip Soames chuckled.

"*Exactement*," inserted Jean.

"Are you seeing Father to fix his head?"

That brought the laughter to a standstill.

"Charles! Shush." Winnie's voice broke the silence. Her wistful, hopeful gaze turned to me.

I looked at Edward and then turned to his son. "Well, here's the thing, Charles. Your father is an amazingly strong man. The strongest I know. I think you don't need me to tell you that, do you?"

He shook his head.

"Well, the thing of it is this, your father doesn't need to be fixed. He's perfect just the way he is. He's just seen a few too many bad things. Scary things that would give any of us nightmares."

"War," Charles said.

"Yes, war."

"Dead people," he continued.

"Yup," I said. "So what do you do when you have a nightmare?"

"Run to my Dad's bed."

"And what does he do?"

"He lets me climb in and tells me he will protect me and fight off any monsters whilst I sleep."

"And how does that make you feel?" I shot Edward a glance when I saw him roll his eyes. He looked about as uncomfortable as a sunburned man in a hair shirt.

"Safe," Charles piped up. "Settled."

"Right," I said. "So just think about that, okay?"

His eyebrows scrunched and his sister cupped her hands and whispered something into his ear.

Edward opened his mouth but his uncle beat him to it. "Children, Mr. du Roque and Lily have offered to give you a ghost tour of the villa after dinner. Would you like that?"

A chorus of excitement ensued. Since when had my daughter learned any ghost stories about Madeleine Marie? I looked at her, sandwiched between Jean and Magdali. She winked.

"Does your family have any pets?" Winnie asked me. "I really like animals."

I loved working with children. Their lack of guile and focus mimicked my own these days. I was beginning to worry if I'd ever be able to focus again after the stress of the last few years.

"No, we don't," I replied.

"Not yet," Lily interjected.

"Excuse me?" I said.

"You always said I could have one—one day. Mom, it's one day now."

"I hear it's all the rage among head doctors," Edward deadpanned.

"This is not the—"

"A girl must have a dog," Jean added.

I was feeling outnumbered. "Really? I just don't think now is—"

"Winnie and Charles—you should both come with me and my great-grandfather next week. We're going to the nearest animal shelter and picking out a dog."

What? "What?" I looked at Jean, who at least had the grace to look embarrassed. For a moment.

"Come on, Kate," Edward Soames said. "Smart people know when they've been outmaneuvered. Even head doctors."

A crack of thunder rent the air and the chandelier flickered.

"Oh dear," Phillip Soames said. "We're in for it now."

"This is just the beginning," I said. "It's not supposed to really hit until after midnight. Right now it's time for the dessert."

All mention of the storm was put on hold as the members of the dinner party immersed themselves in the serious business of *soufflé à l'orange*. The rain upped the intimacy of an evening filled with laughter, camaraderie, and fellowship. Sort of like the *Titanic*.

But thank God for it.

The storm played havoc all around us. It circled around the town several times as the wind, rain, and lightning advanced and retreated like the tides. The wind whistled under doorways, forced branches into a staccato beat against a window or three, and attacked at every angle. Finally, the rain let loose in earnest, the roar punctuated only by the rips of lightning. It was the perfect backdrop for the ghost tour. As I listened to my grandfather and daughter recount stories of my ancestors amid the portraits in his chamber, I motioned to Magdali to step back from the group.

"I think I should go in the attic and see if there are any leaks."

Edward stepped beside me. "I was thinking the same. Where's the entrance? Got any torches?"

Magdali led the way and handed us flashlights.

Dust covered everything from one side of the low room to the other. Discarded furniture and boxes of every shape and dimension littered the floor. A lone porthole at one end flashed bright each time lightning struck outside.

We found two leaks near the window.

"It could be so much worse, I guess," I said.

"Any buckets in the villa that—"

A brilliant flash illuminated the attic at the exact same moment that a thunderous boom rent the air.

The entire villa reverberated in response.

Except that it didn't stop. It sounded as if a train had hopped its tracks and was heading straight for us, gaining momentum.

Edward grabbed my arms and shoved me down the attic stairs. Everything went to slow motion as I saw Lily herding the children down the red-carpeted, winding staircase. Youssef followed, my grandfather in his arms, as Magdali helped Phillip Soames. It was only after Edward half tossed me out the door that I realized he'd been gripping my left arm so tightly that I couldn't feel it.

The rain was coming in sheets and the temperature felt like fifty degrees as I involuntarily shivered. But the shaking had stopped.

"Was that an earthquake?"

Edward's dark eyes met mine. "Maybe. But I don't think so."

I shielded my eyes from the rain and looked toward the roofline. "Did lightning strike the house?"

"No," he said. "That I'm sure of."

Magdali held her daughter in her arms, and Lily guided the children to protection under the eaves.

And like the military man he was, Edward finally ordered everyone back into the marble foyer a few minutes later. He barked orders left and right.

No one dared question him as the children were dried off before a roaring fire Youssef lit in the salon. Magdali retreated to the kitchen to make hot chocolate and Edward pulled me aside.

"I'm going out to assess damage and figure out what happened. Don't let my children or my uncle leave here. I'll return shortly."

"Got it."

Jean was silent and refused to be drawn into any conversation. Even Phillip was shaken.

Only Lily was her jovial self, amusing the children with card games and books.

I felt someone tugging my shirt.

"Where's Father?" Charles's eyes were huge in his face.

"He's going to be right back. He went out to see what that noise was."

"It's something bad, isn't it?"

I refused to sugarcoat it. "Possibly. But I think it was an

earthquake. They happen all the time in this area. And it's over now."

I could hear old Mlle Lefebvre calling for her cat outside.

"Charles? Could you please help your sister with her cards? I'll be right back."

"No," he pouted. "I want to go with you. I don't want to be left behind anymore."

"Okay," I replied. "Let's get our coats." I told Magdali and we went in search of Mlle Lefebvre.

"*Minou, minou, minou!*" she cried into the rain and wind.

"Mademoiselle," I shouted. "You can't stay out here! It's too dangerous."

"*Non,*" she replied. "I must find my moronic cat."

The set of her jaw made me realize she was not going to budge. "Okay, could you please go to Madeleine Marie and settle my grandfather and Mr. Soames? You're the only one who they will listen to. Charles and I will find your cat."

She finally acquiesced, or rather, grumbled her assent.

I grasped Charles's little hand and he skipped to keep up. I called for the cat in our drive and crossed into my neighbor's front garden. No luck. The cat was probably lounging somewhere inside her large house without the spinster's knowledge.

Bending our heads against the spray of rain, we walked past her gate and crossed the cliff road to look at the turbulent sea.

It was the most beautiful, violent panorama I'd ever witnessed. Charles wrapped his arms around my legs and I held him to me. The sea was a turgid, slow-moving mass retreating, retreating into a wall of water and then slamming forward with brutality over the wide shelf of gigantic boulders, which were doing nothing to protect the road at the bottom of the cliff. Everything on the Côte des Basques would be flooded or destroyed: the little hotel, the three restaurants, the lifeguard station, the port around the corner. It was heartbreaking. Just stunning, the power and destructive nature of the elements. I started to turn to look at Madeleine Marie to try to see the roof, and then stopped turning.

There, up the road from me, maybe a thousand yards away, the road was no more. A portion of the cliff had fallen into the sea. A telephone pole, with its tangle of wires and cables, was at an odd angle, hanging off the side of the cliff. It appeared just like the scene of a disaster that CNN would typically report, and a chill raced up my spine as I grabbed Charles's arm and dragged him back over the road and toward Madeleine Marie.

A few feet from the door I felt someone tug my own arm and I swung around to find Major Soames.

"What the hell are you doing out here?"

"We're just going back in," I yelled against the rage of the storm.

He yanked open the door and pushed us in. "I told you not to leave this house and not to let my family leave," he shouted, his eyes furious.

"I'm sorry. I had to get Mlle Lefebvre inside. Charles wanted to come."

"You shouldn't have let him," he said starkly.

"Daddy," Charles moaned. "It's my fault."

"We don't have time for this," he said, swinging his son into his arms. "We've got to get everyone out of here. The cliff isn't secure. You have ten minutes to get everyone outside with coats and ready to march out. Roger?"

"Yup," I said. "Got it."

It took only seven minutes. Edward loaded up his uncle's Range Rover with his family and Jean and Youssef. I climbed into the old Peugeot with Lily, Magdali, her daughter, and Mlle Lefebvre, who got in only after the major threatened her with words that she could not have understood.

The windshield wipers of the Peugeot could not move fast enough to dislodge the water. We followed the black Range Rover down the road and I couldn't seem to breathe properly until we'd curved down to almost sea level.

Edward's brake lights lit up and he came to a halt. What in hell was he doing? I opened my window and stuck out my head to see a pool of water in front of his car. He exited and ran to my door as Youssef got out of a rear door and went around to Edward's driver's seat.

"Everyone out," Edward shouted at me.

"You," he grasped Lily's shoulders. "Get in the back of my car along with everyone else."

We squeezed Mlle Lefebvre onto Lily's lap, and Magdali and her daughter squeezed into the boot of the Range Rover, as Edward shouted instructions to Youssef, who drove into the waist-deep water and miraculously made it a hundred yards away to rejoin the road.

Edward grabbed my arm. "Come on. We're going on foot. We'll meet them on the other side of the Route Nationale."

I opened my mouth.

"Don't have time. Just follow me."

And I did. We bypassed the deep water and raced up the warren of small streets in the village. Lightning forked the sky, raining veins of light toward the earth. Twice more we were stopped by flooding and, with no alternative, he half-dragged me through the fast-moving water that was now as deep as the first impasse. I prayed the Range Rover was far beyond us. We avoided streets with wires down and climbed over an enormous uprooted tree with branches that looked like medieval torture devices. There was not a soul in sight, and I had a sinking feeling that we had somehow missed an order to evacuate. We must have been the only family not watching Canal+. The Route Nationale was deserted; the Range Rover nowhere to be found. Edward shouted an obscenity that would have made a newsroom editor blush.

"Where do you think they went?" My voice was carried away in the storm and I tried again. "Edward?"

He turned. "There," he shouted, and pointed his arm toward the church. "Come on."

He grabbed my arm and we crossed the deserted road flanked by huge gullies of water. We slogged against the wind and the icy rain and passed the restaurants and shops going up the hill. We were heading for the road that led to the church, whose bell was tolling, most likely from the force of the wind.

We were running now and I just couldn't keep up. Edward finally stopped and forced me onto his back. A massive gust of wind buffeted us and we were tossed against a car sideways in the road with such force that we bounced off the top of the Renault and fell in a heap. Wind roared in my ears, snatching Edward's shouts as I untangled myself from him.

And then I saw his leg at an unnatural angle as he lay in the road, sheets of rain drenching everything in its path. Another gust howled passed, taking my breath with it.

He was motioning toward the church, urging me to go on and I shook my head. His curses I heard perfectly.

I crab-walked toward one of the large tree branches that littered the ground in every direction and broke off a section. Using my rain jacket, I fashioned what was the most ineffective, primitive splint known to mankind. He made not a sound as I tightened and knotted the ends of the jacket arms.

"Get up," I shouted.

He pointed to the church. "Go!"

I shook my head.

A flash telescoped above us and we were transfixed by the bolt's descent. It struck the steeple and an explosion of sparks lit up the ancient church. I could barely hear after the explosion—everything was muffled and the air was filled with the acrid scent of burnt stone. And I was blinded by the flash.

"Come on," I shouted again. "Lightning never strikes twice in the same place."

I got him up, cantilevered him against my hip, and we dragged ourselves the last eighth of a mile up that hill. Not a soul greeted us as we fell inside the arched doorway of the church.

It was eerily quiet in the incense-infused, red-domed beauty of the space. The only light came from a bank of candles lit in memory of loved ones lost. A host of saints with tortured faces stared down at us.

I could not seem to catch my breath, but finally I forced myself up. And that's when I saw that there was something wrong with Edward's other leg. The foot was all wrong.

"Where the bloody, sodding hell is everyone? The children . . ." His voice was thin and choked with emotion.

"I—I don't know." I called out for help, the tremors of my voice echoing off the thick walls.

His voice thready now, he whispered, "It's an old wives tale about lightning not striking the same place twice."

I shook my head. "Really? You're going to argue with me now about this?"

He was panting and white as a sheet. He closed his eyes. "Kate, you've got to find . . ." He slumped and his head hit the stone floor made up of dozens of horizontal tombstones of the religious who'd prayed and pontificated in this church the last six hundred years.

I shook him. "Find what? Oh God, wake up. Edward, no. Come on, wake up!" I scooped some holy water from the font next to the door with my hands and splashed it on his face.

Nothing. I felt like I was in a B-grade horror movie and I was the worst actress in Hollywood.

I checked his pulse. Strong as an ox. Of course. I looked at his legs again. Blood was seeping from my raincoat over the makeshift splint that was falling off.

In my head I was saying every curse word in English, French, and Basque as I eased off the poor excuse for a splint. I needed to get his trousers off. I rifled his pockets and came up with a British Army pocketknife. Slicing through the soaked gray broadcloth, I saw far too much blood, open flesh, muscle, and cracked shinbone. I looked away when a ring of pulsating black started closing off my vision. I focused on his belt and tugged it off to make a tourniquet, hoping the pressure was correct. I felt his other leg, all the way down to his foot, which was swollen and obviously broken, but not through the skin.

I shouted again, hoping someone would come, but no one did. Only the echo of my voice and the incessant clang of the bell broke the silence.

Again, I checked his pulse and slapped him in an effort to wake him, all to no avail.

I had to find a doctor, and I had to find everyone else. Dammit.

The wall of wind battled my efforts to open the door, but I made it through only to have the breath sucked out of me. I choked. There were no lights as far as I could see. Power gone. But I suddenly remembered I had my iPhone in my pocket. How idiotic. Leaning against the church, I pulled up favorites and punched Lily's name. A recording by a calm French woman informed me that telephone service was unavailable.

I had no idea where to go, but I started back down the road anyway. I formed a plan. Look for the black Range Rover and knock on every door along the route, retracing our steps. The wind kept knocking me down as there was no windbreak between buildings. Adopting a walking Downward Dog position on my feet and hands, I sang the "Marseillaise" to get a grip. I sang it over and over for so long, that by the time I reached the main road, it had somehow morphed into "Tainted Love" by Soft Cell.

What was wrong with me?

The Route Nationale was nearly impassable now. I lost one of my rubber gardening boots crossing the raging water of the first gulley. I lost the other climbing back over the broken branches of the uprooted tree a quarter of a mile away.

The problem was that I could barely see through my tangle of hair and the driving rain. I almost yanked a chunk out in frustration.

My fists felt nothing as I pounded the doors of dark houses. Where had everyone gone? I would have given everything I owned to see the Range Rover or a doctor. But there was not a car in sight except for a handful that had gotten caught in the rising water.

I just didn't dare cross anything higher than my upper thighs now. It was too fast-moving and my limbs were not working the way they should. And so I climbed the side streets heading back uphill toward the pharmacy and butcher shop.

Grabbing the largest rock I could lift, I bashed the lock of the pharmacy's accordion iron protective webbing until it broke and then threw the rock at the glass sliding door, smashing it into a thousand pieces.

What the hell was I doing? I had no idea.

I grabbed a huge beach bag that was on sale and went into

the back room, scooping up anything that looked like a pain killer, antibiotic, or antiseptic. Then I grabbed bandages and tape. I grabbed a phone receiver I spied near the register and dialed Lily's number before I realized it was dead.

I looked toward the gaping hole that had once been the sliding glass door and finally realized the reason I couldn't really see. I was sobbing. I forced myself to stop by screaming so long and so loud that I couldn't breathe.

And there in the doorway was Jojo the mayor, with Pierrot behind him.

"Qu'est-ce que vous fais là?!" Jojo held an ax in one hand and an ancient pistol in the other.

I sagged to the floor. "What am I doing here? Broken leg. Losing too much blood. Major Soames." For some reason I couldn't form a sentence. "Ambulance. The church. Send it to the church. My family, have you seen them? In a black Range Rover, heading to the Route Nationale."

"They're probably at the train station. We diverted all traffic there."

"Thank God," I whispered as I slumped back. I could finally breathe. "I have to see my daughter. Please find out if she's there."

Pierrot peeled my fingers from the bag's straps and took it to the back room again. "Hey, I need that for Edward Soames."

Jojo took off his yellow rain jacket, got to his knees, and I watched as he picked up my shaking arms one by one and put them in the armholes. I hadn't noticed but there was a long, deep gash on one and the skin was too white. Maybe from that tree? As he zipped it, I noticed blood had soaked the front of my cream silk blouse now transparent from the rain. I looked away.

"Don't worry, Pierrot's a trained medic. Did his *service militaire* a long time ago with me. He's making sure he has everything he needs. *Alors, chérie*, do you know your blood type?"

"Oh, okay. Um . . ." *What did he ask?* "I—what?"

"Blood type?"

"Oh. Yeah." I sighed. "I mean, O. It's O."

"Positive?"

"Mmmm. Yeah. Why?"

"Shhh . . ." He stood up, walked to a Dr. Scholl's revolving stand and selected a pair of rubber thongs and walked back to me.

What in hell was he doing?

I looked at my feet.

Blood and shards of glass.

The last voice I heard before the ring of black closed me from reality was Jojo's. "*Viens vite, Pierrot! Elle est en choc.*"

Funny how shock sounds the same in both languages.

And why fear it? It's actually such a lovely, comforting feeling to float away. I was drifting high in the clouds above the Pays Basque in the night air. The storm withdrew in on itself and disappeared like a magic trick. I was looking down at the mountain peaks of Les Trois Couronnes, and the lady's black hair steamed down the sides and fell into the sea. She was crying, or maybe it was just the rain. I wanted to comfort her. Tell her everything was going to be okay. But there was a black ball of fear lodged in my throat, and my arms wouldn't obey my command to reach out to her.

She opened her eyes.

And I woke up screaming.

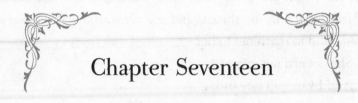

Chapter Seventeen

It was zero to six hundred miles an hour in an instant. Every cell of my body was in revolt as I returned to consciousness. I just couldn't force myself to open my eyes. I didn't want to wake up.

Until I heard Lily's voice calling to me. "Mom. Mom. Mommy . . . Please wake up." And, "No. Don't you dare put that stuff under her nose again. Mom? Please?"

She was patting my hand. I could feel her breathe on my face and her lips on my forehead. She whispered in my ear, "Mom, come on."

I breathed in and opened my eyes. It was a little too bright and everything was out of focus and the sharp scent of rubbing alcohol permeated the air. "Wha . . ."

"Mommy," she said, a smile in her voice. "I told you she was coming to."

"*Finalement*," the growly voice of Pierrot reached my ears.

"You should be proud of your mother," Jojo's voice began. "She's *une vrai*—a true French hero. Major Soames is here because of her. And she sang and sang the 'Marseillaise' the entire trip in the ambulance. Although she didn't have all the right words or verses quite correct." He patted my hand. "I will teach you the words. And maybe let you use my microphone to sing it at the next *boum* in the village square."

"Mom . . ." Lilly said. "Why are you crying?"

I couldn't work my mouth.

"Shhh . . . Don't ask her to talk, Lily," Pierrot said. "It's going to take some time. Madame, you are going to be fine, but you lost quite a bit of blood. You ruptured your spleen, which the surgeon removed. And you have almost a hundred stitches, mostly on your arm and elsewhere."

"Mmm . . . mmm." I wanted so much to ask something. "Maaay . . . Maaay." I stopped.

"Major Soames. You want to know about Major Soames, of course," Lily said. "He's going to be okay. He had surgery too. Longer than yours. He also lost a lot of blood—almost too much. He was lucky you found help in time. They set his leg in surgery. And his other foot is in plaster. But he's already complaining about being in a wheelchair. Granddaddy made him stop complaining."

My eyes were finally regaining focus, and I looked at Pierrot—Basque terrorist, neighbor, liar, swindler, and savior. "*Esk . . .*"

He leaned down to my lips. I whispered, "*Eskerrik asko.*"

Lily's eyes were wide. "What did she say? Is she okay? She's slurring her words too much."

Pierrot smiled. "She said thank you. In my language."

"Oh," Lily said. "I didn't know she knew Basque."

"I didn't either. Your mother is remarkable," Pierrot said. "I shall teach her the Basque anthem. All seven of them."

It was lovely to just listen to all of them and not have to talk. I felt so tired, but I didn't want to sleep. I just didn't want to move.

"Mom?" Lily said with hesitation. "They said I shouldn't tell you, but I know you'll be mad later if I don't tell you now."

That woke me up. "Wha . . ."

"No, messieurs. I know my mother better than you. Before she became a French and Basque hero." Lily's hands were on her hips. "Mom, Mr. Soames's house is gone. It fell with the cliff. That's what that horrible sound was last night. No one was in it, luckily. The servants had evacuated. But he's lost everything." She paused and searched my face.

I swallowed and nodded for her to keep going. *God.*

"Mr. Soames refuses to move in to Madeleine Marie with Winnie and Charles. Granddaddy has not been able to convince him. He says it's already too much that we have to take in Major Soames when he is released from here, and that you have to recover too. Now he's talking about moving back to London. Permanently. And Granddaddy is very sad. We have to do something."

I nodded.

"I knew you'd agree," she said. "So I have an idea. Can we sell him part of Madeleine Marie?"

She looked so hopeful. I didn't want to break her heart. But there was something inside of me that would not agree with her idea even if it would solve all our problems. I shook my head no.

She looked crestfallen. "Then what? What should I do?"

Pierrot leaned in, "Get close to her mouth. She can whisper. It's the breathing tube from surgery. Sometimes you lose your voice."

She leaned in.

"Give him . . . say bedrooms in Madeleine Marie are a gift," I whispered.

Her eyes were round as a two-euro coin. "You want me to say you are giving him bedrooms in Madeleine Marie as a gift?"

"Yes. Must say gift."

"Um, Mom. That's a big gift."

"Tell him it will give me joy." I closed my eyes. He would remember our conversation of over a month ago, when I refused his gift and he'd chastised me. "He won't be able to refuse me." I was already drifting. Couldn't hold it together . . . But Lily's words to the others floated in my conscious.

"Is she okay?" Lily whispered harshly. "Does she know what she's saying? Does she really want me to gift bedrooms to Mr. Soames?"

"I just said your mother is a national treasure. Do what she says," Jojo commanded.

"You said she was a French hero," Lily corrected.

"Treasure. Hero. What is *la différence*?" Jojo said.

"And a Basque hero," added Pierrot.

"Here is an *ideé*," Jojo said. "Yes, I'm certain. If M. Soames doesn't accept Madeleine Marie and these bedrooms, I'm certain your mother would want to give it to the village in honor of me saving her. The *mairie* is *foutu*—destroyed. We need a new *mairie*."

"I saved her," Pierrot argued. "I should get the whole house."

I opened my eyes. "*Non*. And hell no." I closed my eyes again.

Lily laughed. "Okay, then. Got it."

IT'S A FUNNY thing about life. That our vulnerabilities are actually our greatest strengths because they make us human, but that showing vulnerability requires courage. Phillip Soames taught me that. He learned in return that following one's own advice "is just a humiliating pain in one's own arse," as he put it succinctly the day I returned to Madeleine Marie to find him ensconced in our biggest guest bedroom. It was across the hall from my grandfather and as I was convalescing, it gave me great pleasure to hear them bickering like an old married couple in separate bedrooms.

It gave me even more pleasure, the first evening, when he knocked on the door and said he understood my message and would not insult the kindness by offering lodging fees in return. It was understood that he and his family could stay forever and a day and that it would give us only joy if he never left. It was also understood that he would pay for a few household expenses such as food and I would accept it.

The morning after returning, Lily brought a luscious breakfast made by Magdali on a tray. Charles and Winnie, as solemn as two church mourners, brought up the rear, bearing enormous, untidy bouquets of ragged flowers picked from the storm-tossed garden.

"Oh," I said. "How lovely. Thank you."

They stood there, uncertain what to do.

I patted the bed. "Come sit with me. I have a story to tell you." They ran to the bed and carefully kept their muddied shoes off the duvet as they sat down. Lily arranged the tray on the bedside table and pulled up a chair.

"I spoke to your father when I left the hospital. He said to tell you that he's sorry in advance."

"Why?" They asked in unison, shocked.

"Because he is going to be as ornery as a bear and twice as mean when they unlock the hospital cage he's in."

"What?" Charles said.

"He did not say that," Winnie announced. "That does not sound like Daddy at all."

Well, I had never been good with lying. And why was I trying to start now? "Okay, children," I started over. "The doctor said your father will be released early next week. So I just want to prepare you."

"For what?"

"For the fact that he is probably going to be the absolute worst patient known to mankind. He's already making the nurses cry and he barely had two words to say to me. So that means he's going to be short-tempered here too."

"Mom!" Lily was laughing. "You're scaring Charles and Winnie."

"Am I?"

They shook their heads no.

"See? They're not scared." Lord, I hoped they wouldn't be. "So, I just want you to be prepared. You know I'm a head doctor like you said, Charles, right?"

"Roger," he said, just like his father.

"So, we're going to do something nice for your father because I just happen to think he's one of the nicest people I know—other than Mr. Soames, of course."

"What do you want us to do?" Winnie said wistfully.

I worried about this little girl. She was not at all like the bold, outgoing girl Edward had described.

"We'll do anything," Charles added. "He almost died giving up his space in the car. And you too, ma'am."

I placed my hands on either side of the covers and spread my fingers wide. "It's really hard to be weak when you've always been strong. Just like it's really hard to be strong when you've grown used to being weak. Does that make sense?"

They both nodded.

"And when something is hard it's easy to become frustrated. And when that happens, people sometimes say and do things that they regret later."

"I know that," Charles said. "That's what happens all the time with Mum and Dad."

I lifted his chin and looked into his eyes. "I know you're worried about that, but sometimes you have to say to yourself that that is their problem to solve, not yours. Roger?"

He nodded.

"So all you have to do is go to your father's bedroom every morning, make him look you in the eye, and tell him you love him and need him. And do it again in the evening."

Silence filled the room. Lily was laying out clothes for me.

"That's it?" Winnie was fiddling with the red ribbons on the ends of her braids.

"Yes, that's it."

"But, he knows that already," Charles said.

"Knowing it is not the same as hearing it," I said.

"Roger," Charles said.

Lily gathered the children and picked up the tray. "Mom, Magdali said she'll be right up to help you bathe."

"Thank you. The toast was perfect."

I watched her walk out the door and picked up my list of a hundred things to do. It was daunting. Just mind-blowingly daunting. The roof, according to Magdali, was now a sieve with half the tiles blown off in the storm just like every other house in the area. The next rainstorm would flood the entire villa. And the hits just kept on coming.

There was a knock on the door.

"Magdali? Come in."

Lily entered.

"Forget something?" I looked around the bed.

She walked straight to me, leaned over, placed her hands on

either side of my face and looked at me. "I love you, Mom. And I need you."

I breathed through the ache in my throat. "I love you too, Lily. I'm the luckiest mother to have you for a daughter."

"I'm sorry," she said.

"Shhh . . ." I said.

"No," she said. "I'm sorry I ran away. Sorry I scared you by staying away. Sorry I refused to live with you."

I reached up and pulled her to me with my one good arm. "Well, I'm sorry I didn't protect you. And I'm sorry I got stuck and couldn't figure out a way to get us out of there. I should have done things differently. I should have been bolder and taken a risk, like you said. I'm more sorry than you'll ever know."

She began to cry and I did too. I stroked the downy softness of her hair.

She finally sat back up. "Mom?"

"Yes?"

"I just want you to know that I would go through it all over again because I know who I am and I like who I am. And I wouldn't be me unless I had experienced it all. I wouldn't trade places with anyone."

"That's just about the greatest thing a mother could wish to hear."

A sly smile crept into her expression. "So now might be the perfect time to tell you that Granddaddy, Youssef, and I went to the animal shelter in Bayonne and brought back a dog."

"What?"

"You're going to love him. And we decided against a puppy.

Max was on death row and he refused to be ignored. He is just the cutest."

"Max? Like my client?"

"Yup. They've got similar personalities."

I sighed. "How big?"

"Seventeen pounds, if I did the conversion from kilos correctly. There's only one thing."

"Yes?"

"He has to sleep under the covers or else."

"Or else what?"

"He howls."

"Roger." God. Now even I was talking like the major.

THE DAY BEFORE Edward Soames was released from the hospital, I was finally allowed to venture outside the cocoon of Madeleine Marie. All had tried to warn me about the extent of the devastation, but it was a shock. I'd returned from the hospital at night and hadn't imagined the carnage.

Mother Nature had had her say, and it had not been understated. On the beach below the cliff, every restaurant, every establishment of any kind, including the boutique hotel, had been rendered to tattered skeletons or swept away completely. Downed trees, branches, and electrical wires were in every direction, albeit crews were out dealing with the mess. I slowly walked toward the barricade in front of where the Soameses' house had once stood, and there was nothing there other than a huge gap. I could not will myself to look down the cliff to see the wreckage.

The French National Guard had been called in immediately after the storm to cordon off areas, distribute food and water, and provide temporary accommodations for anyone left homeless. The entire area was a disaster zone. The Soameses' villa had been the last one on the cliff road but had appeared impervious due to the structural improvements Phillip had undertaken years ago. Why was our villa still standing and his was not?

It just made no sense.

I walked back toward Madeleine Marie and looked down to glimpse at my arm. Ignoring it had not worked. It was simply the ugliest scar this side of the Pyrenees. Jagged and long, stretching from shoulder to wrist. At least it was my left arm, and I was a righty. The scar on my chest was not nearly as bad, and the scar from the spleen surgery would fade and always be hidden under my clothes. But that arm? It would only impress a pirate. My vanity was going to be sorely tried on that one. At least the cuts from the glass on my feet had not been nearly as bad as I'd thought. All that walking on the beach had left my feet tough.

Mlle Lefebvre was standing next to her gate in front of her house as I walked by.

"*Bonjour*, Mme Hamilton," she said with a rare one of her smiles. "Very 'appy to zee you out walking."

I bent down to kiss each of her wrinkled cheeks. "*Merci*. I am so happy to see you too. Did you find your cat?"

Her face instantly changed to her usual dour expression. "*Non. Ma pauvre minette.* I fear something grave has happened to her."

"Please don't give up hope. Sometimes animals go into hiding before and during a disaster. Your cat must have smelled the storm coming. I'll ask my daughter to organize a search party. And will you reserve a night next week to come for dinner? I know my grandfather would love to see you."

"*Ah, oui? Vraiment?*"

"Absolutely. Really. Say next Sunday?"

"*D'accord!*" She turned and slowly walked back to her house. I could hear her muttering something about old goats and distinctly heard my grandfather's name.

I crossed the pea gravel and looked up. The storm had not removed a single strand of ivy, which had protected the lovely old walls of my family's home.

My home.

And as I tugged on the heavy door, and wedged myself through the opening, I could have sworn I heard a whisper of a meow.

I called out, "*Minou, minou, minou,*" as I had heard Mlle Lefebvre call on many evenings.

I turned my ear toward the drive and stood stock-still.

Nothing.

It must have been wishful thinking.

Whispers from the Cliff . . .

It was just too tight for three of us down here. Oh, who was I kidding? It would have been idyllic if it was just Yowler and me. It was the Barker that was making everything uncomfortable.

Sure, he'd changed. Or so he said. I had my doubts. No one ever changed unless they chose to change. And this Barker, who insisted his race came from some place called the United States of Amuricah, had not found religion. The only thing he had found was a better life. He'd explained it all whilst the storm raged outside.

But let me back up. I didn't tell you about that fall.

I thought I was going to die. Yes, in fact, I think I did die a little. Yowler said she gave me one of her lives. Grudgingly.

It was a fall like no other—a straight twenty-two-foot shot from Ground Zero under the old boxwood to the Barker's furry back below. Yowler said I was lucky the Boxer—her word— was lying—

"You're not still thinking about that silly little fall, are you?" Yowler stood in her corner a few feet away. "You know that no one likes a whiney *culotte.*"

"I am not a whiney pants."

"He's a whiney pants," yapped the Barker.

Yowler sniffed. "As if you're any better. All you do around here is complain about a few little pinpricks."

"He left fourteen quills in my back," Barker whined.

"What's a few needles? Some would call it le acupuncture *and pay a lot of euros for it.*"

I couldn't help it. I laughed. I knew exactly what that was. There was a Two-Legged who used to come to the house where I lived across the water and he would stick needles in the lady Two-Legged who lived there.

"See," Yowler said to the Barker. "Quilly knows how to

laugh at himself. That's the key to happiness. Being able to laugh at yourself."

"He's laughing at me—not laughing at himself," the Barker insisted.

Yowler shrugged. "Again, another complaint. All problems from the past have an expiration date. And yours expired the day you jumped over the fence and escaped from your stupid, bullying older brother."

"Maybe you're right. Things are different now. And I'm different too," he insisted.

See? I told you he thought he had changed.

"And I like the new me. Life is beautiful," he insisted a little too violently. "I've got it made. I sleep here, under shelter, instead of outside. And I find as much food as I like in the dumpsters on the beach." He stopped. "Until now. What am I going to do?" He wailed and he tried to tuck his butchered tail between his legs.

"Find new dumpsters to raid," Yowler said. She was obviously losing patience.

I peered toward the narrow, horizontal window-like space of the massive concrete bunker embedded in the cliff face. It was the only way out and my legs were not made to jump up walls like Barker, or climb vines like Yowler. Which meant that if I couldn't climb back up the small air vent shaft, which of course, I could not, then I was imprisoned here forever or until I died, whichever came first. I could feel tears forming in my eyes.

"Not you too," Yowler moaned. "Stop. We'll find a way to

get you out of here. Stop worrying so much. You know that's a completely useless emotion."

I sniffed.

Yowler circled around me and sat beside me, her tail curling near my body. *"If you quit feeling sorry for yourself, I'll drop down the pipe a few of those disgusting things you like so much along with the cat chow my pet is leaving outside. But, Quilly?"*

"Yes, Yowler?"

"They taste worse than that purple road cleaner. I really don't know what I see in you."

"I don't either," I said.

"Don't look at me," Barker said. "I think you're both nuts."

"It's simple," I said. "Yowler? Can you please lower your face to mine?"

Her big, beautiful orange face reached my level a few inches from the dank, concrete floor. My paws were so little that they sank into her orange fluff and my nose rested on hers. "I love you, Yowler. You're my best friend."

"Um . . ." she said. *"Now you're becoming sentimental? Now? Just when I was becoming* un petit peu *intrigued by this* drôle, *emotionless attitude from the other side of the pond. You know this opposites attract rule seemed to be working well for us, but now I see you are a bit like me and that will be boring. So how's that going to work?"*

Barker paced and panted. "Don't look at me."

We both looked at him.

"I'm sorry," he continued as he lowered his haunches to the

floor, "but I am totally confused. I'm at the top of the pet lik-ability scale, and you two dingbats are coasting the bottom at probably a minus fifty factor together. I'm a plus ten. Everyone loves dogs since we're down with the whole servant-master thing. You two don't do anything for our masters."

I immediately brightened. "What's a master?"

"A concept neither of us should ever learn." Yowler groomed her face with her lovely paws, managing her long whiskers with dexterity. "Why are you suddenly looking so happy, any-way, Quilly?"

"Because I'd rather be a minus fifty with you than a plus ten Barker all alone."

"Sentimental fool," Yowler whispered as she lowered her face back down to mine.

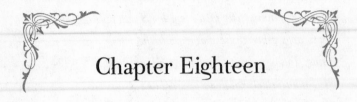

Chapter Eighteen

It was a shock to see Edward in a wheelchair.

The moderate progress we'd made in addressing his PTSD was forgotten. Becoming dependent on others was just not something in his wheelhouse. The result was a retreat into himself.

"I don't want to talk about it," he said when I came to see him in the bedroom Magdali chose across from my own. "I only want to thank you for opening the villa to us temporarily."

"Of course," I replied. "I know you and your uncle would do the same."

His face was as closed off as the barricade up the road.

"What's the prognosis?"

"Eight months in pins, likely. One more operation—although I'll go back to England to see an Army Specialist and have the surgery there."

"Will you come back here?"

He shook his head. "No reason."

I breathed deeply. "Right."

"Right."

Awkwardness compressed the air in the room. "Um, so Phillip informed that your wife is arriving this afternoon."

"She is," he said.

From the set of his face I knew I could not ask him how he felt about that. "Magdali and I made up the room next to yours for Claire, unless you would prefer for her to be in here with you. I thought that with your leg and the pins you'd—"

"Yep," he interrupted.

"Okay. Youssef will help you in the mornings and evenings."

"Perfect. But as I said, we won't be here much longer."

"Okay, then." I paused, uncertain how to go on. "I'll just go now. I must tell—" I backed toward the oak door.

"Kate?"

I stopped. "Yes?"

"Thank you," he gritted out. "I mean it. Thank you for going back into the teeth of that storm and finding help. I owe you. And there's just no way to repay that debt."

"Edward?"

"Yep?"

"I actually owe you. I—"

"Utter shite," he interrupted. "Don't start with the psychobabble. Please. I beg you."

"Shush. Just suck it up and listen. You did me a favor. I've felt like a pathetic failure the last year and a half and actually much longer—concerning my daughter. While I hate everything that happened during that storm, at least I didn't fail someone this time. I didn't fail you. And for that, I am grateful. But I also know you can't stand the fact that you had to rely on someone else. And I'm sorry for that."

He raised one brow. "You have got to get a bureaucratic French job."

That was not the answer I expected. "Why?"

"You spend far too much time worrying about everyone else and what they're thinking. A short stint at the post office—refusing to make change, closing early, adding weight to packages, and just generally being foul to everyone who enters—will change your life."

That was the man I knew. The man who used humor to cover up any emotion greater than gratitude.

"Okay," I repeated. "See you at dinner. Got to go check out hairnets and support hose at Gallery Lafayette if I'm going to apply for that job."

"Good girl," he said.

But as I left, his forced smile dissolved under the sunlight streaming in through the window. Blankness filled its place.

His wife's Ryanair flight was late from London Stansted. Phillip went to the Biarritz airport with the children to collect her, while Magdali and Lily prepared a family reunion dinner for the Soameses at Madeleine Marie. I escaped to a surfing festival at the Grande Plage organized to help those affected by the storm.

"*Alors*, Kate," Jojo said, racing up to me on the beachfront. "You know I have *un grand problème*. I must find a space to work while the current *mairie* is repaired. Have I told you I've arranged for the insurance to pay for every last *sou* of damage? But it's impossible to get through to any of the agencies *a ce point* since hundreds of customers are calling. Would you like me to try to place a call for you? They always take calls first from *le maire*. Perhaps we can come to some sort of *petit arrangement*? You hit my back and I hit yours? That's the American expression isn't it?"

"Something like that."

"So, do we have an understanding? You also might have another *petit problème*. I wonder if your villa, with all the prior poor condition is eligible. But, with one call from me. . . . Well, you know how it goes."

"Your kindness knows no bounds," I said archly.

His face was scrunched up in obvious incomprehension.

"Okay, I'm sure I can arrange something. At least temporarily. And yes, could you call? No one has returned my call. But I'm certain with your *expert* help, Jojo, perhaps you'll arrange to get them out to assess the damage pronto—if you don't want your future files in the villa damaged by flooding." I had no doubt the insurance company would fix the roof. I wouldn't fall for Jojo's French bureaucratic nonsense. On the other hand, the man would get them out there all the faster if he was in the villa.

He beamed like the sun in August. "*Parfait*. And I have an idea for some immediate money for you. Allow me to introduce you to my friends from Australia, the newest visitors to our great Pays Basque."

"No introduction is needed."

Jojo arched a black eyebrow.

Pierrot walked up with the Australian surfing contingent and before I could say, "Raspy, bitchin', gnarly waves, mates," I had agreed to take in three Aussies who were desperate for lodgings, having lost everything when the hotel at the Côte des Basques was ravaged. Every undamaged hotel in fifty miles was packed to the gills with people affected by the storm.

"I will warn you guys, the villa is not a hotel nor can we do anything except give you clean sheets and towels and a simple breakfast."

"Great. Perfect! We only need rooms for the next three weeks. You sure are a lifesaver, Kate." The team captain, Russ Nation, winked at me.

"Right," I said.

Jojo puffed out his chest and stepped in. "Madame is giving you a very good rate—one hundred-twenty-five euros a night per person with breakfast. May I suggest that you help her any way you can? Are any of you talented with carpentry or roofs?"

I could have kissed Jojo if I didn't know he probably was going to want a kickback.

"No problem," Russ said, still looking at me. "Cody and I know all about roofs. Watcha need, sweetheart?"

All right. "Um . . . how about if we take a look at it after you move in? Likely just a makeshift tarp until insurance and roofers can be arranged." I refused to look at Jojo, who was probably smiling again at all the ways he could use influence to arm-twist me.

"You got it, Kate," Russ said. "Now how about we check out that barbeque? Do Frenchies even know how to barbeque? You Yanks sure do. Had some mighty fine ribs in La Jolla last season. Shall we?" His eyes were clear and his interest obvious.

Why was I fighting it? I looked at Pierrot and he nodded in the direction Russ was looking. It seemed everyone in France was on a mission to set me up on a date.

Except me. "Thanks, Russ. I'll catch you a bit later."

"Suit yourself, Katie," he said with a huge grin. "Come on, mates." The threesome headed toward the large makeshift grills.

Jojo and Pierrot made faces at me.

"Don't you start," I said, shaking a finger.

"*Mais*, Kate, *alors*!"

"But what?"

"It's time to dance *la* dance," Pierrot said.

"I can't dance. And I don't want to dance."

"Ah," Jojo said with a grin, "any man here would love to teach you!"

"Any man would be a fool to try," I said as I waved good-bye.

I wasn't hungry anyway.

THE NEXT MORNING, at six thirty, I awoke to the sound of voices beyond the door. Youssef's deep baritone singing and laughter floated in. He was likely giving Edward a bath since he always sang while attending to my grandfather's bath.

The man was just a saint and a lesson to us all. Only Magdali was not enchanted. Youssef was not deterred and it had to be only a matter of time before she would crumble in the face of such goodness. I had been dreaming about a wedding for Magdali in our garden for the last month.

There was a knock, not on my door, and then Youssef's jovial voice encouraged someone to enter, followed by, "I'm just leaving, madame. Your husband has finished breakfast." The sounds of a jostled tray and dishes followed. Youssef whistled a tune and it faded as he walked down the hall.

I put aside my ever-present list on the bedside table and gave myself a sponge bath, avoiding all the stitches that were finally beginning to dissolve. The Aussies were coming, and I had to go food shopping and towel and sheet shopping, help Magdali make up more beds, set up the large front salon as Jojo's temporary *mairie* office, and explain it all to my grandfather and the Soameses.

At this rate, for the first time in likely a hundred or more years, Madeleine Marie's fourteen bedrooms were going to be almost all in use.

Quickly dressing in jeans and a long-sleeved shirt to hide the scar, I opened the door to the hall. They were in the midst of an ugly argument beyond Edward's door. It was funny how you didn't need to hear words to know. It was the tone, the urgency, the hissing. I froze and then backed into my room to pick up the forgotten list on the bed. At that moment, Edward's bedroom door opened and a woman's back appeared—her posture rigid and her hand on the doorknob.

So this was Claire.

"I'm sorry you don't like my gift, Edward. I found it at the airport and thought it would be useful for your future employment." She held a briefcase in her other hand and leaned over to put it beside the bedside table I knew was near the door.

Edward's eyes met mine before he refocused on his wife. I stood still, uncertain what to do.

"I can see you don't appreciate all I've done. As usual," she continued. "Well, you can ring up Mr. Dodd yourself and tell him you don't want the job he's offering. I still don't understand why you won't try it. He said you could telecommute the first six months after all." She paused for a response. None was in the offing. "Edward, you have to do something if you're going to leave the Army. I'm sorry this happened to you, but you can't just let this defeat you like your last deployment. Everyone else has troubles too, you know. I'm taking the children back as soon as possible. It's too much to ask these people to house all of us. It's up to you to decide if you want to live in the house with us or not when you return. But if you do, things must change. I'm not living like before anymore." She turned to go out the door and stopped when she saw me. "Oh, I'm sorry." She had the grace to look embarrassed as she shut the door behind her.

I stepped forward into the hall to shake her hand. She had a beautiful heart-shaped face framed by dark auburn hair curling to her shoulders. Her large green eyes slanted down slightly, above her unsmiling lips.

"I'm sorry too," I said. "I didn't mean to have the door open. I was just coming back for this list." I held it up like a guilty child. "Sorry, I should introduce myself. I'm Kate. Kate Hamilton."

We shook hands. She studied me.

"You're the psychologist."

"I am."

"Phillip said you're helping my husband."

"We've spoken a few times," I deferred.

"I see," she replied, her lips tight. "Well, I thank you for your efforts. And for your very kind hospitality. As you probably heard, the children and I will soon be out from underfoot. I'm sorry for any inconvenience." She looked away.

"Not at all. It has been a pleasure to have everyone."

"I'm sure."

I tried again. "Phillip helped us so much in finding Youssef. And offering financial advice. And in case no one has told you, I am indebted to your husband for ensuring my family was safely evacuated during the storm."

"Yes. I heard all about it," she said. "And you saved Edward."

"Have you had breakfast?" I rushed on, "Shall we go to the kitchen together?"

"Hmm . . ." she murmured, and then finally relaxed her mouth into a smile. "Yes, of course."

Her children were already seated at the large informal table in the kitchen, where Lily and Magdali now cooked. The immense Aga stove took center stage in the large room, and earned its space by giving off lovely heat to ward off the chill of the morning.

Winnie and Charles laughed when Lily screeched upon discovering she'd burned a few pieces of sliced baguette. "Magdali, what am I doing wrong?" Lily groaned.

"You have to babysit them," Winnie said with a giggle. "That's what Mum says."

Claire stepped forward. "Those stoves have to be coddled into doing what you want. Kind of like a mean, old person with a good heart. Here, let me show you." Claire expertly sawed down the center of a baguette and stuck them under the broiler.

Magdali caught my eye and raised a brow before returning to a sink filled with dishes.

Within minutes Claire had perfectly prepared toast, cocoa for her children, and tea for Lily before making her own. I hovered over the churnings of the Nespresso machine before joining the party at the table.

Max the mutt had his adorable gray wire brush face and one paw in Winnie's lap.

"Max has not figured out that I am his master," Lily said with a chuckle.

"That's because Win knows how he likes his toast buttered," Charles said with a grave expression.

Winnie leaned over and rested her little face on top of Max's. "He's just the best dog ever. I wish I was his master. I miss having a pet."

Max let out a low whine to voice his opinion and his big brown eyes gazed adoringly at his favorite cook.

"Well, perhaps, just perhaps, we can adopt our own dog when we go back to England," Claire said.

A chorus of delight suffused the kitchen as Winnie and Charles each promised to do whatever it would take to make this so.

While Lily and the two children chatted about everything canine, I leaned toward Claire Soames. "You are an amazing mother. You don't need me to tell you that, but you are."

"Why would you say that?" She asked with surprise.

"Because you raised your children alone while your husband was deployed, and it's obvious Winnie and Charles are extraordinarily well balanced."

"Mummy," Winnie begged, "May we take Max for a walk with Lily?"

"Of course," she replied. "Put your dishes in the sink first."

"Magdali," I inserted in the bustle, "do you have time to go shopping with me? We are taking on a few boarders this week and need to make up three rooms. And M. le Maire is taking over the front salon for a few weeks. We'll need to move furniture." *I suddenly remembered I still hadn't gotten rid of the old blue sofa. It was growing on me. It was all just part of the tragi-comedy (becoming more the latter by the minute) that was my ridiculous story.*

"What can I do?" Claire asked.

Magdali and I looked at this beautiful woman.

"Nothing," I said, "you've got your children to look after and you're a guest here."

"Nonsense," she insisted with all the authority of a military wife. "Give me part of your list. I can work with Youssef in the salon and see to the bedrooms if you show me the linens."

I looked at Magdali, whose smile radiated back at me as she replied, "I'll be right back with the sheets."

As she departed, I looked at Claire. "How can I thank you?"

"Send Edward back to England a better man. A better husband."

"But he is a good man."

Her bright green eyes glittered with restrained emotion. "Not anymore."

"I see." I didn't see at all. "I understand he's leaving for England soon for more surgery. Have you considered joint marriage counseling?"

"I don't need counseling."

Psychology 101: Don't force an issue when it's obvious someone doesn't see a glaring problem right in front of them. "Claire?"

"Yes?"

"You don't know me, and I don't know you. The only thing I do know is that men and women who serve their countries during war generally have a higher rate of divorce. Absence, PTSD, trauma, resentment, and more contribute. Please forgive me for stating the obvious. But—"

"You are, indeed, stating the obvious."

"I'm sorry. If you want me to stop, just say the word."

Edward's beautiful wife stood silent for so long, I wasn't sure she'd speak. And then, finally, "Go on."

"A marriage's resilience is based on the amount of desire both have to work through issues great and small. It doesn't matter whose problem it is or who is to blame. All it takes is one person to give up. Don't give up."

She stared at me, daring me to continue.

"I'm divorced," I said quietly. "My marriage was a failure almost from day one. I had no clue what to look for in a partner. I had no choice but to divorce. You have a choice. Your husband is a good man."

Claire picked up her saucer from the table and took it to the sink. "Do you know what to look for now?"

"Sorry?"

"In a partner?"

I hesitated. "Yes."

"Are you looking then?"

I joined her at the sink with my plate and cup. "No. Now is not the time for me. I've got a villa and a family to rebuild and provide for."

She placed her hand on my arm. Her fingers were surprisingly warm and gentle. "There's never a good time, Kate."

I studied her beautiful eyes. Why was everyone hell-bent on this subject? Did I have a poster on my head that instructed "Marry her off, please"?

"I don't need a partner, Claire. I have a family. That's all I need—all I ever really wanted." I stopped myself before I said, 'I've served my sentence.'

"Everyone needs someone, Kate."

"You're right," I replied slowly. "Do you need Edward?"

I saw her swallow and turn on the faucet, her eyes downcast on the task at hand. Finally, she nodded, yes.

"All right then."

There was hope for them. A small pinch as of now. With luck and desire, it would grow. I hoped they would both find the strength and courage to untangle themselves from the web of anger, resentment, and sadness that kept them apart.

"Claire?" I reached for a dish towel and began to dry the pot she'd used to make cocoa.

"Yes?"

"Thank you for helping us today. We couldn't do it without you, I fear."

Her gaze met mine. There was not an inch of a smile. Her unhappiness was palpable. "I'll help earn all our keep as long as I'm here."

"WHERE'S LILY?" MAX's voice boomed over the laptop speakers, distorting the quality of the sound. Heather was nowhere to be seen. "Such a great girl, you've got there, Katie-girl. Restores my faith in the next generation."

"Why that's the nicest thing you've said to me in a long time, Max. Where's Heather?"

"Just finishing up one of her classes. Did I tell you I built her a studio here?" He leaned forward and lowered his voice to a thousand decibel whisper, "She is a self-feeder. Never had one of those. Such a relief, although . . ."

"Yes?"

"Well, I've got to be nice now. Got nothing to entice her to stay otherwise. It's kind of a pain in the ass to be honest. But I don't want her to leave." His eyes, magnified by his Porsche Design eyeglasses, blinked.

"Seems like you have a problem, Max. You've got to decide if you want to work at being nice so you can be happy. Or . . ."

"Yes? What's the *or*?"

"Or being a serious pain in the ass, and be alone."

"How many decades have I been chatting with you, Katie-girl?"

"Um, maybe two and a half years, Max."

"Seems a hell of a lot longer than that."

"I know."

He shouted a laugh. "I'd a left a lot sooner if you didn't make me laugh now and again. Wish it was more often."

I waited. I knew he was about to let loose with something important. It was a sixth sense; a look clients had when something became self-evident.

"All this hokey talking about God knows what," he continued. "It was leading to this, right?"

"What precisely?"

"That I gotta be nice to people to be happy."

"Well, let's put it this way, generally people are happier when they are surrounded by others who are content. And kindness promotes happiness in others."

"But I'm a fucking narcissist, Kate. I don't need happy people. I just need sucking up. A lot of sucking up. Let's face it, the more the better."

I kept a calm, professional face and took a deep breath. "Max, do you—"

He burst out laughing. "Got you!"

I shook my head with disgust. Narcissists were just such a pain to deal with. I'd take a restrained psychopath over a narcissist any day of the week. Except Max. He was a special case. Perhaps he had had a great caregiver at some point when his mother—

"Now, don't start asking me about dear old Mom again. You've got that look. Mommy dearest is dead and buried forty-seven-feet deep at Forest Lawn and will never rise again." He rattled the ice cubes in his glass of Chivas. "The stake will make sure of that."

"Okay, well, now might be just the perfect time to ask how that stock is doing."

His face became stone-cold sober and he leaned forward. "Okay, look, it's not rising as fast as I'd hoped."

"Just tell me it's not falling." *When would life stop sending financial red herrings? Just once I wanted it to all work out neatly.*

"It's not falling."

"And?" I waited as he flopped open an iPad. "I need to liquidate, how soon can the money be wired?"

He looked away from the iPad. "Why do you need it so fast?"

"I've got to buy out my uncle pronto, Max. He's breathing down my neck. I think he's worried the villa will collapse before I buy him out. He's scheduled his lawyer to meet me at a notary's office in just a few days. So I've got to sell everything, right now. Thank God the house in Connecticut sold in a bidding war the first week. Between that, the twenty-five I wired to you plus whatever miniscule gains, and every last dime I've got in retirement, and a loan from Barclay's with a ridiculously high rate, I will have enough." I wouldn't tell him that I'd have literally seven hundred fifty dollars to my name afterward. I was risking it all, and for some reason it felt like no risk at all. Except the part about not sleeping at night.

"Hmm . . ." He was staring at his iPad.

"What? Did the stock drop?"

"Nope."

"Max?"

"Yeah?"

"I'll email you my Barclay's routing number for my checking account. Can you arrange for the money to be wired by tomorrow?"

"If you say so, but—"

Lily entered the bedroom office with Russ behind her. He was too large for the doorframe. She giggled and waved as she ran up to peer at Max on the laptop. "Where's Heather?"

"She's coming. Who's the dude?"

"Russ Nation, mate. You?" He looked at me and winked.

"Max Mulroney. You from Oz?"

"And proud of it. The Dutch accent gave it away, didn't it?" Russ had a megawatt smile and he wasn't afraid to use it. "Sorry to interrupt, but Kate, I need a word. The guys and I have rustled up a few tarps. You okay with us laying them on the roof at first light? There's massive sets of gnarly forecast to roll in tomorrow and we want an early chance to have at 'em before those mates from the North Shore fly in for the competition next week."

"No problem, Russ, I—"

"You ever considered acting?" Max asked without a single perfectly capped tooth showing. I'd never seen the man so serious. He looked like a viper had him in a death bite he was so still.

"Excuse me?"

"Acting? Ever done any?" Max paused. "Ever seen a movie?"

Russ laughed and it was, I supposed, a gnarly, bitchin', tubular sight to behold if you were a surfer chick. He was just plain radical. At least that is what I thought was going through my daughter's head given the fact that she was staring at him with utter adoration. Funny. It had no effect on me. Okay, maybe I could appreciate his strength, but that was only because he'd need it to put down the tarp. And thank God he must have great balance. Those tiles were slippery with probably three centuries of moss.

"Yeah," Russ said. "Course. Me and my mates see movies all the time. Hey, they're showing a rerun of a golden oldie at the theater in Saint-Jean-de-Luz tomorrow. *The Endless Summer.* Wanna come with us, Kate?"

"The roads aren't even completely clear yet."

"Sure they are. Besides, you and I can take my motorcycle. No problem with my Triumph."

"I really think—"

"Do it!" shouted Lily and Max at the same time.

Heather came onto the screen and pulled up a chair next to Max before planting a kiss on his forehead. "Oh, it's a party," she said, smiling and looking every inch the gorgeous yoga instructor that she was. "Who's that?" She blinked, her eyes fastened on Russ, the man of the hour.

"Russ Nation," Max said, lighting up a cigar. "Remember that name."

Heather immediately extracted the cigar and put it out. "Why?"

"I think it's time we take a little trip to see Kate Hamilton in the flesh, oh, and catch a surfer flick with Mr. Nation. Plot out a movie there. Got a spare bedroom, Kate?"

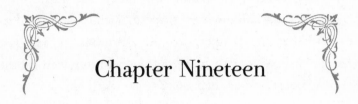

Chapter Nineteen

Five days, three enormous tarps, and two very brief rainstorms later, I carried a *64*-emblazed beach bag into the notary's office in Bayonne. Sixty-four was the postal code for the region and a brilliant clothing company had snatched the magic number and plastered it on every possible item that could be sold in a store. Of course, the beach bag had not been made to carry business and financial files in it, but then again there were few items in the du Roque villa these days that did not serve one, two, three, or rather thirty-eight different uses.

Magdali, Lily, Claire, and Youssef were so exhausted from the extra work of the Aussie boarders and Jojo's temporary *mairie* that I'd finally broken down and asked Magdali to hire a maid for three hours a day.

And thank God for Russ Nation, who'd managed not to fall through the ancient, delicate tile roof while temporarily patching it with huge tarps. A promise to actually go see *The Endless*

Summer had been his only request in return. That was tonight. I was praying for an epic, tubular, raspy hurricane instead.

The banker, M. Landuran, stood as I entered, as well as Jean-Michel and the Basque *notaire*, M. Zarantxu, and a lawyer, Mme Dulonge, whom I'd hired sight unseen to review all the documents prepared by the *notaire*.

It was going to be uncomfortable. My uncle did not disappoint.

"Kate, *chérie*, you have brought *le chèque*?"

"Of course. M. Landuran, you have it? Certified?"

"But of course."

"Jean-Michel, have you read the documents essentially removing you from any future rights to the Villa Madeleine Marie after your father dies?"

The *notaire* spouted a haze of French legal words that made little sense to me. I looked toward my lawyer, whose CV had had more law degrees and meritorious mentions than any other lawyer I knew. She nodded her assent and I followed suit.

Jean-Michel extracted a silver Cartier Panthère fountain pen and carefully uncapped it. "You know, Kate, this is a very sad day. You have effectively broken over three hundred years of tradition with this. You should be ashamed."

I loathed conflict. It was my Achilles heel. Oh, I could do it, and hide it, and always would, but still. I was clearly not a du Roque. "I would appreciate it if you would sign the document as agreed, Jean-Michel." I stared him down, waiting for his painstaking signature to be drawn. His scrawl of old French names was costing me a half million euros. The exchange rate had only made it worse. I was down to zilch and had no backup plan. It was the most financially disastrous thing I'd ever done. I'd have to work the rest of my life since my pathetic retirement account was wiped out.

M. Landuran unearthed a check from his beautiful black leather briefcase and passed it to me. I studied it, and then handed it to Jean-Michel. His effort not to smile was impressive. The notary informed all that copies of the document would be legally filed and we would be sent our own copies.

I looked around the long table, and again felt like a foreigner in a foreign land. Would I ever feel like I belonged in this country?

"I hear the villa sustained heavy damage in the storm," Jean-Michel said. "It's really too bad my father stopped the insurance."

The hairs on the underside of my arms prickled. He couldn't be right. It was just another pathetic attempt to infuriate me. I refused to rise to the bait. "Well, then you should be glad that I was willing to honor our agreement. Then again, one should always be kind to the black sheep and petty criminals on one's family tree. Oh, sorry. Your branch has been lopped off."

His mouth opened but I cut him off.

"Good-bye, Jean-Michel. Or should I say adieu? Don't ever come to Madeleine Marie again or I'll set the dog on you." Yeah, and he'd be licked to death. I turned without waiting for his retort. "*Merci*, everyone." I walked out the door without another word. Exiting the elevator, I was met by M. Landuran who had hastened down the stairs to meet me.

"Bravo, madame," he said with a sly smile. "You reminded

me of your lovely mother. How is she? Will she be joining you at some point?"

"I think not. She's in São Paulo or somewhere equally exotic at a guess."

He opened the door for me in the beautiful formal fashion in which all French gentlemen excelled and we walked toward the underground parking.

"Mme 'amilton—"

"You may call me Kate."

He pushed forward his lower lip and shrugged his shoulders. "I am so sorry. I cannot. Mme 'amilton, I am sorry to mention again that I am quite worried about your finances. You realize there is only seven hundred sixty-three euros in your account. And what about this business regarding insurance. Your uncle was incorrect, *non*? You will not default on the loan?"

"You forgot the twenty-three centimes. And I wouldn't worry about my uncle's words. Sadly, he cannot be trusted."

"Madame," he reproached. "How will you go on?"

I stopped at the parking pay station. He extracted a two-euro coin from his pocket and handed it to me. "Allow me, madame."

I accepted it and paid the parking fee. "Don't you worry, M. Landuran. As long as the villa doesn't fall down the cliff, everything will be fine."

Liar, liar pants on fire. I couldn't drive fast enough back to the villa to track down Jean, happily ensconced in front of the television, listening to the loud whispers adopted by gold announcers worldwide.

"Insurance?" he said.

"Yes, it's up to date, correct? You paid it each year?"

"Of course. Jean-Michel paid it the last few years. He said he would take his own personal check to the *agence*, using the proceeds from the sale of items each year. He might be an embarrassment to me now, but never forget that he would have been a fool to stop paying the insurance as he expected to inherit and wouldn't take such a risk."

I shook my head. "I'm going to call again. Or ask M. le Maire to call for me. They still haven't returned my call and it's been three weeks. This is ridiculous. If we were in America, there would have been estimators out within three days."

My grandfather's face had become ashen, and the veins in his hands more prominent. He'd been looking so much more vivacious lately. I'd chalked it up to Lily being there.

I touched his shoulder. "Don't worry so. You're right. He just said that out of spite. I'll get it straightened out."

"Kate?"

"Yes?"

"Tell Mlle Lefebvre. And Jojo. They will help you."

"I don't need help. Really. It's not that complicated."

"I know you can do it. But sometimes, yes oftentimes, it is more comforting to have someone with you, even if it just feels like they're supporting you silently."

"And sometimes, it's easier to just do it yourself."

"You only say that because you've never had anyone support you in your life. Perhaps you should practice."

COULD THIS DAY get any worse?

Yes, of course it could.

I've found that bad things do not come in threes. They come in thirties. Not that I'm a pessimist, you understand. Introverts are not pessimists necessarily. I'm just rosy picture challenged. At least I wasn't alone in this state. The oh-so-not-cheery Edward Soames as of late was the prince of moods.

His room was semi-dark, the shades half drawn. The light of a forty-watt bulb burned by his bed after he informed I could enter.

"Don't say it."

"Say what?"

"The obvious."

"Fine. I'll just say the second most obvious thing then. I think it's time for you to join us for lunch and dinner. Youssef said he could carry you down the stairs."

His blue-gray eyes were etched with too many hours of interrupted sleep, and his three-day growth of beard was darker than his slightly balding head. His one leg was elevated; the steel ring with pins ominous. "Don't be ridiculous. I'm far better here and I'll herniate the man's back. If you haven't noticed, I weigh a stone more than him."

"Well then, we'll move you to a room on the ground floor."

"Don't bother. I'll be gone within two weeks at most. And the *maire*'s voice would send me over the edge."

"All right. Then I'm going to coordinate a round robin of people eating up here with you."

"Kate?"

"Yes?"

"Stop. Just stop. And stop telling the children to come in here to comfort me."

"I haven't told them that."

Silence prevailed.

"Okay. I told them once. Only once." I dragged a faded up-holstered chair next to his bed. "So, look, I might have a bit of a problem and you're an engineer."

"Don't start trying to make me feel useful."

"Shut up," I said harshly. "Just shut up. Stop feeling sorry for yourself."

"I don't feel sorry for myself, Kate. I feel sorry for anyone trying to help me. I don't want to be helped. How many fucking miles did we walk and you still don't get it."

What was this? Why was fate always tossing my mirror image via a recalcitrant British Army dude? "Got it. Get it. I'm not trying to get you to feel useful. You might not have the answers but I have to start somewhere. So here it is: I don't know if my idiotic uncle paid the house insurance and I'm still waiting for a call back. I bought him out this morning. So, if I have to buy a new roof, how much will it cost, do you think? I need estimates for materials and labor."

"Pass me my mobile."

I did as he asked, left briefly to get a notebook and pen, and then opened the shades to let in the light. He gave me a dark look but said not a word as he was already talking to someone on his phone.

I turned the oblong window lock and pulled open the two long windows, which groaned from disuse. A gush of warm air poured around and behind me into the stale room.

And I could see her.

The lady lying on the peaks of the Pyrenees. Les Trois Couronnes. The Three Crowns. Wisps of clouds draped above her as she slept. She was just so beautiful and peaceful-looking. I wondered if I'd ever truly find long lasting peace. I could talk the game of fulfillment to clients, but it was harder to hold on to than anything else in life.

Below me, Mlle Lefebvre had trespassed the front entrance and was looking under our hydrangea, still calling for her cat.

"*Minnou, minnou, minnou!*"

"Have you searched behind the villa?"

She looked up at me and shaded her eyes with one hand. "Of course. I 'ave walked all five hectares. Three times. Nothing. But sometimes I 'ear her. And something is eating all the cat food I leave out each night."

I heard the crunch of footsteps on pea gravel before Russ Nation, wearing a half-peeled Billabong wetsuit and carrying a surfboard under his arm, came 'round the side of the villa. "I thought I heard you. Hey, we finished checking the tarps. They are completely secure, so no need to worry yourself on that score."

"Thanks, Russ."

"The guys and I are heading out to surf, but I'll be back to collect you for tonight, Kate."

"Great," I said with as much enthusiasm as I could muster.

"And, madame, I think I know where your cat is. I sometimes hear a cat mewling and a dog barking when I take the shortcut down the cliff. I'll take another look-see right now."

"*Hein? Qu'est-ce qu'un* 'look-see'?"

"He's going to try and find her for you," I called down.

Russ looked up at me, gave two thumbs up, and winked. "See you later, Katie."

It was getting harder and harder not to like Russ Nation. If he could just be less jovial, a decade older, and . . . oh, who was I kidding? He was just the nicest, easiest-going guy I'd met in forever and a day. But I wasn't ready. I just wasn't. I sighed.

"Didn't you once tell me to fake it until I make it?"

I swung around to see Edward studying me.

"Really? This the voice of experience in faking telling me what to do?"

"Yep."

"It's a total waste of time," I said quietly.

"Maybe not," he replied. "Or maybe it is. You won't know until you try."

"He's more than a decade younger than me."

"How old was your husband?"

"A decade older."

"So age doesn't seem to matter. Wankers come in all shapes and ages."

I walked over to him.

"Kate, you're still young, attractive, plenty of life left in you."

"Oh my God. Did you just say something nice to me? You're not dying are you?"

"Are you going to just work like a fiend here all day? Go out there and live a little. If I can't, you should. Come back and tell me all about it. On second thought, I don't want to hear. Oh, and . . ."

"Yes?"

"Carry condoms."

"I would hit you if you weren't so pathetic lying there."

"Finally a chastisement. No one dares anymore. I think that's the worst part of this."

I sat in the chair and looked toward his notes.

"Okay, then. My buddy James is going to get back to me. He'll do a little research for us. Until then, sit tight."

"But, what should I—"

There was a knock on the door.

We both said, "Come in."

Laden with fresh sheets and towels, Magdali entered with Youssef on her heels.

"Sir, are you ready for us?" Youssef's blindingly white smile overspread his dark face.

"I am."

Magdali was already in the bathroom collecting towels and Youssef joined her.

"By the way," I said quietly.

"Now what?"

"I've noticed you're not drinking. Magdali confirmed it."

"You just haven't discovered my stash."

"In case no one else knows, I just wanted to say I'm impressed you're sticking to your word. If anyone had cause not to, it's you."

"Have I ever not kept my word with you, Kate?"

I shook my head and only the sounds of Magdali and Youssef in the bathroom could be heard.

"Your wife still cares about you, Edward. No, don't ask. I just know. And I think, in the end, she's willing to work to save your marriage. Have you decided if you're going to move back into your house in England when you return?"

"I am."

"Good. I think—"

"Leave it. I said I'd go. I am not sure I'll stay. We shall see."

I was about to speak when he stopped me.

"For a therapist, you don't know how to quit when you're ahead." He reached forward and tugged a strand of my hair before breaking into the first genuine smile I'd seen since the disaster.

THE OUTING—NO, I refused to think of it as a date—with Russ was everything I knew it would be. He was funny, and had a master's degree in business from the London School of Economics, and more importantly, a PhD in emotional intelligence.

And halfway through the quintessential surfer movie, he put his arm around the back of my seat as if he was working on a doctorate of romantic moves. For the rest of the movie I tried to remember the last time someone other than my ex had kissed me. Had it really been almost twenty years ago? Did people even kiss the same way? He had better not try in the movie theater. And he'd better not try to French kiss me at all. I shifted in my seat. This was just insane. I was not going to kiss an Aussie surfer in his thirties.

Oh, but I did.

Here's how it went:

We were walking down the main avenue in Saint-Jean-de-Luz after the movie, and hundreds of people were all around us, celebrating some sort of weekend festival. Everyone was wearing white with red sashes and red berets and espadrilles. Confetti and the salty tang of the port filled the air. And suddenly, Russ tugged me into the shadowed, protected entrance to St. Jean-Baptiste Church to avoid collision with a rowdy group. His eyes were twinkling just like in some cheesy romantic comedy, and he said, "You're not going to slap me if I kiss you, are you?"

I guess I must have laughed, which he took as permission. The next thing I knew, his lips were caressing mine with a softness I hadn't been prepared for.

And then it was over. I looked over my shoulder to see if anyone had seen us. I'd been divorced for a long while but it still felt like I was doing something wrong.

"Come on. Let's ride back to Biarritz and get a drink at Le Royalty. You look like you could use one." He laughed.

Thank God he didn't seem to take anything personally.

"By the way, I found your neighbor's cat. And also someone's dog. But it's going to take a seriously large jack hammer to get them out."

"Where are they?"

"In some sort of fortified concrete bunker on the cliff face right in front of the villa. It's got an extremely narrow horizontal opening covered with heavy vines. God knows how they squeezed themselves through that opening. No one would guess it was there."

"It must be one of the old Nazi bunkers built during World War II. We just need to figure out how they got in to get them out."

He scratched his head. "Yeah, well I searched as much of the cliff face as I could. Any side entrance is gone. And I searched the villa's courtyard. Nothing. Except an air hole the size of a large fist. I told the lady and threw in a lot of dog and cat chow for them. I promised her I'd get them out tomorrow."

I looked at his ridiculously handsome face shadowed by a streetlamp and pulled him down to kiss me again. Nothing. I felt nothing. But at least I was back in the game again. Maybe with practice, something would come back.

The problem was I wasn't sure I could remember what something felt like. Maybe I never had.

Chapter Twenty

It was late when we got back. We kissed one long last time just inside the front vestibule. And I bade him goodnight, using the excuse that I had to see to something in the kitchen. He grinned and nodded before darting up the stairs to his room. There was just no way I was going up to the bedroom level of the house with him.

The kitchen door was ajar, and I went in to find Magdali sitting at the table, writing out a list. Youssef, grinning, crouched behind her, his large hands massaging her shoulders while he pressed a kiss on her head.

Magdali looked up and they both froze.

"Sorry to interrupt," I said, not sorry at all. I looked first at my sister and then to Youssef, who had discreetly stood up, returned his hands to his sides and then taken a step to the side. Did they really think I hadn't noticed? I refused to pretend I hadn't. I opened my mouth, unsure what would come out of it only to have—

"I've asked Magdali to be my wife, and she has finally agreed," Youssef said, his grin returning.

"Finally?" I whispered.

"I only had to ask five times," he replied.

Magdali had yet to meet my eyes. At least she had set aside the pen. "Magdali?" I rushed to the other side of the table and dropped down to hug her awkwardly.

She finally looked at me; her large eyes were filled with emotion, something I hadn't seen in them since childhood. And in that instant I realized that my eyes, my face, were probably very much like hers. We, neither of us, shared our true emotions with others. I tugged on her arm, and she stood as I pulled her into an embrace. We both began to cry.

"Oh, Magdali," I continued when I got a grip. "Oh, I am so happy for you, and for Youssef. When did this happen? And when will you marry?"

"As soon as possible," Youssef interrupted, with a laugh. "Before she changes her mind."

"I will not change my mind. I never change my mind," she retorted, standing tall. "And we will marry when it is most convenient for all. Perhaps two or three years from now."

Youssef stopped laughing.

"Magdali, you don't need to wait that long. You marry exactly when you want. You're my sister and I don't want you to wait for happiness."

She looked between the two of us. "You're taking his side on this. Not at all like a sister of the Himba tribe. I knew you'd take his side."

He held up his hands. "I should check on M. du Roque and Major Soames." He started backing out of the room and just before he disappeared, he winked at me and said, "Thank you, madame."

"Kate. You will call me Kate if you're to be my brother-in-law."

"Yes, madame."

I grasped Magdali's arm and nodded to the kitchen door and we walked out arm in arm to stare at the night sky.

"Why did you say two or three years from now?" I asked gently.

"There's no reason to rush."

"You're right."

"There really isn't," she insisted.

"I agree with you."

"Youssef wants us to marry right away."

"I see."

"But like I said, there's no reason to rush."

"If you like I can keep saying 'you're right' and 'I see' if it will make you feel better."

She leaned down and picked a tiny white hydrangea blossom from a massive cluster.

"Why are you scared?"

"How can I not be?" She turned to face me. "It almost always ends badly. Your grandfather had three marriages. Your father had two. You had one. Your mother had two. Even Major Soames is unhappy. And my mother was perfectly happy with no husband and so was I. I refused to marry my daughter's father. I knew he wouldn't be a good husband and I didn't need him to raise Solange. There's no reason to do this."

"Then why did you agree to marry him?"

"Because he wouldn't stop asking."

"And?"

"And . . . and . . . I like him."

"Magdali, perhaps it's a little more than that. You love him."

"Just because someone loves you today, it doesn't mean they will love you tomorrow. People in the Western world place so much importance on romantic love. My mother always told me that family and village come before anything else. And I believe it. Look at you, Kate. You're here. You must see it, feel it. Love comes from family, from your friends and neighbors. It doesn't come from a man."

"But it all starts with two people."

She shook her head and sighed.

"Magdali, you're right and I am too. I would never tell you what to do, but I will say this. Of course there are no guarantees. But, you have chosen well. There is no question that Youssef is a man of excellent character, is there?"

She shook her head.

"And if anything goes wrong, you won't stay in the marriage. You are my sister and I will always be here for you. You have nothing to fear except him breaking your heart, but that could happen if you marry or not. And I will be here to carry you either way."

And for the first time ever, it was Magdali who opened her arms and I went into her embrace. "You're right, Kate. I will do it. I want Solange to have a brother or sister. I don't want her to be alone like we were."

I nodded and rested my cheek on her thin shoulder. "And like Lily is."

"Do you want more children, Kate?"

"I don't think I could even if I wanted too. I didn't conceive easily."

"I know I shouldn't say it," Magdali said quietly, "but I wish you would find someone like the major."

"Don't, Magdali."

"All right, I won't. How was the movie with Russ Nation?"

"Long. Three hours of surfing was even too long for me."

She laughed and tugged my arm to take a walk around the front of the villa. We continued in silence until we stood on the cliff road. The winking lights of Hondarribia, Spain, shone far away into the night.

"He's a good man too," she finally said. "He supervised all his friends for two straight days to make sure the tarps were attached properly with sandbags he poured himself from the beach. And I showed him how to run the old sewing machine to make the bags. Do you know how many people have come here asking him to do the same thing for them?"

"We're lucky he's staying here."

"We're lucky he likes you," Magdali said with a coyness I'd never heard in her voice.

"You're better at changing the subject than my clients. So then, what kind of wedding do you want? Are you going to let me have the reception here?"

"No! There is no need. That is too much and I don't like crowds. We'll go to the *mairie* and be married."

"Um. That would be here then."

She laughed again. "True. But no crowds. Just a little lunch *en famille* after would be nice."

This from the woman who had invited half the people of the village to come to meet my daughter when she arrived. Two could play at that game. "And will you and Youssef and Solange stay here? Or will you want to move to your own house or apartment somewhere else?" I tried very hard to sound neutral, but I had no clue if I was successful. What would I do without them?

"I just told you family and friends and village are everything important to me. I want to stay in the only home I've ever known, if that is okay."

I let out my breath. "Don't worry. I think I might have gotten down on my knees and begged you to stay if you had suggested something different."

She caressed my cheek. "I am so glad you finally know the truth. I think I always knew you were my sister when we were growing up. You liked to play the same silly games I did and we could be in a room together for hours and not say a word to each other and be perfectly content."

"I know," I replied. "You were the only one with whom I could be myself as a child."

"But when you became an adult, you put aside the masks, yes?"

I thought about it a long time as we returned our gazes to the Spanish coast in the distance. A bank of fog was rolling off the coast and the sea was almost perfectly flat, with only the wavelets reflecting the now hazy lights in the distance.

"No. The reverse was true. I built an impressive false front. Perhaps it's what introverts like us do, Magdali."

"I didn't know we were introverts."

"But, you know now, here? I've finally forgotten to be anything else but myself," I realized it as I said it, unvarnished by any of my past filters. Despite all the financial issues weighing on me, I felt lighter and freer than I'd ever felt in my life.

Magdali turned away from the vista to look at me. Her beautiful smile glowed in the darkness. "That's because you're among people who love you without question, without condition. My mother always said that in Africa your entire village is your family, so there's no use trying to hide anything because the truth will always come out."

"Uh-huh," I said. God, I wished I could afford to send them both somewhere fabulous on their much-deserved honeymoon. And I knew where. I wanted to send them to Africa so my sister could see the places she'd heard about her entire life. "Speaking of family and truth, will you go on a honeymoon right away?" I inhaled deeply.

"*Absolument pas*. No!"

"We shall see," I whispered.

"Youssef and I have very simple needs, and we don't need much to be happy. Perhaps a little weekend away will suffice when there is less work to be done."

"There's still time to think about it. Well then . . . shall we plan the wedding for three weeks from today?"

"*Quoi?!*"

What, indeed.

Chapter Twenty-One

The next afternoon a cool wind blew from the Pyrenees, and Russ, true to his word, had assembled his mates above the cliff face with a massive amount of rope, pulleys, and an impressive jackhammer he'd wrangled from one of the construction crews that had swarmed into the region immediately after the disaster.

That I hadn't been able to line up a crew myself was beyond frustrating. And even Jojo hadn't been able to get past the answering service of our supposed insurance company. I tried not to think that they were not returning our calls because we were no longer their customers, possibly. But even if we were, I was still going to have to front the money to a roofer. Money I didn't have. Thank God Russ Nation knew how to lay tarp.

And thank God for three mothers who had jointly showed up at Madeleine Marie this morning to ask if I would counsel their children as they were having nightmares every night—

fallout from the storm. They also said the headmistress of their school had asked if I would stop in to discuss issues with many of the children. No one seemed to mind that I didn't have a French medical license. They said no other therapist could see them; they were all booked up. This would never really work. I knew that. But maybe just for the short term and for donations for the villa instead of a medical fee.

Russ's shout to lower him down to the narrow ledge in front of the bunker brought my thoughts back to the scene in front of me. He held the jackhammer in his arms as they fed line into the pulley to lower him.

Grandfather was in his wheelchair at the edge of the pea gravel bordering the gates. Mlle Lefebvre was so nervous she had her withered hand on his shoulder. La Comtesse de Bergerac stood discreetly next to the baker, who handed her what looked like a raspberry macaroon before wiping his hands on his large white apron. Even one of the German cyclists had stayed behind the pack to lend a hand. Lily had Winnie and Charles by the hand while Youssef and Magdali had Solange's hands in their own. The only people who were not there were Claire and Edward Soames.

I turned and shaded my eyes to look at the third-floor window. And I could make out their faces. He in a chair and she standing beside him. What would become of them?

It was hard to know. Each would have to give more than they probably had any idea they would have to contribute to save the union. Pride would be the bitterest of all the emotions to swallow. And having to give what the other needed when the past had shown they would receive less than what they specifically needed in return was a close second. Could they lower their defenses and allow love to grow up the columns to their hearts? Only time would tell.

The earsplitting pounding of metal against concrete echoed all around. I walked to the stone guardrail of the cliff wall and looked down. Russ wore dark glasses and a navy bandana to guard his nose and mouth from the dust. He'd pushed aside a veil of vines and a practically impenetrable bunker nearly flush with the cliff was slightly exposed. The Nazis had even drilled an uneven trail of crisscrossing lines to camouflage the bunker. It was going to take hours to make a dent in it.

I checked on my grandfather, who assured me he wanted to stay with Mlle Lefebvre. She was beside herself with worry for her cat. The relative quiet of the villa beckoned and I mounted the stairs.

Edward's bedchamber door was open and a brown herringbone patterned piece of luggage sat inside his room next to Claire's feet. Her gaze rose from her husband seated in the wheelchair we'd secured for him yesterday.

"Are you off, then?" I took a step in their direction.

She nodded. "Won't you come in?"

I did as she bade.

"Phillip is driving me to the airport, but it seems we have a slight alteration, if you agree."

"What can I do?"

Edward wheeled the chair closer to the door and his wife followed. "Claire has agreed to return alone and leave the children here with me until the doctors say I can return to England for the surgery. May Winnie and Charles continue on here too? I realize it's an imposi—"

"Of course they can stay," I interrupted. "There's no question. I was dreading when they would leave!"

Claire pursed her lips. "Thank you, Kate. We're much obliged. I think it safer if they're here whilst I have all the temporary ramps installed in our cottage, and they do have a few more weeks of holiday."

So he was going back to her. I smiled.

His face was tight, but he nodded. "Until I leave, I'll continue to try to solve your roof problem. But I should warn you that the lowest price I could find was roughly forty-eight thousand euros."

I swallowed.

"It's a rather large surface, Kate."

Claire's gaze ping-ponged between us. "Alright then, I shall leave you both to it. Phillip is waiting to take me to the airport and I must say good-bye to the children." She leaned down and pressed a quick kiss on the top of her husband's head, but didn't wait for his kiss in return. She took my hand and kissed my cheek. "I shall pop a proper note in the post, but I do want to thank you again for your warm hospitality."

"Claire, you've been indispensable here and I really don't know what we're going to do without you," I replied.

"Yes, well, bye-bye, then." She clasped the handles of her small valise and started down the carpeted stairs.

I turned to Edward, who was staring at his wife's rigid back descending the steps. "Would you like me to bring you some tea?"

"You know I only drink coffee. And, yes, please."

"Right. Black. Just came up for a sweater. The season is ever changing. It's getting much colder in the afternoons."

"You've been spending too much time among us."

"Why would you say that?"

"You're starting to talk about the weather. It's an unfortunate English trait. Instilled at birth."

"Got it. Will refrain from small talk."

"Especially to deflect uncomfortable topics."

I burst out laughing. "Well I would say you're spending too much time with me since you seem to have mastered the art of diving right into the potentially embarrassing and obvious. So you've chosen to go back to Claire."

"I have."

"I'm so glad."

"I'm not."

An awkwardness grew. I let it.

"Sometimes you have to defer happiness, Kate. You know that. You taught me well by example. I won't risk my children's sense of security. They're far too young to understand that their parents would be better off apart. I've done a lot I am not proud of. But I won't do that. If nothing improves by the time they leave for university, I'll depart then."

"So you'll limp along."

"Yep. Figuratively and physically." He smiled and it was the first time I'd seen him do that in a long time.

"I understand. More than you know. And I respect your decision even if I think you should give counseling a try if only to make things more bearable."

"Always trying to promote your profession I see."

"If you say so," I retorted, joking. "But I'd rethink your course to martyrdom. And that is a major concession from me."

"Is it? Why?" His eyes were in a ray of light coming in from a window. They were more blue than gray.

"Because you've taught me the opposite. That it's truly all right to go after what you want and to take no prisoners or have regrets when you do."

He scratched the back of his head. "Soon you'll start chastising and then where will you be?"

"Let's hope not in a war zone."

He wheeled closer to me. "Isn't that what marriage is?"

"Not one I'd ever participate in again."

He studied me, looked as if he was about to say something, but then changed his mind. "Okay then, go along and get my coffee, please. And don't forget your jumper."

I wondered if he would ever allow himself to be vulnerable longer than a sentence or two. Maybe it was just the starchy Brit in him. Well, I had a few more weeks to rub a little sentimental cowboy into the prig. Then again, I wasn't sure he wasn't more content in his own private world of thought where he probably only unleashed his emotions alone in the cool, dark hours of the night.

I gave him a mock salute and he shook his head. "You'll never get it bloody right, Hamilton. Stop trying so damn—"

At that second, the mayor shouted from below. "*Viens vite, madame!*"

Come quickly? What now?

"Go," Edward ordered. "Forget about the coffee. Here, take my jumper." He tossed the huge gray sweater from his shoulders.

I KNEW IT was something bad. I knew it as I flew down the stairs. And yet, the worse things got in life here, the calmer I became.

Phillip's car was gone and the crowd of onlookers had swelled. From the top step of the entry, I could see Lily handing the massive hissing orange tabby cat, with her tail and paws swinging like a prizefighter, to Mlle Lefebvre, who was screeching with joy and calling the cat some very interesting names. Our other neighbor, Pierrot, had a boxer on a leash and I wondered if this was the one that had gone missing.

I called to Youssef. "Youssef? Could you tell Major Soames about this? And bring him some coffee? I'm sure he's worried."

"Of course, madame," he replied.

Russ was being hauled over the side of the now crumbling cement barrier of the cliff. He was bare-chested, drenched, and held what looked like a bundle in the confines of his dripping shirt.

His eyes met mine and he grinned. He was not a man I could ever imagine having an unhappy day. It did not appear to be in his genetic makeup. And it made me smile as I walked to him.

Jojo was jabbering at my side. "We have a very, very *grand problème*, madame. I do believe M. Nation has ruptured a water line. There is water flooding from the bunker. And, I am sorry to say that this is on Madeleine Marie's property. So you are *responsable*." He clucked a few times like the cockerel he was.

"This cannot be my problem or responsibility," I said calmly. "It's not on our property. It's part of the cliff."

"*Alors*, Mme Hamilton, that is not correct, actually. I am intimately aware of the site plan for the villa and there is no question this is your *problème*. Your family owned all of this land before there was even a dirt path for donkeys. You also own the very small park at the bottom of the cliff. The only thing you do not own is the road."

"And why are you intimately aware of the villa's site plan?"

Jojo had the decency to look embarrassed. We both knew he had probably measured every last square foot of the property to attempt to buy it out from under our noses.

Youssef returned with Soames's wheelchair and parked it next to my grandfather before returning to the villa.

Russ held out the bundle of his shirt toward me just as Youssef wheeled my grandfather closer, Lily and Charles on his heels.

"Well, whoever is responsible for fixing this should probably act quickly. There's quite a bit of water seeping into the bunker. But at least I saved this little guy. I don't know if he's another pet or just local wildlife, but he looked tame, and out of place," said Russ as he handed the bundle to me.

I grasped the ends of the shirt. "What is it?"

Russ smiled. "Not a joey, I can tell you. That's a baby kangaroo, by the by. Never seen one of these. I think it's a hedgehog."

"Let me see," said Jean. "We used to have *un hérisson*, a hedgehog, in the gardens. They are harmless and actually quite wonderful in the garden as they keep out slugs."

"Winnie! Winnie!" Charles called out behind him, looking about frantically. "Where's my sister?"

"Charles, what's wrong?" Worry marked Lily's forehead.

"That's Michael. I just know it! He went missing when we came here the last time. He somehow escaped his cage whilst in Great-Uncle Phillip's garden. Oh, Win will be so happy. Where is she?"

"I'll find her," Lily said already half running. "I think she's in the back garden."

"So what happened, Russ?" I placed a hand on my grandfather's wheelchair.

"That bunker was made to withstand a nuclear bomb I think. Never seen so much concrete and interior iron scaffolding. I was hammering at what looked to be a weaker spot on one side near the opening. I just needed enough space so I could slip inside. I can't figure out how the dog got in there to begin with, until he slithered out like a snake before I was even in. That damn cat was not coming out, and I could see the outlines of a creature next to her. I thought it was a kitten or two. Anyway, she wasn't leaving without him. I can tell you that. What I can't figure out is how he got in there."

Youssef appeared, carrying Soames, and placed him in the empty wheelchair. The major's face was white with pain.

Russ made room for him in the circle.

"Mlle Lefebvre thanks you, M. Nation," Jean said. "I thank you. I've never seen her so happy."

"Hey," Edward said, "is that my daughter's hedgehog? By God, it is." He picked it up from Jean's lap. "Michael? Where have you been? On a great explore? You bad hedgehog, you."

Winnie came tearing around the corner of the villa, her red-ribboned pigtails flying and her legs churning through the pea gravel, Lily and Max brought up the rear. Winnie stopped short of the two wheelchairs. "Michael? Oh, Michael! Oh, please let me have him. Is he okay, Father?"

"Better ask the man who rescued him. Mr. Nation." He handed the hedgehog, which was curled in a tight ball with only his little snout peeking out, to his daughter.

"Oh, Mr. Nation!" Winnie said, her eyes shining. "Where did you find him? I looked everywhere! Thank you, thank you. Oh, I can never thank you enough!"

Max whined and pawed Winnie's pant leg.

"Max is jealous, Winnie," said Lily. "May I hold Michael? I've never seen one."

"Of course," Winnie said, and handed her the shy, little creature. Max immediately jumped into Winnie's arms, all seventeen pounds. She dropped down under the weight and began laughing as Max licked her.

"Look how adorable he is, Mom," Lily said.

I examined the little snout. "He fits right in here. A complete introvert, literally," I replied.

"Is someone going to please pay attention to the water issue," Jojo moaned. "*Alors.* I fear for the stability of the cliff."

"*What?*" What the hell was wrong with me? Dallying with hedgehogs—

"What is he talking about?" Edward's voice cut through the chatter.

"While I was hammering at the concrete to get inside," Russ inserted, "water began pouring onto the floor. Little critter could have drowned. Don't know what I hit with the jackhammer."

I darted to the road and peered over the side of the barrier fence. Water was seeping out of the mouth of the bunker. Not at an alarming rate, but fast enough for a neophyte like me to understand that it should be fixed as soon as possible.

I pulled out my iPhone and searched for the name of the cliff engineer the banker had told me about what seemed like eons ago. Right, a Mme Jaragoltxe. I dialed her, and then hoped she wouldn't take offense at my attempt to pronounce her name.

Not only did she not take offense, she laughed.

"I speak English perfectly," she said. "And I live not three minutes from your villa. I know it well and will come right away."

I ended the call and, as I did, the sound all around me seemed to close off as I looked up and saw the tips of the blue tarps capping Madeleine Marie flapping in the breeze. I turned and peered down at the water running down the cliff.

And then I tried to call the insurance company again, for what seemed like the hundredth time. A busy signal.

"It's going to be all right," Lily said from behind me. "You know that, right?" I whirled around to face her. Magdali and Mlle Lefebvre, holding the enormous cat, were beside her.

I knew a good mother would comfort her. Would pretend everything was, indeed, going to be all right. That's what I'd always done in the past. Yeah, and look where that had gotten me. "No, Lily, I don't know that. Right now I'm worried about the stability of the cliff. You saw what happened to the Soameses' villa."

Youssef wheeled up Edward.

"Lift me out of this damned chair," he said, looking at Youssef. "I need to see how bad it is."

Youssef and I hauled him out of the chair seat to see the cliff face. He studied it then turned toward the villa. It looked like he was mentally calculating the distances. He was sweating despite the cool air.

"Edward, stop," I said. "The engineer will be here any minute. I called a Mme Jaragoltxe, who apparently is an expert on the cliff and—"

"Evacuate everyone," he said quietly, firmly.

"What?!"

"Now," he replied.

It's funny how, looking back, I realize that was the precise point when I lost my legendary ability to stay calm in any situation. I suspect I looked something like a cartoon animation when they run past a cliff and their legs are spinning in thin air. Well, that's what it felt like. Little did I know then that it was only the beginning.

Chapter Twenty-Two

It felt like we were preparing Noah's Ark. Magdali, Lily, and I lined up everyone from the villa, and all the animals two by two. Jojo was in his element—bullhorn in hand, shouting at all onlookers to disperse *immédiatement*, calling in police with yards of yellow danger zone tape. Pierrot had announced he and his wife would not leave their villa. Mlle Lefebvre was sticking with us, but was worried for her cat, so was hand-feeding her sardines out of a can.

"No, you cannot go back into the villa, Grandfather," I shouted. "Youssef, get him in one of the cars. Now!"

Thank God, Phillip Soames had made it back from the airport.

"But where are we going to go?" Charles moaned.

"He's right, you know," Russ said. "There's not a hotel room to be had anywhere."

I thought quickly. "Well, the way I see it, we have two choices.

We can either go to the church, or we can stay here, but camp in the acres beyond the most distant flower beds."

"Do you own that land?" Edward asked.

"We do. It's just gone wild. It's the largest parcel in the region. The size of maybe five football fields? I'm no good with distances."

"Oh, let's camp," Winnie said. "I love camping."

"Well," said Mlle Lefebvre, "I do not like camping and I suspect neither will your grandfather or M. Soames and Major Soames. I have just enough bedrooms for them so they are invited to stay.

A moment later, it was settled despite grumbling from Edward. Youssef was tasked with getting all of them organized.

Mme Jaragoltxe walked over to our group, a notebook in hand. "This is going to need extensive repair. That is the bad news. *La bonne nouvelle*—the good news—is that it is not a water main break. There are no water lines that close to the end of the cliff. This is something else."

"What?" said three people at once, including me.

"I believe it is *une source*."

"A spring?" I whispered. "And?"

"I won't know more until I get someone I trust to go down to take a look. But that won't be until tomorrow."

"And if it is a spring? What would have to be done? And how much would it cost?" My mind was spinning. Forty-seven thousand for the roof. Now what?

"Ah, madame, it is very hard to say. If it is a minor issue that can be plugged up, perhaps under sixteen thousand. Much more if it is—how you say in America?—*le* tip of the ice nugget? But you see, you will need to reinforce and rebuild to give stability after. This is *très importante, oui,* after what happened during the last storm?"

Okay, sixteen thousand was a lot but it all seemed preposterous at this point. "*Oui,* madame."

"And since it is so important, and it is a large portion of the cliff, the reinforcement will cost at a minimum another fifty thousand euros, madame."

Crickets . . .

"Madame? Are you all right?"

"Me?" I began to laugh so I wouldn't cry. "All right? Oh yes, I am just perfect."

Lily tugged my hand to come with her toward the villa.

"Wait. Magdali, will you please escort everyone to beyond the gardens? I'll be collecting important things from the house with Lily." The tone of my voice appeared to have scared everyone into submission. At least there was a silver lining to madness.

We barely made it into the kitchen before Lily wheeled around to confront me.

"Are you going to make us go back to the States, Mom? Just tell me now so I can be prepared to return to Miss Chesterfield's."

"I honestly don't know, Lily. I don't know where I'm going to come up with that kind of money. I'll go to the bank and try to get a second loan and I'll call Antoinette. I'll call every last person I can think of. That I can promise you. And if I need to,

I will go back to the States and work my tail off to try to raise the money. Is that an answer you can live with?"

She ran into my arms and began to cry. "Yes," she sniffled. "And I'll try to raise money too. I want us to use my college fund. We'll find another way to get the money. I'll get perfect grades and get a scholarship."

I smiled. "Actually, you are a French citizen like me, and if you are able to win a place at a university in Europe, it would not cost us nearly anything. But, and this is a big but, I want you to have the choice to study here or back in the States, so we are not going to touch that money."

"But, Mom, I really think—"

"No," I interrupted.

"Wow. You never interrupt."

"Yes, well, I've changed. And some of the changes might not be for the better in your eyes. Come on then, let's fill up these baskets with food. Then we've got to go pack some bags with clothes, blankets, pillows, and the like. Start praying that it doesn't rain. And I've got to move the cars in case the cliff gives way. And tomorrow I'm looking for other lodging."

"Mom?"

"Yes?"

"I like the changes."

I stopped rushing around the kitchen stuffing baguettes and cheese in the baskets long enough to give her a huge hug and kiss. "Thank you, Lily. I like how you've changed too."

"There is one more thing, Mom."

"Yes?"

"I like Russ. He was cool, saving the animals and everything. And by the way, you never told me about the movie."

"It really isn't any of your—"

"I know, I know," she interrupted, laughing. "Just saying."

A NIGHT UNDER the stars was not what I expected. We managed to string up a tarp, leftover from the roof work, between four trees marking a square. Russ and his friends built a campfire and we all picnicked like kings and queens on saucisson, cheese, butter, and Serrano ham on baguettes. There was chocolate from Miremont, and very good wine. Might as well bring the best bottles as the place might not be standing tomorrow.

I tried not to think about it. Youssef and Magdali and I had emptied the rooms of the best of the paintings, photographs, and anything of true value, not that there was much. I'd even pinned the French Legion of Honor medal on my grandfather's lapel. I'd never seen him look so grave, despite Phillip's efforts to keep his spirits up. He'd even invited Jean to come to London.

I'd whispered to my grandfather, "It's not going to happen. We did not come this far to have Madeleine Marie fall."

"Life does not always have happy endings, *chérie*," he whispered back. He grasped my face between his hands, "But as long as we are all together, that's all that matters."

"Don't worry. We will be. I promise."

He'd finally relaxed and had even been laughing as I let myself out of Mlle Lefebvre's little villa.

Her cat was standing by the door and darted out between my legs despite my best effort to keep her inside. But she was an outside cat and by the looks of her, the weeks she'd been gone had not made a dent in her superior size.

I, on the other hand, was losing weight. I couldn't figure out why. I'd been eating enough butter, bread, and cheese to make me the size of the bakery.

After the campfire burned out, the children snuggled together and, one by one, dropped into slumber. Magdali and the Aussies soon followed. Except Russ, of course. I saw him approach from the direction of the villa far behind us.

He sat next to my makeshift bed. "Just went to check on her—your villa. All is well, Kate."

"Thank you. I think it's going to be fine. It's just a precaution."

"That's the thing that's always impressed me about you," Russ said.

I waited.

"You're the least fearful person I think I've ever met. And yeah, I heard enough about you to know your background."

"What do you know? Is nothing sacred?"

"Not in a French village. I know enough. So what is your secret?"

"I'm a fine one to ask when you're the model of carefree happiness. How do you do it, Russ?"

"Well, I learned a long time ago that you have to consciously choose to be happy. Far too easy to look at the negative. But choosing happiness is a great risk, isn't it? 'Cause it's setting you up for disappointment. But happiness is my religion. Disappointment is my penance. Thank God, I've had little penance. But you, Kate, what do you think? How do you keep so calm?"

"I think I finally figured out that you have to choose to stop being afraid. Bad things will always happen, but good things will too. A long time ago I was floating in life. Kind of like a person in a stormy sea. And I hated that I wasn't trying to swim to shore, but now I know I would have never been able to do that. So I'm glad I just conserved energy and floated. But I think I had the whole picture wrong. This might seem strange, but I think now I was more like the sea in the scenario. And everything else is like the weather—good and bad. There will always be storms and calm, but it will never change my essence ever again."

"Good philosophy, Kate." He smiled and then pulled me to him and kissed me. It was a simple kiss, meant to comfort in fellowship. "May I tell you something? Something that might be hard to hear?"

"Of course, Russ. You've been so kind. What is it?"

"Take care. Take great care around Soames."

"Why would you say that?"

"Because he cares for you. More than you probably know. But blokes can see it. It's in the way his eyes follow you. And he's married."

"You're wrong. It's just that he cares for me because we've talked quite a bit. It happens occasionally. But it's temporary.

Soon he'll be back in England and he'll sort out his life just like the rest of us."

"And what about you, Kate?" He caressed my hair and I leaned back, enjoying the feeling.

"What are you asking?"

"Does anyone have your heart?"

"Yes," I answered immediately.

He laughed. "I know it's not me. You answered far too quickly."

I kissed his cheek. "My heart belongs to my family. I am rich in family now."

"Is there any room for someone else?" His question was quietly whispered in my ear.

"Maybe," I whispered back. "But that will be a long time coming. I'm just not ready, Russ."

"I know that," he replied. "I do. But a man can keep trying. And I love this place. I'm going to stay until the end of the season if you'll continue to rent me a room. But I'll keep coming back every year. I'll have to anyway."

"Really? Why?"

"Because there's always going to be something to fix and never enough money to do it right. That's where I'll come in. Eventually I'll warm the cockles of your heart and wear you down."

I looked at him. In the darkness, his pupils were very large. "I hope you do." I almost meant it.

"That's a girl," he said. "What are cockles, anyway?"

❦

I DREAMED OF the Pyrenees that night under the stars. A cold wind blew above us, and I sometimes drifted semi-awake in the darkness only to snuggle deeper under the duvet I shared with Lily, who had joined me at some point. I could smell the milk and honey shampoo she used in her hair and I inched closer to her. I could have almost cried from happiness to have her next to me. It had been such a close call. I'd almost lost her and lost myself in the process.

I drifted back to the mountains, dreaming of catching wind currents with the ospreys and songbirds. I was high above the lady draped across the peaks. Her hair was growing lush and long, filling the crevices, until it reached a stream that was flowing toward the sea. Animals of every kind rushed to drink from the icy flow, and suddenly . . . I shivered and came wide awake.

And sat up.

Lily groaned. "Mom, it's freezing."

"Shhh . . ." I whispered. "Go back to sleep. I'll be right back."

And in the way of most teenagers, she didn't question me, she just went back to the oblivion of sleep.

I grabbed my gray sweater, put on my faded blue espadrilles, and headed toward the villa. I couldn't be right. It was just a foolish idea. Just a stupid Basque legend that Pierrot had probably conjured up all in the initial effort to get what he believed to be a rich American to cough up some cold, hard cash.

I dodged right at the cliff road and made my way to Pierrot's house. I looked at my watch. Perfect. Three in the morning—in any language.

I knocked on the door.

Nothing.

Thirty seconds later, I began pounding.

"*Eh, ho! Qui est-ce?*" Pierrot shouted. "*Mais quelle connard. Et quelle . . .*" His florid curses segued into one of the incomprehensible Basque languages. He was not giving me compliments of any kind, I was sure. He opened the door, finally.

I had to laugh. He was wearing an honest-to-God nightshirt. I'd never seen one before. And a red-striped nightcap. His blue eyes bulged.

"Hiya, Pierrot," I said. "I have a question."

"Do you realize it is three in the morning?"

"Yes. Is there a problem with that?" I was good at keeping a straight face.

"Well, yes there is. It is very rude to wake your neighbors. Maybe it's different among cowboys, madame. But—"

"Pierrot, were you just telling me a little false Basque legend when you came to Madeleine Marie all those months ago? Or was there a grain of truth in that blatant attempt to hose me out of a lot of money? You know. The tale about the lost well? About how centuries ago there was some sort of extraordinary water source somewhere here?"

He scratched his head and the cap fell off. "*Absolument pas!* I do not make up stories."

I raised my eyebrows.

He smiled. "Would you like a little Manzana Verde? Come

in. You know Manzana Verde? Finest green apple liqueur in all of the world. Now, let's discuss this legend. I know it well."

Half an hour later, I had to hand it to Pierrot. He was a man who could hold his green apple liqueur, as well as a third and fourth round of Armagnac, and still tell a grand story.

The question was if it had any merit. He guessed why I wanted to know somewhere between the first and second round. I was convinced by the fourth round. By the time I stumbled back to the makeshift camp, visions of Evian and Perrier danced in my head.

But as I snuggled against Lily's back, I prayed with all my heart that for just one time, this one time only, this one dream would be a reality. I knew I didn't have a right to ask for it, because really? I had everything I ever wanted. But, still, I wanted this for my daughter. And for Magdali, and her daughter. And for my grandfather, and . . . everyone in this little corner of paradise. I wanted it for them.

Okay, then, but I was done playing the saint and martyr. I wanted it for me too.

Everyone loves icing.

Chapter Twenty-Three

And so there was icing.

Winnie, Solange, Mlle Lefebvre, Lily, and I liberally spread it all over the thirty cakes the baker prepared for Magdali and Youssef's wedding eight weeks later. The kitchen had expanded into the garden, where a long row of prep tables held the fruits of three local chefs, two bakers, one butcher, and the local wine merchant. All had worked nonstop for three days to prepare for the nuptials of one of their own.

"*Alors*, here you all are! Some welcome." I knew that voice all too well. I couldn't believe she'd actually come.

Antoinette tugged at the fingertips of her chic black gloves one at a time to extract them from her hands. "Ah, *bonjour* Mlle Lefebvre. *Comment allez-vous?*" She kissed each of the older lady's cheeks elegantly. "Oh, and my beautiful Lily. How you've grown! And dear Kate, of course."

Mom. God old Mom. The opposite of every other mom of

my friends from childhood. While other mothers were getting manicures, going to PTA meetings, playing tennis, or baking cupcakes, my mother had divorced my father and then built a business all while immaculately dressed in haute couture with never one hair out of place. I suddenly thought how incredibly strong but lonely she must have been. So different from all the other mothers, so completely a fish out of water in America. I finally understood, and in that moment, my heart melted.

"Thank you for coming," I said simply and gave her an immense American hug, refusing to let her give me two pecks on the cheeks.

"*Mon Dieu*," she said, "what has gotten into you, Kate?"

"Absolutely everything," I said, hugging her again.

Lily towered over my mother when she too gave her an American hug. Antoinette now seemed frailer and thinner than I remembered.

"Where is Paolo?" Lily wondered.

"Pretending to be a gaucho on an Argentinean horse," Antoinette replied. "Baf, you know how these men must be macho from time to time. And where is my dearest Magdali?"

Arranging a last little bouquet of white roses in an old silver pitcher, I held it up to examine it better. "She's upstairs, packing for her honeymoon. Come let's go up together. She'll be so happy to see you."

"Perfect. Will someone please take my luggage to my room?"

I grabbed the ancient Louis Vuitton suitcase, and Lily led the way up the long staircase.

Max Mulroney and Heather exited one of the bedrooms as

we entered the long upper hallway. Their surprise arrival three days ago had stretched the villa's occupancy to the limit. Apparently, I had my daughter to thank for their invitation to the wedding, and their immediate acceptance.

A flurry of introductions ensued. Antoinette was completely nonplused by the Hollywood contingent. The same could not be said for Max, who was in his element, using his three-week French Berlitzolian efforts to much comedic relief.

"Madame, *quelle* pleasure to make *votre* acquaintance," he said with exaggerated flourish. A red Basque beret hung at a precarious angle and matched his red espadrilles. The only thing missing was a navy and white striped shirt and a rope of piments d'Espelette, the famed red peppers of the region, to complete the portrait of casual Gallic perfection.

"Hi, Antoinette," added Heather, in her typical yoga gear and wonderfully oblivious to the formality that was before her, i.e., my dear mother.

"*Enchantée,*" Antoinette replied with her nose tilted at an angle that suggested she felt the opposite.

"Hey, Lily," Max said, "have you seen Russ? He promised to take us to watch the surfing at that spot, Parle-whatever."

"Parlementia," Lily corrected. "Yeah, I think he's waiting for you in his VW bus with the million surfboards on it."

"You're leaving?" I asked.

"*Oui, oui,* Katie-girl," he replied. "But we'll be back in time for the wedding. It's in three hours, right-o? We're going house hunting after."

God help me if they became neighbors. Then again, the

Pays Basque was one part old-world aristocracy and three parts foreign mutt. They'd fit right in. And Jojo was Max's new best friend. It was a well-known fact that legend suggested there was an American living in every French village. I would happily relinquish my role.

Max tousled Lily's hair. "God, you're gorgeous. And so tall! Had no idea when we Skyped. Okay, you've got to come to Hollywood as soon as you graduate, deal? I'm going to set you up with some people I know at ICM. Have you ever taken any acting lessons? You would be a natural."

Max the dog came bounding up the stairs with Winnie at his heels.

"Whatever is this?" Antoinette said.

Lily burst out laughing. "That's Max."

Antoinette leaned down and scratched his ear, but with a look that suggested he would regret it if he dared jump up on her.

"They named him after *moi*," Max said proudly.

"Why?" Antoinette gave a last pat to the dog and straightened.

"Because he's really sweet even if he's scruffy and he likes to sleep under the covers with anybody," I replied.

"Exactly," Max said, and then beamed. "I liked him from the get-go. Okay, off we go. See ya later, Antoinette."

My mother sighed as she watched them descend the staircase. She looked at me and said in melodic French, "Are these the sorts of people you have for friends these days? Barely civilized."

"They are precisely the type of people who are my friends these days," I replied. "And no, they are completely uncivilized. Just like me."

She made a classic French half gurgle, half exasperation noise in the back of her throat. "And you put them in my room."

"I didn't know you were coming."

"Never mind. I shall take the room across from you."

"Um, that's taken too," I stated. Winnie was hiding behind me in awe of my mother. "By this young lady's father, Major Edward Soames. You can meet him later. Come, you can stay in the room at the end of the hall."

"But that's the *nursery*."

"Yup," I replied. "Last empty room in the villa. Has the same excellent quality horsehair bed as the one in my room. In other words, incredibly lumpy." I picked up Antoinette's luggage and continued walking, choosing not to see my mother's jaw drop.

I could barely hear her hurried steps behind me. "But why are there so many people staying here?"

"As I told you, there are very few hotels reopened since the storm. I've been letting them out to people who were stranded. Even the mayor is using one of the salons as his office."

"Joel Boudin is here?" Antoinette said, with no shortage of shock.

"Yup. Jojo is my new bestie." I deposited her suitcase just inside the nursery. "Ceremony starts in three hours. Do you want me to bring you some tea or are you going to take a nap now?"

"I shall take a lie-down," my mother said with that hint of a

British accent imparted on her by all the English nannies she'd endured.

I kissed her on the cheek and headed down the hall before she could ask me to unpack for her. At the last moment I knocked on Soames's door.

"Come," he commanded.

A blast of sound—of metal against rock—drowned out conversation for long seconds after I entered.

"I thought you said they were giving it a rest today," Edward said from the chaise longue we'd moved to his room. He was able to sit for much longer periods now, so much so that he was leaving for London tonight, along with his children.

"No," I replied. "They're only stopping at noon. Half a day. You know the bride. My sister wouldn't have it any other way. She is a maniac."

"She is, indeed, exactly like you."

I shook my head, but smiled nonetheless.

"We haven't had a chance to speak much lately, other than about this damn spring of yours. Are you excited to be at the helm of this new venture, or do you think you'd prefer to have a company buy you out in the end?"

"It's too early to say, Edward, as I told you. But I think I really want this joint venture with Magdali and maybe with Lily, if she decides she wants to be involved after university or later in life after she's lived a little. It's exactly what I never knew I wanted. A family business in France. It will take years to get French degrees to be able to practice psychotherapy here. But now I have a great luxury. I have options."

"And the people here will love you for it. Think of the jobs Du Roque Spring Water will create."

"The only thing that mars my joy is the amount of pipeline construction required, and the hours of French bureaucracy it will take, but I refuse to complain. Okay, only a little. It is you, and I know you love it when I complain."

He shook his head. "I wish I was going to be here to see you and Magdali tied up in red tape for the next decade."

"Red, white, and blue tape, and every document in quadruplicate with notary seals," I paused to straighten the duvet on his bed nearby. "Just don't forget the offer Magdali made. There will always be a need for top-notch engineers here. Or someone in London to work on export to the English-speaking world if this spring is as great as Jojo's experts suggest."

Edward looked at me, but said not a word. His face was like a blank slate—as it was the day I'd first met him over chocolate biscuits and unsipped tea.

"What's going on in that thick head of yours?" I murmured.

"You're one to talk," he said quietly, finally. "How are things progressing with Russ?"

"You're changing the subject. I thought we'd stopped doing that."

"I told you, I'd think about it, but I'd prefer to figure out my next steps on my own," he said. "But if I can help you, I will."

"Got it."

"Your turn. Answer my question," he said. "Please."

I looked at him and sighed. "Everything is fine. Russ agreed to lend us his best production manager from his surfing corporation to work with us the next six months. And Phillip has promised to find us the best professionals. You know that."

"Why isn't Russ offering to stay here?"

"I didn't take him up on the offer. And he should go back to Australia anyway. He's got some important deals coming up, and he misses his family, and the waves are better in—"

"Kate, what's really going on? What's wrong?"

I walked to the chaise and sat on the end. "Look, I'm a tiny bit stupid and scared in this department, okay?"

"You don't look scared. What are you scared of?"

Why not just say it? I couldn't say it to anyone else. And he was leaving. "That no man will ever really know or love me," I said so quietly he had to lean forward. "The real me—the one before I was married. The person before everything went so wrong. The one I was as a child here before I wasn't allowed to come back. There are moments I sometimes don't know who I am, Edward. And you know, I'm just fine alone but surrounded by my family."

"Why are you worried about this? Honestly. You think far too much."

"Your compassion and empathy is touching. As always."

"You don't need compassion. You're bloody strong and don't need some namby-pamby cuddly talk."

"Don't worry. I know I'll not get that from you."

"Then just who are you, Kate? How can you not know? I do."

"I don't know. I used to know a long time ago, but now sometimes I don't."

"You're fooling yourself," he said. "You know exactly who you are. That's not your problem."

"Really? Then what is my problem?" I didn't know if I was getting angrier or more interested. This was going to be good, I was sure. I was even more sure that whatever he said was going to be his own core root issue, not mine.

"The problem is you don't trust people enough to show the real person under the mask."

"Perhaps I'm not the one wearing the mask here. You are."

"You don't trust me, do you Kate? Even now, after all we discussed and aired grotesquely. Are you ever going to trust anyone ever again?"

"I do trust you. Shocking, isn't it? I trust you with every fiber of my being. The problem is that you don't trust yourself. But here's the thing of it. You just have to find a new purpose. A reason to get up every day. And a way to stop numbing the pain. That's the first step. Loving someone, your children, and always having something to look forward to, are the last two key ingredients to happiness. And then things will fall into place eventually and start making sense again. And damn it, Soames, I'm counting on you to do it. To inspire me as you always do. Because you deserve happiness more than anyone else I know."

He shook his head.

"Stop it," I said.

He looked at me questioningly. "I didn't say a bloody, fuck-ing thing, Hamilton. What has gotten into you?"

"Listen to me. You. Deserve. Happiness. Now go to it."

"There are times I think you need to change professions. Don't you know anything about therapy? You're supposed to let me draw my own conclusions."

"Edward Soames, you are sometimes the absolutely most impossibly blind idiot. You were never a client. You were my friend, and still are."

He reached out his hand and I placed my own in his. "Best friend, actually."

I swallowed against the tightness growing in the back of my throat, but could do nothing about the tears starting to balance on my eyelashes. So I nodded instead.

"Oh God," he said with exasperation.

"What?"

"You might need to reconsider joining the business world."

I reached for a tissue and blew my nose very indelicately. "Why?"

"There's no bloody crying in business," he said. "Only in therapy."

"You just told me to take off my mask. Now you're telling me to put it back on. Make up your bloody mind."

"I knew you'd finally learn how to curse properly if I stayed here long enough. Perfect. My job is done. Go on then. One of the Aussies is coming any minute to help me dress."

I stood and brushed the wrinkles from the apron covering my jeans. "I should start too."

"Kate?"

"Yes?"

"I'm no good at good-byes."

"I know," I said. "I'm not either."

"So I'm not going to say good-bye when I leave later this afternoon."

"All right."

"But I want to thank you. And I,"—he paused and looked aside for a moment before continuing—"want to say some important things to you, but I'm not in a position to say them at this time. So I will just say farewell, Kate Hamilton. Until we meet again."

I bent over and placed a hand on the side of his face to lean in and kiss the top of his head. "Yes. Until we meet again."

And then, I was out the door to the comfort of my room, where I could cry a few tears in peace.

MAGDALI WAS THE most beautiful bride I had ever seen. Her gown was made of a long length of pale pink gossamer fabric, wound around her body and ending in a long train-like stretch of fabric flowing behind her. To show her love of Lily, sprigs of lilies of the valley threaded the tight bun of her hair. To show her love for her daughter, Solange was the only attendant. Granddaddy and I served as the required witnesses.

Jojo conducted the civil ceremony with great pomp and circumstance, of course, and Pierrot made the first toast during the feast.

Russ, whose chair was back-to-back with mine at the next

table, leaned over to say something. "I finally got through to that ridiculously inept insurance company this morning."

"And?"

"They gave the usual bureaucratic pathetic excuses, but yes, they're on the hook. Apparently someone has been sending the yearly payments from an American bank. That's all I could get out of them. Bottom line? You're covered."

I watched my mother wending her way to the table. "Of course. It was Antoinette."

"Your mother is something else. And I say that in the nicest possible way," he said and then laughed.

"I know. She's impossible to categorize."

"Unlike you. You are easy to categorize. One part ingeniously French, and three parts fearless American."

"Russ, how am I ever going to thank you? For all you've done for us."

"Maybe by giving me a good price on my room at Madeleine Marie next summer?"

I smiled. "Of course."

"And letting me teach you how to surf when I come back. You do know it's done standing up, right?"

I liked him. Everyone liked Russ. How could one not? "Absolutely."

"I'm for Sydney day after tomorrow. You will answer my emails when I write to you? You know, the nonbusiness-related ones?"

"Of course, I will." I laughed.

"Good. Perfect. Wonderful. There is going to be dancing today, right? Will you give me the first dance?"

I nodded, and he tipped back his chair slightly to kiss my cheek. "Excellent."

I turned to survey the room.

Antoinette had been remarkably quiet, lost in the crowd of more than eighty friends and villagers who had descended into Madeleine Marie's vast gardens, awash with tables dressed in white linen and flowers of every sort imaginable—white roses, sunflowers, lilies, roses, and hydrangeas.

It was autumn, and Mother Nature, in her fickle way, had decided to grace us with a lovely, hot Indian Summer sort of day.

And as everyone carefully navigated their way through a five-course lunch, culminating in wedding cake and a groom's cake of chocolate gateau Basque, Magdali rose from her seat between Youssef and me and addressed the crowd.

"*Mesdames et messieurs,*" she said. "I am honored you came to celebrate this day. I am proud to be a member of this village, and to be a member of this family. I would like to thank three people particularly. First, M. du Roque, for his kindness to my mother, me, and Solange. Second, Mme Antoinette du Roque, for her gift of a honeymoon to the country of my mother's birth, Namibia. And lastly, Kate Hamilton, for she has given me the most precious gift of all—the gift of sisterhood in the past, an equal partnership for the future, and love always. And to all, I give this Namibian proverb: If you want to travel fast, go alone. But if you want to go far, travel together. Youssef?"

"Yes, my beautiful wife?" He was so handsome in his morning suit.

"Thank you for choosing me with whom to travel."

He kissed her, bending her nearly backward in his passion, and the crowd stood and roared its approval.

Antoinette came up behind me and leaned in. "*Chérie*, what a scar. Perhaps a dress with longer sleeves would have been a better choice? That's the sort of scar that only a man can pull off well. *Mon Dieu.* Does it hurt?"

Grasping her arm, I steered her to the edge of the crowd and then beyond, toward the bed of lilies near the old, stone potting house. "Mom?"

She nearly reeled from the shock of me calling her *Mom* instead of *Antoinette.* "*Oui?*" She eyed me suspiciously. "Why have you dragged me away from the party? I was just having the most fascinating conversation with M. Landuran."

"Well, when you go back, do you think you can sweet-talk him into processing our new loan a bit faster? It appears love moves mountains here in France instead of cold, hard business facts."

"*Mais bien sûr.* Is there another way?"

"Well, that brings me to my main question."

Her eyes rounded. "I do not like answering questions."

"I know. Trust me, I know. Forty-something years with you has proven that many times over."

"I can't imagine what you mean," she said indignantly.

"Did you have any idea when you harangued me into coming here a few months ago that I would end up staying? Actually making a new life in France?"

Her smile began slowly, beguilingly, vivaciously, as her slightly slanted, impossibly mysterious aquamarine eyes studied me. "What do you think?"

My mother was one of the most stunningly beautiful women I'd ever known—apart from my daughter, who looked just like her. It was easy to see why half the men in Biarritz were in love with her. The other half were farsighted. And she reveled in the attention. I wouldn't let her sidetrack me. "Come on, *alors*, tell me. Why did you really ask me to come here and sort out Madeleine Marie? This is your villa really . . . not mine. You're next in line."

"*Chérie*, it was never mine. Far too many horrid war memories. It was always meant for you. Consider it a little divorce gift. I do like them so much more than wedding gifts, don't you? Always a fifty-fifty chance that someone will need one. This one is yours. You deserve it after a decade and a half of hard labor."

She would never admit it. It just wasn't her way. Just like she would probably never tell me or any other woman that she loved them. But she did it the real way. She showed love through her actions.

It had just taken me too damn long to figure that out. Just like everything else in life.

"And giving Magdali and Youssef that trip to Namibia was just about the nicest thing I can imagine."

She pursed her lips and raised her eyebrows in that insouci-ant fashion that pretended indifference. "Enough of that. All right then . . . Paolo is going to cause a frightful scene, but I suppose I must give you a bridge loan until dear M. Landuran approves *le cash* for the business in full. But I will require the business loan back within a twelve-month period. I am not *that* generous, you see."

I pulled her stiff form into my arms, partially against her will, to be sure. I just didn't care anymore. She was going to have to feel the love whether she liked it or not. She finally relaxed. "*Maman*," I whispered in French, "*je t'aime*. I couldn't have gotten through it without you. I was starting to lose my mind."

She pulled back. "You only thought you were. I knew you weren't. Du Roque women do not ever lose their minds. We don't have that luxury, which is really too bad. But it seems his-tory has always felt the need to challenge us. But, *ma chérie*, aren't you secretly a little glad for the trials and tribulations life tosses our way? It makes us better, don't you think?" She broke away completely from my embrace, and tried to brush out the wrinkles in her immaculate blue linen Chanel suit. "Do you think you could refrain from that dreadful American habit in the future?"

"Which one?"

"The one where you feel the need to crush my clothes? Even the barbaric English know the art of restraint. Agreed?"

"Nope."

"Ah. Well, then, whatever."

Aside from French and British English, my mother had the most unusual grasp of Americanese, using the choicest cutting-edge terminology found only on college campuses or in *Urban Dictionary*.

Last Whispers from the Garden . . .

"Don't get any ideas, Quilly," Yowler whispered to me whilst we crouched behind the potting house.

"What do you mean?"

"Don't ever think we should embrasser *like the humans do. It's just crass."*

"Crass? What does that mean?"

"Tasteless and unrefined." She stretched out a hind leg and did that cleaning thing that made me want to yak.

I was too polite to ask her to curtail that awful habit. If you love a friend, sometimes you just have to put up with some of their less attractive qualities. Although, as far as I could tell, Yowler didn't really enjoy putting up with my eccentricities. But I was good at putting up with the fact that she didn't like putting up with anything. I guess that was one of the parts of me that she liked best. What I liked best was her grit, her sense of adventure, her fearlessness, and how she pretended she didn't like me as much as I liked her. Deep down inside, I knew she adored me—an odd thing in our world. And now that we were best friends, it was funny . . . the thing that I had first been infatuated about—her scent? It just wasn't as important anymore. It was lovely, still, of course. But it wasn't as wonderful as everything that was Yowler, the most beautiful, orangiest, softest, most brilliant cat with too many names

*in the world. Oh, you didn't know cats have three completely
separate names? Well, there once was a famous Two-Legged
author on the other side of the pond who wrote all about that.*

"Quilly?"

"Um, yes?"

"Is your head in the clouds again? I was talking to you."

"Right. Sorry. What can I do for you, my dearest, darling
Yowler?"

"I was just saying that perhaps you might start trying to
like sardines. It's so much more amusante to skulk around
the port in Guéthary, and slink into the boats in search of a
lost little fish."

"As opposed to?"

"Sniffing the leaves in this garden, hunting those horribly
slimy creatures."

See? I told you she didn't like all the parts of me. "Yowler?"

"Yes?"

"I would be happy to go to the port with you. Besides, I
am worried that the little Two-Legged with the red ribbons in
her hair is going to change her mind and try to take me back to
that horrible life of the light switches and the indoor running
wheel that goes nowhere."

"Well, I think it was very smart of the humans in the villa
to suggest a trade: you for that pathetic excuse for a canine,
Max."

"Don't say that. I sort of liked him. He never tried to
bite me."

"That's only because he was too busy sleeping the day away inside. The opposite of a moron if you ask me."

Yowler lowered her head to mine. And for a moment, her eyes seemed to glow and soften.

"What?"

"Nothing. I just thought you might be hungry. Come on, let's go back to the lily patch. Forget the sardines."

See? I told you she loved me.

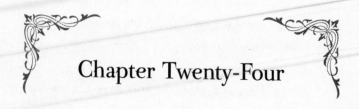

Chapter Twenty-Four

The bells rang again. My watch showed ten to four and for once I knew precisely why and for whom they tolled—my beloved sister and Youssef. Long ago, I'd stopped counting and wondering. I loved the mournful, sweet, ancient sound echoing from high on the hill of the village.

Here, in the garden, now that Magdali and Youssef and the last guests had departed the wedding feast, the doves cooed their contented song, the hedgehog—a few quills peeking from a rustle of fallen leaves near the potting house—napped in the warm shade of the poplar, and Mlle Lefebvre's huge marmalade cat, tail and whiskers twitching, stood guard whilst she eyed the two boxers with murder on their minds, but cowardice in their hearts.

Lily's feet, lighter and faster than all others in the house, were skimming the pea gravel. I turned to wait for her.

Sometimes now, late at night, between cycles of sleep, in that haze of semiconsciousness, when dreams become dreams and reality creeps in to examine those old trunks still in the attic of my mind, I notice the old pine floor is swept clean; and all the items are neatly arranged in a pretty pattern. Underneath each polished leather lid are mementos and clothes not of this season, lovingly wrapped in tissue. Never to be worn or used again, they are still part of the fabric of my life, part of me, the once fragile and secret parts now outgrown in an era of boldness.

I am not afraid to look at them anymore.

They are not beautiful, but I love them in all their glorious, hideous imperfection—sort of like the jagged scars I now carry inside and out.

And as I watched my beautiful, glorious daughter run toward me, my throat grew tight with emotion. In that moment, I knew. I knew I was the luckiest, happiest person on this sometimes Godforsaken place called Earth.

"Mom! Mom! They left . . . The major and his children. Didn't you want to say good-bye?"

She stopped in front of me, panting, her hands on her knees.

"No, it's all right. I already did earlier."

She nodded. "It was beautiful, wasn't it? The wedding."

"It was."

"Where are you going?"

"To get the car parked behind the potting house. I'm going to drive to the base of Les Trois Courrones and hike to the top, remember?"

"Right. I forgot. Is anyone going with you?"

"No. I want to do it alone. But don't worry, I'll be back by the time darkness falls."

"Perfect. Can we watch *Zombie Apocalypse* in French again tonight? Nothing is funnier than French zombies."

I hated zombies. "Of course."

She hugged me, and the lovely, natural scent of her warm hair made me want to cry again from happiness. What was wrong with me? I had to get a grip. Didn't I possess any of that cool, French blood at all? Getting used to a full range of emotions would take time.

"Love you, Mom," she whispered.

The tears couldn't be held back any longer. "Not as much as I love you."

THE DRIVE AND climb to the jagged profile of the lady I always envisioned asleep in the mountains was not as difficult as I feared. There was a small path cutting through the pine trees. The low, mournful tones of cowbells echoed off of the mountain the higher I climbed. Breaking through low-lying clouds of mist, I finally reached the granite top of the mountain. Westerly stood the other peaks that made up her profile.

A gust of wind slid off her massive nose, enveloping me as I stood on her lips. I imagined her gasping and whispering in French her first little words of wonder upon finally coming awake for the first time in a very long time. I was suddenly cold, but alive, dancing inside with the frenzy of the wind and the fast-moving clouds sweeping past me.

I feel everything now.

And yes, it's a wildly empowering sense of freedom from any kind of fear.

But perhaps that's what it means to be alive. All the pieces of me are coming back together in a different, more vibrant pattern now mixed with new pieces—and I'm at ease with all that might come my way in its own time. Yes, I was home. And I was awake at last.

The earth trembled. Roots groaned.

I ONCE MET a woman on a night flight to Paris. And in one bizarre instant, I allowed myself a brief moment of intimacy with a stranger. Intimacy is not something most men do well, if you must know. But there was something about this woman that resonated. It was in her expression, her posture, her inability to focus on anything for longer than a minute or two. She was teetering on the edge.

Just like me.

Coupled with anonymity, that made her safe.

And so I asked her. I asked her the question that I'd asked myself a thousand times before I boarded that plane to the Old World. What are the boundaries of family obligation—of one human to another? She was as clueless as I, even if she wore some doctoral badge of professionalism like a Band-Aid on a sucking wound. But I had to admire her for her brutal honesty, whether she knew I overheard her or not. It's absurd how a brief encounter with a stranger can change a life.

But does anyone really know how to live a good life?

I still don't know. I only know that the answers in life are different shades than just black or white, and that trying to figure out the best color for any given moment is life's work and journey; resilience its drive.

The top of this unusual mountain peak on the French-Spanish border I was climbing was a mere forty-five minutes of rough going, tops.

There was a hazy shadow of someone else up there through the swirling mist.

The earth suddenly shook and I grabbed the trunk of a sapling just strong enough to bear my weight. Rebalancing myself, I gazed up.

The figure was gone.

About the author

About the book

Read on . . .

Insights,
Interviews
& More . . .

Meet Sophia Nash

Sophia Nash was born in Switzerland and raised in France and the United States, but says her heart resides in England. Her ancestor, an infamous French admiral who traded epic cannon fire with the British Royal Navy, is surely turning in his grave.

Before pursuing her long-held dream of writing, Sophia was an award-winning television producer for a CBS affiliate, a congressional speechwriter, and a nonprofit CEO. She lives on the coast of the Pays Basque and in the Washington, D.C., suburbs with her two children.

Sophia's novels have won twelve national awards, including the prestigious RITA® Award, and two spots on *Booklist*'s "Top Ten Romances of the Year." ◠

Story Behind the Book

An important question most people ask themselves at some point is: What is the purpose or meaning of life? It's usually during a dark hour, when life appears most bleak. Socrates at his trial for impiety claimed "the unexamined life is not worth living." He believed that the first step toward finding the meaning of life is to know and deeply understand ourselves. But when people get stuck at the juncture of major change, and reflection yields little, sometimes taking a small step toward the new and unknown launches a journey of discovery.

The Pays Basque, the mystical land half in France and half in Spain, has always been the place I go for reflection. The traditional Basque houses reflect the importance of nature: whitewashed and trimmed in red to signify earth and blood, or green to reflect the crops and mountains, or blue to denote the sea and the sky. Steeped in history, inhabited by Basques and a slew of nationalities, it is, in this author's view, one of the most beautiful and poignant places on Earth. Specifically, the stretch of coast from Hondarribia, Spain, to Biarritz, France, and the breathtaking Pyrenees are the backdrop and inspiration for *Whispering in French*. Whilst all the characters and events in this story are fictional, this part of France is, indeed, my homeland. I find inspiration here as have hundreds of painters and writers before me. Indeed, this is the stomping ground of Hemmingway and Picasso among many others. It is almost impossible not to be moved by coastal walks on the littoral, swims in the freezing Bay of Biscay, or hikes to little known peaks in the mountains. But by far, my favorite view has always been that of Les Trois Couronnes—the Three Crowns in the Pyrenees near the coast. It appears to change every day, and in every type of weather. As a child, I loved to imagine that the slumbering lady draped over the peaks would one day wake up and go on to fulfill her centuries of dreams. Hence, a full story was born nearly forty years later.

Occasionally, readers ask me why I write. It's so simple. To write is to be on a journey of discovery. Often challenging and infuriating, storytelling is also sometimes, if one is very lucky, uplifting for writer and reader alike. All is fair in love and storytelling. Yes, I always hope to entertain, but the goal is to inspire and question life's purpose. I do so hope *Whispering in French* accomplishes that goal by reconciling some of life's harsh realities so that redemption might be found. ◠◡

Also by Sophia Nash